CU00661238

The Unforgiving Sea

The Searight Saga, Part Two

Rupert Colley

Rupert Colley

Rupert Colley was born one Christmas Day and grew up in Devon. A history graduate, he worked as a librarian in London before starting 'History In An Hour' – a series of non-fiction history ebooks that can be read in just sixty minutes, acquired by Harper Collins in 2011. Now a full time writer, speaker and the author of historical novels, he lives in Waltham Forest, London with his wife and two children.

Works by Rupert Colley:

Fiction:
My Brother the Enemy
The Black Maria
This Time Tomorrow
The Torn Flag
The White Venus
The Woman on the Train
The Unforgiving Sea

History In An Hour series:
1914: History In An Hour
Black History: History In An Hour
D-Day: History In An Hour
Hitler: History In An Hour
Mussolini: History In An Hour
Nazi Germany: History In An Hour
Stalin: History In An Hour
The Afghan Wars: History In An Hour
The Cold War: History In An Hour
The Russian Revolution: History In An Hour
The Siege of Leningrad: History In An Hour
World War One: History In An Hour
World War Two: History In An Hour

Other non-fiction:
A History of the World Cup: An Introduction

The Unforgiving Sea

Historyinanhour.com

Rupertcolley.com

Prologue

A Village in Devon, Southern England,
August 1944

I never felt so relieved to be home. I looked in the hallway mirror and thought how I'd aged. What did I expect? But from tonight, I was starting a new life, a quieter, more peaceful existence. I'd had enough adventure to last a lifetime. All that was behind me now.

I called for Angie, my little Jack Russell. Mr Jenkins, the headmaster at the village primary school, had been looking after her during my long absence. She came to me, wagging her tail. She hadn't forgotten me. I picked her up and ruffled her coarse fur and, laughing, turned my face away as she tried to lick me. Jenkins had been my first visitor, earlier in the afternoon, the dog at his feet. He shook my hand firmly and welcomed me home. He seemed sorry to have to return Angie to me. My next visitor, within minutes of Jenkins leaving, was Joe Hamilton, the village shopkeeper, wearing his habitual apron and bearing a basket of foodstuffs to 'keep me going'. How kind. I thanked him profusely. I'll have to settle up with him soon.

The third person to call was June Parker. She kissed me on the cheek and hovered at my doorway declining my offer to come in. The wife of a soldier, she wore a long dark coat despite the warmth of the afternoon sun and lipstick of the brightest red, her blonde hair curled at the back.

'You're to go the pub tonight, Robert,' she said in a conspiratorial tone. 'The White Ship, but no earlier than eight o'clock, you hear?'

'That sounds intriguing.'

'You'll find out. Come and pick me up at eight and we'll go together. That way I can keep an eye on you. Pleased to be back?'

'I can't tell you how pleased I am.'

'And we're all very pleased to have you back. It must have been awful.'

After she'd gone, I went up to my bedroom, the dog overtaking me on the stairs. The room was sparse – pastel flowery wallpaper, just the single bed, an ugly wardrobe, a bedside table. What does one expect from rented accommodation? Above a dresser was a pleasant moorland painting depicting Highland cattle with their long horns. And above the bed, a wooden crucifix supporting a metal figurine of Christ. I unhitched it off the wall and noticed the shadow of the cross left in its wake on the wallpaper. Sitting on the bed with Angie lying behind me, I studied it. It was heavy but crudely produced, the extended arms overly long, his nailed hands out of proportion with the rest of him. It was cheap. And ugly. The idea of his contorted face staring down at me every morning was unnerving. I hid it in the top draw of the bedside table.

Across the landing from my room, the second bedroom – Clarence's room, a mirror image of my own. Although the same height, Clarence had been thinner than me, and looking in his wardrobe I found a number of his clothes that would fit me now. I'd lost so much weight that my own clothes, down to the last pair of trousers, were all too large for me. I stretched the fingers of my right hand. With a bit of manoeuvring, I slid the gold band off my index finger. It had lost none of its shine in the intervening weeks. I tossed it around in my palm. With this ring, I'd made a promise. To deliver it to a woman. A woman who lived in the village. It was all I had to do. To deliver this ring. Tomorrow. I placed it in the bedside table drawer – next to the crucifix.

It was almost eight now and having washed and shaved and changed my clothes for Clarence's, I was ready to go. I wore a navy blue jacket and a plain dark green tie. The tie at least was mine. I swept the dashes of Angie's white fur from my trousers and checked myself in the mirror one more time. Yes, I thought, I looked fine. It was time to reacquaint myself with the ordinary world encapsulated in this tiny Devonian village, a world I often thought I'd never see again. I patted Angie, promising her I wouldn't be too long.

*

The front door of this little house opens straight into the village square. In front of me, at the opposite end of the square, the church, too big, I always thought, for a village this size. The air was still warm, the evening fully light, the last hints of sun fading away leaving long shadows. A small group of children were playing around the bus shelter, most of them on bikes, cycling between the parked cars. The church clock chimed eight as I strolled down the lane towards June's. I felt almost giddy with contentment. A tractor passed me from the opposite direction, the farmer waving at me enthusiastically. I could feel my shoulders relax as I breathed in the country air, the smell of freshly-cut grass drifting in on the breeze. I slowed down and listened to the silence. Somewhere, from within one of the houses, a peal of laughter; the rumble of the tractor fading into the distance; the children playing; a swallow whooshing overhead. How I'd become accustomed to silence when, for days on end, I lived in a world without sound, and how awful and oppressive it felt, the menace of the quiet. But not this, this was heaven-sent and I felt pathetically grateful for it. Nothing mattered to me now. I was twenty-three years old. I had my whole future to worry about but none of it mattered. I refused to be hurried, things would fall into place bit by bit. At this point, I had only the one task, a simple one but a difficult one... to deliver the ring.

*

I knocked on June's door. It opened and I was momentarily taken aback. Standing in front of me was a girl of about sixteen dressed in a swirling yellow dress with small red spots. For a moment, I thought I'd come to the wrong house but then I remembered – this was Abigail, June's daughter and only child. The last time I saw her she was still a little girl. Not now.

'Is that you, Abigail?'

'Yeah. Mum will be down in a minute.'

I nodded and waited on the doorstep, half expecting to be invited in. Instead we stood in awkward silence. 'Enjoying your summer holidays?'

'It's all right.'

'And erm, how's your father?'

Her eyes scanned the village square behind me. 'Yeah, he'll be back in a few days.'

Fortunately, the sound of footsteps coming down the stairs relieved of us both of further conversation. 'Robert, you look nice,' said June, appearing behind her daughter.

'And you, June, you look lovely.' She did – wearing an attractive mauve dress, her hair loose at her shoulders decorated with a yellow bow.

'Abigail, you could have asked Robert in, poor chap.' Abigail stepped back into the house and disappeared up the stairs. 'She's expecting Dan, her boyfriend,' said June in hushed tones.

'Dan? I don't remember a Dan.'

'From the next village. Walks with a limp. Shall we go then?'

As we walked the short distance to the pub, I asked about her husband.

'He's out in Italy. But he's got a week's leave – the first since he left some two years ago.'

'You haven't seen him in that long? You must be looking forward to his return.'

'Of course.' She leant towards me as we walked. 'I'm a little nervous about it, if truth be told. I've got so used to him not being around. Sounds awful, I know.'

I remembered Pete Parker all too well. I too wouldn't relish his return.

We reached the White Ship and I noticed how dark it was and how quiet it seemed from the outside. 'Is it open?' I asked.

'Why wouldn't it be? Come.' To my surprise, she took my hand. She pushed open the heavy doors. Following her in, I found the place to be in complete darkness. It was still light outside but someone had closed all the curtains. I knew what was coming next…

June, standing behind me, slid her arm round my waist and said, 'Welcome home, Robert.'

The noise of cheering and applause broke upon my senses. Lights came on, curtains drawn back, and there, in front of me, a gathering of smiling faces and raised glasses. Hanging high from the wall behind, a banner that read *Welcome home!!* I stood, open-mouthed. Although I may have anticipated this seconds before, I was still taken aback. June laughed out loud, 'Oh, Robert, your face.' Someone on the piano slammed down a couple of introductory chords then started playing *For He's a Jolly Good Fellow*. Everyone in the pub, it seemed, joined in while I stood there, abashed, but my heart brimming with pride.

'Get that down yer,' said Pearce, the village blacksmith, thrusting a pint of something in my hand.

As the music came to an end, Mr Jenkins stepped out of the crowd, offering his hand, beaming. 'Robert, dear man, on behalf of the village, I'd like to formally welcome you back home.'

My audience cheered and again raised their glasses. 'Aye, aye. Cheers,' came the shouts.

I lifted my glass and took a gulp. Ale. Foul stuff. 'Thank you, thank you, everyone. I'm touched, I really am; I'm quite lost for words.' All these people that had turned out for me, this gathering of villagers, many of whom I'd known for years without knowing them at all. I knew of course they weren't really here for me – I was simply an excuse. But I was touched nonetheless.

I'd been an infrequent visitor of the pub for years – low

ceiling, sturdy wooden beams painted black and decorated with a row of horse brasses, polished wooden floor, and a large oil painting of a black pot-bellied pig. Others came to say hello, shaking my hand, slapping me on the back, asking how I was, whether I'd settled back in. I felt quite overwhelmed as I acknowledged people's greetings and thanked them for their good wishes. Gradually, the crescendo faded, people returned to their seats and to their conversations. Jenkins beckoned June and me over to his table where he was sitting with Joe Hamilton and an old cove with a pipe, Bill Fraser, who was disappearing into his chair.

'So,' said Hamilton, 'what's it like to be back?'

'Wonderful.'

'Well, cheers, Robert,' said Jenkins. 'We're all glad to see you safe and sound.'

June raised her glass and smiled at me. 'We were worried for you, you know, when we heard that the *Academic* had gone down, we all thought, well, you can imagine…'

'It must have been terribly difficult,' said Jenkins.

'Yes. It was. Extremely.'

'Do you want to tell us about it?' asked Fraser, sucking on his pipe.

'Bill, really, that's not the sort of thing one can ask,' said Hamilton.

'Listen,' said Fraser, jabbing the table top, 'I'll be eighty-eight next birthday, so I can ask what I bloody well like.'

'You've only just turned eighty-seven—'

'Still.'

'It's a long story,' I said. 'Too long.' And not, I thought, for the likes of pub entertainment. It was my story and I knew that before I could move on, I would need to confront it, come to terms with it, to replay every ghastly detail and tonight was not the night to do it.

'You might get a medal,' said June.

'Just for surviving? I doubt it, I'm afraid.'

'Well, I'd give you a medal. Now, gents, if you'll excuse me…'

We all stood politely as June left us and joined another table. Still watching her, Fraser muttered, 'They say he's back soon enough.'

'You mean Pete Parker?' asked Jenkins.

'He's bad news, that one.'

'Yes. I remember him at school,' said Jenkins. The headmaster had been at the school for so long that he could lay claim at having taught virtually every villager under the age of thirty. I remembered Jenkins myself – his face continuously flushed, strands of his thinning red hair always out of place. When he came up close to, one could smell his breath. I still can't smell kippers without thinking of Jenkins. One of his more recent teachers was Joanna, and it was Joanna I was hoping to see. I asked Jenkins whether she was around.

'No, she left.'

'Oh.' I hadn't expected this. 'Do you know…'

'Nope. She just upped and left one day. Not a word. Didn't even have the decency to hand in her notice. The house is empty. Frightfully inconvenient. Luckily, I've found a new teacher before the term starts in September.'

In the background, the piano started up again, a raucous tune.

I caught a glimpse of June standing at a table a few feet

10

away. One of the seated men had his arm round her waist. She made no attempt to remove it. Hamilton started talking about the war in Russia and Jenkins interrupted with his views on Stalin. I only half paid attention.

'What do you think, Robert? Has Herr Hitler overstretched himself?'

'Sorry, it's a bit noisy in here. Is that Gregory on the piano?' Gregory Linden-Smith, an old friend of mine, a talent at the piano with a love for the classics – Beethoven, Liszt, Chopin, composers that were continually usurped by demands for *Roll Out the Barrel, Knees up, Mother Brown* and other pub favourites.

'That's Gregory, all right,' said Hamilton.

'Silly bugger,' growled Fraser. 'Tried to get into the army. They wouldn't have him, of course.'

Yes, I thought, that would figure. Poor stuttering Gregory, always trying to do what was best and invariably failing. Bright as a spark but very few were clever enough to realise it. To most, he just came across as a fool, the village idiot.

'We've organised a football match,' said Jenkins. 'The men of our village against another. For charity. Half of the proceeds will go towards restoring our church roof, the other half to them to do with as they like. I'm to be referee.'

'Men?' snorted Fraser. 'No men left, apart from the imbeciles.'

'Nonetheless, it's in a good cause. Now that you're back, Robert, perhaps you could play?'

'I doubt it. I don't think I'd be up to a football match.'

'Parker will be back in time, though, won't he?' asked Fraser.

'Yes,' said Jenkins. 'He'll be wanting to play, that's for sure.'

I heard my name being called. A group of men around a table beckoned me over. They'd got me another drink, they said. As long as they didn't ask me about my war, I thought.

*

Two or three hours later, I found myself staggering home with June. I was drunk and perfectly aware of the fact. Before leaving the White Ship, I'd made a point of thanking everyone, lurching from table to table like a demented fool, becoming more emotional with each 'thank you'. And now I was lumbering the short distance home, holding onto June for support.

'I never knew you could sing,' she said.

'Sing? Was I singing?'

She laughed. 'Of course you were, like a good 'un.'

'Good God, I was, wasn't I?'

'Oops, mind your step. Don't want you collapsing now, do we?'

'Where we going?'

'Back to yours, of course.'

After a couple of failed attempts at opening my front door, I had to give June the key. Angie came bounding over to me, her tail wagging. 'Good girl,' I said as she jumped up.

'Will you be all right?' asked June.

'Probably not. You'd better come in.'

She smiled knowingly. 'I think I'll leave you to it. I'm sure you'll be fine. Good night, Robert, and welcome home again.'

*

I staggered upstairs into the bedroom, and fell onto the bed. Eventually I managed to stir myself and get undressed and into my pyjamas. Lying on the bed, feeling nauseous, I stretched over, opened the drawer of the bedside table and found the ring. A simple ring, just a gold band. I twirled it round my palm. Simple but so important.

Part One

The Boat

Chapter 1

Karachi, India, Two Months Earlier

It is dark, but voices surround me. They sound faraway, as if from underwater. The words are but a blur yet distinctly female. I listen out for the noise of water lapping against the boat but, for once, I can't hear it. I open my eyes and expect to see the sky above me, expect to feel the torturous burning of the sun on my blackened skin. Instead, I see a ceiling, an actual man-made ceiling with a whirring fan. Flies buzz round. And then it comes back to me – I'm not on the boat any more. What, until recently, I thought would last forever, is no more; I was rescued. I am not on the boat. I repeat it several times in my mind, hoping the words will be a source of joy. They are not. I'm too tired for joy or indeed any emotion whatsoever. I feel nothing at all. I am not on the boat. Instead, I am on a bed. Oh, the luxury of lying on a bed, looking up at a ceiling, watching the blur of the fan blades whishing around. My fingers brush the sheets, lovely clean sheets. I feel my chin – the beard's gone. Someone has shaved me. I have no recollection of it happening. A face appears within my vision, a woman's face looming over me. She's young, a girl – dark complexion, long eyelashes. I hear her speak. 'Are you awake?' The words form in my mind – yes, I am awake, but the words don't come. The inside of my mouth feels as if it's been stuffed with cobwebs, my tongue a heavy pebble. I may have emitted a croak, I'm not sure. A second woman appears, older, a deeper voice. 'He's awake. Second Mate Searight,' she says much louder. 'You are alive. Welcome back.'

*

I slept so much in that first week or two in Karachi that the days merged into one. I sat in an office that looked out over the sand dunes and beyond that the sea; a large, spacious office, white walls, large windows, another ceiling fan, a set of bookshelves to one side, a portrait of the king. Outside, a lorry passed, a cloud of sand in its wake. Behind a desk in front of me were two men and a woman. The younger man, perhaps in his forties, was a medic, a doctor perhaps, wearing a cloak so white to be almost painful on the eye. The woman, an army private named Sophie Jones, sat to one side of her companions, her legs crossed, a notebook and pen poised in her hand. She was young, probably no more than twenty. The major, sitting in the middle, introduced himself as Bryant and the medic as Doctor Karr. I recognised the doctor from one of the many quacks that had stood next to my bed. I'd become a bit of a curiosity amongst the medical staff and indeed everyone in the camp. I could imagine the talk – *hey, come see our new patient. This is what you look like after two weeks on a lifeboat.*

On first sitting down on the chair placed in front of the desk, I complained apologetically that the chair was too hard. They understood – I still had no flesh on my buttocks. Private Jones fetched me a cushion and pointed to a glass of water on the desk. I thanked her. Major Bryant leant forward, his fingers steepled. He was a gaunt man, his eyes large, a red mark on the bridge of his nose. With his head cocked to one side, he asked how I was. I told him I was fine, that I was feeling much stronger. And it was true – the staff had been feeding me up slowly – bowls of watery soup replaced by thicker soup, then dishes of rice with little bits of chicken and vegetables. I savoured every mouthful. Never again will I take food for granted. But, I told the nurses, I didn't want any more chicken. In fact, I never wanted to eat meat again. I told them about my diet of pills and Doctor Karr confirmed my daily intake of vitamin and protein tablets. Private Jones took notes.

'By the way, Searight,' said Major Bryant, 'it says here your first name is George.'

'Yes, sir. But I've always preferred my middle name.'

He looked at me as if I was a circus oddity.

'We want you to tell us everything,' he said.

'It's a long story.'

'That's fine. We have all the time in the world. We need to know everything.'

'Everything, sir?'

'There were forty-two men on board the *Academic* plus a couple of Indian coolies – you were the only one to survive. It's important we establish the facts, as far as you can remember them, so we can account for the ship and the men that went down with her. We know you suffered a terrible ordeal so if you think you're not up to it yet…'

The three of them looked at me expectantly, waiting for my answer. Major Bryant may have offered me the option but somehow, having gathered together, I knew they would prefer not to wait. Anyway, I thought, there was no point in delaying it. I knew I had to tell the tale at some point, so I might as well get on with it. Who knows, perhaps at the end of it I would feel better.

'I think, sir, I'd rather tell you now.'

I felt the sigh of relief. 'Good. Well, there's water if you need it, and if you get tired as you go along, we can always take a break. Feel free to smoke.'

'I did smoke, sir, but with so long without I don't feel the need to any more.'

'Understandable. Right…' He glanced at his companions. The doctor nodded. 'So, these are the facts as we know them…' He picked up a sheet of paper, and reaching for a pair of spectacles began to read. 'The HMS *Academic* left Gibraltar on 11 May heading here, for Karachi, a distance of some six thousand miles, expected to take four weeks. You were hit by a torpedo fired from a German U-boat some nine hundred miles from land. Correct?' I nodded.

'And it says here that although you had a companion ship, the HMS *Heritage*, you were unescorted.'

'Yes, sir.'

'And you were transporting mules – six hundred of them.'

'Yes, odd as it sounds. They were destined for Burma to move supplies through the jungles there.'

Doctor Karr chortled. 'What was it like with six hundred mules on board?'

'Smelly and noisy.'

'I bet it was.'

Bryant turned the sheet of paper. 'So, the *Heritage*, which was carrying some five thousand tons of coal, had to turn back after two days because of... it says here jammed steering gears.'

'Yes, sir, it was unfortunate.'

'Unfortunate indeed. So you were out on the seas without any escort of any kind?'

'Yes, we'd been in that situation before, and it's not a pleasant experience. We knew we were sitting targets for any U-boat in the area, although we'd been assured that they were few and far between in that stretch of water. But of course, that's exactly what happened.'

'Yes, of course. And that's where I want you to start, Searight. What was exactly the sequence of events that allowed you to live while every one of your forty-one comrades perished?'

I looked at the three of them, Major Bryant with his eyes fixed hard on me, Doctor Karr, his arms stretched behind his head, and Private Jones, crossing and uncrossing her legs. A shout from outside distracted me. A group of soldiers were jogging along the sea front, a sergeant on a bicycle yelling at them. Two middle-aged women, arms linked, stepped aside to allow them to pass. 'I don't really know where to start, sir.'

'Just start at the beginning. What time of day was it? What was the weather like?'

'You want to know that much detail?'

He nodded. 'I think it's important. Don't you?

Chapter 2

Another Month Earlier

It was, I remember, the twenty-first day of our journey. The sky was clear and the Indian Ocean as still as a sheet of glass. Idyllic as it may sound, it was a cause for worry – the calm conditions were ideal for U-boats. As much as it was unpleasant to be working in foul weather, one at least felt safer from attack. It was seven in the evening and I had four hours off ahead of me. I'd had my dinner and retired to my cabin, which I shared with seven others. There was a porthole designed not to be opened, and the lack of fresh air, and the stench of sweat, unwashed bodies and damp and dirty clothes coated in seawater made for unpleasant living conditions. But for now my only companion was an Essex man by the name of Bernard Swann, a man mountain of a sailor. He was one of those men made for the sea. He'd been seafaring since the age of fifteen, following in the footsteps of his father and grandfather. A black bushy beard made him look much older than his twenty-eight years. I sat down on the edge of my bunk and sipped my tea, swirling it around in its tin mug.

'You can still bloody smell them, can't you?' remarked Swann, lying above me. 'Even in here.'

'You mean the mules? You'd think we'd have got used to it by now.'

The Indian authorities had given us two coolies to look after the mules, but watering, feeding and clearing up after six hundred of them was proving to be a full time occupation, and gradually the stench permeated every far-flung corner of the ship. We realised the expression 'stubborn as a mule' was not without foundation. The beasts had refused to step on the gangplank and onto the ship. The coolies thought they had the solution but no amount of carrots would tempt them across. And so we had to resort to manhandling them aboard. With a man on each side, we stretched a leather strap across their rumps and with much swearing and sweating in the blazing Gibraltar sun, and that was just from the mules, we physically dragged them aboard ship – virtually every one of the blasted animals. Then, with the help of a crane, came the bales of hay – tons of it. It took the whole day, leaving us exhausted but satisfied with our day's work.

I finished my tea and swung my legs onto the bunk. Above deck, port side, Clarence, my older brother, was due to finish his look-out duty, peering through the dusk with his binoculars, watching out for the slightest movement. Ours was a peculiar relationship when aboard ship. Clarence had signed up to the merchant navy as an officer, wanting to make a livelihood out of it. I, on the other hand, joined up only because of the war, forsaking my job at a bank in Plymouth, the nearest city; therefore I was as low as one could get in the pecking order. The consequence of this was that, on addressing him, I had to call my brother 'sir'. Although he tried not to show it, I think it rather pleased him.

Indeed, without so much as a knock on the door, he showed up. We didn't share the same cabin but he liked to call on me every so often. 'How goes it?' he asked breezily, shaking dry his water cape.

'About to have a shut-eye.'

'Don't you ever knock?' asked Swann.

'And what about some protocol round here? I'm 'sir' to you, Swann. Or had you forgotten?'

'I beg yours, sir.'

'All quiet out there?' I asked.

He took a seat on the single chair we had in the cabin. 'It would be if it wasn't for the captain's jittering. He's convinced it's only a matter of time.'

'He's right,' growled Swann. 'Perfect weather for a U-boat.'

'That's what he reckons. I say, Robert, haven't got a spare ciggie, have you?'

'Well…'

'Go on, man, just the one.'

Reluctantly, I gave him a cigarette from the pack I kept under my pillow. 'You're not going to smoke that in here, are you?' I asked.

'Don't worry, little brother, Father's not here to smell it on us. We can get away with it.'

We both had the image of the canning I got when, aged about eleven, my brother persuaded me to have a cigarette, then told on me. It was wintertime, raining hard. Sheltering in the coal shed, shivering, I smoked my first cigarette, feeling slightly sick throughout but determined not to let it show in front of my brother. Father, when he found out, was furious. He spanked me with the palm of his hand. It hurt not the slightest but the humiliation, knowing I'd been set up, caused me to cry. Clarence claimed Father had smelt it on me but I knew.

Swann cleared his throat. 'What he means, sir, is that your brother knows I can't abide fag smoke.'

Clarence hesitated. 'I'll save it for later,' he said, placing the cigarette behind his ear.

A few weeks after the cigarette episode, I tried to get my own back. Having caught Clarence smoking behind the elm tree at the end of our garden, I told Father. My attempt at revenge backfired – those who told tales, I was told, deserved a thrashing. I never tried again.

'Don't suppose you can smell the mules from where you are, can you, sir?'

'No, Swann, boatswain's aftershave sees to that.'

'Boatswain wears aftershave aboard ship?'

'I was joking, Robert, just a little joke.'

'Of course.'

'My brother was never any good at spotting a joke,' he said to Swann, who was still lying flat out on his bunk. 'Never particularly blessed with a sense of humour was my brother.'

Chapter 3

It came into view – a silver speck on the horizon. So far away, I couldn't tell at first what sort of plane it was, whether it was friend or foe. I radioed up to the bridge, informing the captain that something was heading our way. The word spread quickly. Soon Clarence was by my side. 'Here, let me take a look,' he said, grabbing the binoculars from my hand.

Untangling myself from the strap, I asked if it was one of ours.

He answered, not by addressing me, but by radioing upstairs. 'It's a Condor, Captain.'

The news may have been alarming but I knew he still felt a shiver of satisfaction at being the first to spot it. I saw the crestfallen look on his face as the captain bellowed back down the line, 'We've worked that out for ourselves, Searight, thanks all the same.'

We watched it as it came towards us, yet the nearer it got, the higher it flew. 'That's a Condor, then?' I asked.

'Yeah, a Focke-Wulf Condor.'

26

Soon, it was directly above us, circling like a real-life condor, a bird of prey eyeing its next victim. 'I don't understand, why aren't we firing at it, and why is it not attacking us?'

I feared a scathing response. Without taking his eyes from the binoculars, he said, 'It's out of our range and he knows that. They carry bombs but he's unlikely to hit us from that height.'

'So, what's he doing then?'

'The blighter's reporting our position, that's what he's doing.' Finally, taking his eyes off the plane, he turned to me. Placing a heavy hand on my shoulder, he said, 'He's telling his mates in the U-boats exactly where we are. We're buggered, we really are. Out here alone, unescorted, and whose bright idea was that, on a ship with a single gun that's as much use as a peashooter. We're being hunted and we don't stand a chance. Not a chance.'

*

The hours that followed were torturous. Everywhere I went I saw my own worried expression reflected back to me. The captain first doubled, then trebled, the number of men on lookout at any one time. I took turns with a man who, apart from my brother, was my only link to my previous life. Owen Gardner and I were almost neighbours, both residents of the same village. Unlike me, a relative newcomer and an outsider, Owen had been brought up in the village – man and boy. 'Imagine we were back at home,' he said, 'sitting in front of the fire at the Ship right now with a pint each in our hands.'

We didn't look at each other – we had to keep our eyes to the binoculars constantly.

'It seems a thousand miles away, doesn't it?'

'It probably is.'

We scanned the water near and far, looking out for a conning tower of a submarine, the telltale 'feather' in the wake of a periscope, or the spray generated by an incoming torpedo. Owen, a handsome chap with enviable blond hair, was married to an attractive, older woman called Joanna, a German, who, one day, simply appeared in the village as Owen's wife. No one had known he'd even had a girlfriend, but they seemed well matched, quite the most attractive couple in the village.

When not on lookout, there was little else to do. I wandered the decks preferring to be outside than cooped up inside. The few times I did venture down, I rearranged my few belongings in my locker. I wrote a letter to my parents. I told them everything was fine, how we were making good progress and how we were due in Karachi in just over a week. This much was true; I didn't say that none of us had any great expectation of making it. I told them Clarence was doing well, how the men respected him and the senior officers valued him; I told them about the mules, and how much I enjoyed our stay in Gibraltar and how lovely the weather was there. I told them about life on the ship.

Clarence sought me out numerous times – asking me how I was. We even had dinner together. The lounge area was almost deserted. Everyone seemed to have lost their appetites. We picked at our meal consisting of some form of meat and mashed potatoes. 'It's like a last supper,' he declared. 'Take, eat; this is my body, which is given for you. At least the tea's strong.'

'Drink – in remembrance of me. So, what's the news

from the bridge? They must be expecting something.'

'Nope. Captain radioed through for assistance. They won't be able to get anything to us for at least two days, so they're not bothering.'

'Nothing at all?'

He shook his head while considering a forkful of meat. 'They're leaving us to our fate. Us and the mules.'

'But it's been twelve hours since we saw the plane. Wouldn't they have attacked by now?'

'Perhaps they don't have anything in the vicinity either. But those U-boats can speed along once on the surface. It's only when they're submerged do they slow down. They won't be able to resist an easy kill. They'll send something, mark my words. What *is* this meat?'

'I think it's pork.'

'I reckon it's mule. Either way, it's foul.'

'No, it's not fowl.' I sniggered at my joke.

'Very funny. So, still happy you joined up?' he asked.

'Are you?'

'I remember as a kid during the summer holidays, going into Plymouth with Father. He'd go off to some meeting and leave me to wander round Devonport. You were at home with Mum, I suppose. I loved it. I used to gaze at the ships wondering where they'd been, where they were going to. I'd see the sailors and envy their adventures and their travels. I used to love that smell, you know. That's when I knew I wanted to be on the sea. Father thought it a good idea. He was an army man, as you know.'

'He's never talked about it.'

'I used to ask him about the war but he said you couldn't ask questions like that. He said men like him saw things that no man can put into words. He said no generation should have to experience that again.'

I stirred an extra spoonful of sugar into my tea. 'Uncle Guy was there too.'

'Yeah. I used to think he was such a poor blighter, losing his leg in the war. Now I think he got away lightly.'

'Couldn't have been easy though.'

'No, but, you know, there's a lot of men worse off than him.'

'He's another who never speaks about the war.'

'I know. He wasn't keen on us joining the merchants. The thought of his nephews being out at sea gave him the jitters. I can see why now.'

'Yes.'

'Listen, Robert, I wanted to say…'

We were distracted by the appearance of Swann. 'You chaps all alone?'

I never did get to hear what my brother wanted to say.

Chapter 4

No one saw it. No warning was heard. Clarence, Swann and I had returned to my cabin to fetch my cigarettes. Not due for lookout for another hour, Swann said he was going to have a kip. We may have been expecting it, but when it came it was a shocking moment. The ship roared. I felt myself being lifted off my feet by the blast. I fell back in a heap as the ship screeched and rocked. The intensity of noise filled my ears. The alarms sounded, the lights flickered on and off. I found myself against the cabin wall beneath the washbasin, my nostrils filled by the stench of cordite. We heard distant shouts and screams. Scrambling to my feet, I helped Clarence get up. 'Shit,' screamed Swann. 'They've gone done it.' The ship surged again, as if climbing out of the water as she took another hit.

'Lifejackets,' ordered Clarence.

With our lifejackets secured, we opened the cabin door, only to be forced back by a cloud of thick, black smoke. Swann ripped off three pillowcases, handing them to us to cover our noses. With our eyes streaming, we grappled our way along the corridor, falling against the right-hand wall. Turning a corner, we reached the bottom of the stairway, the only exit to the open deck, to be confronted by a sheet of flame like a curtain. Sweat poured off me; smoke suffocated me. We glanced at each other, the panic written on our faces. Swann was the first – taking a few steps back, he ran and propelled himself through the fire, landing on the bottom rungs of the steps. I saw his feet disappear up the rungs. Panicked voices came from above. Holding my breath, I did the same, my skin burning up as I leapt through the flames. Brushing the sparks from my uniform, I shouted at Clarence. 'Hurry up, for God's sake.' The steps beneath me were turning red, burning through the rubber on the soles of my shoes.

Pacing frantically, Clarence was screaming. 'I can't... I can't do it.'

'Clarence, please...' I jumped back down and felt the heat lashing at my face, the smoke on my throat.

I felt myself being pulled up the steps by my arm. It was Swann. 'You'll fry. Come on.' I fought him off. 'Clarence...'

Clutching his neck, choking, Clarence fell to his knees as the flames whipped above him, melting the ceiling.

Swann was too strong for me, pulling me up the steps by my arms and the lifejacket. 'I can't leave him, I can't leave him,' I screamed.

We reached the deck. My lungs breathed in the air. Everywhere, men were running, shouting, punctuated by the hissing sound of escaping steam. Pushed aside, I fell to my feet, coughing violently. Looking up, I saw three of the fire crew, lugging the fire hose. Hope momentarily filled me as I got to my feet. But the hose fell limp in their hands. 'Steam pressure's gone,' shouted one, as the last drips of water fell. The corridor below exploded in a ball of flame. We staggered back. 'Clarence,' I screamed. 'No!'

The chief officer, a man by the name of Hodgkin, came rushing down the deck, shouting, 'Abandon ship! Captain's orders – abandon ship!'

'Can't we save her?' shouted Swann.

'Hole's too big. It's beyond plugging.'

'What about the lifeboats?'

'Starboard ones are knackered. Go to port.' As he said it, the ship lunged to the right. We fell back against the railings. Peering over the side, my heart lurched on seeing the sea lapping within three or four feet of the deck. There were already men in the sea, their lifejackets keeping them afloat.

The ship, listing heavily to starboard, was ablaze with fire; smoke swirling up. Voices shouted from everywhere, along with a strange strangulated noise, getting louder and louder. 'The mules!' I shouted.

I saw a man consumed in flames, staggering, screeching, his arms flailing. Someone pushed him overboard.

Swann and I, with the fire crew, followed Hodgkin, his figure engulfed in smoke, as he headed towards the portside lifeboats. Slipping with almost every step, I felt as if we were climbing a hill covered in a sheet of ice. I could hear Hodgkin shouting – 'Abandon ship! Captain's orders – abandon ship!'

Passing one of the hatchways, Swann and I heard shouting coming from the storage accommodation below. On peering down the hatch, we saw that the ladder had been badly buckled. 'Help me; I can't get out,' came an echoing voice from within. Swann took the rope hanging on a peg under the hatch and, on securing it, shimmied down. I followed. The place was almost in darkness, most of the lights having blown. We landed in about three feet of water. Bits of wood and flotsam littered the surface. The place was used to store lorries – dozens of them. Despite the size, it felt claustrophobic with its low ceiling. 'Here, over here,' someone shouted. A body, face down in the water, floated by, his shirt billowing on his back. The lorries had tumbled over each other, resembling a massive road crash, windows broken, twisted metal. We followed the voice, Swann in front, wading through the water, going down the incline, the water getting deeper.

We found the man, his face too much in the dark to see. 'I'm stuck,' he croaked. The water here was up to our chests.

'Is that you, Smithy?'

'Yeah. Bloody lorry's got me pinned.' He'd been jammed against the metal wall by the front of a lorry, its hood open. I didn't know the man but guessed he was one of the mechanics. 'I think me leg's broke.'

'Hold on,' said Swann. 'We'll get you out. Searight, I'll shift the lorry; you pull Smithy free.'

Swann shouldered the lorry and pushed. I took Smithy by the armpits bracing myself, feeling his breath on my skin. 'Hold on now,' I said to him. 'If anyone can move it, Swann can. Built like an ox.'

'I can't shift it,' yelled Swann.

'Just get it off me.'

Swann tried again, screaming as he pushed his full weight against the cab. I joined him. But even together, straining every muscle, we couldn't budge it. 'Sorry, mate,' said Swann, breathlessly.

'No, don't leave me, don't leave me, please.'

Swann looked at me. I saw him glance at the shaft of light coming from the open hatch. We could hear men on deck cursing at not being able to free one of the lifeboats. Smithy reached for my hand. His grip was surprisingly strong. 'You can't leave me here to die.'

Swann tried again – a last frantic attempt at shifting the weight of the lorry from Smithy's legs, even if only for a moment. He reeled back, his chest heaving, his whole body deflated. Stepping through the water, he said, 'I tried, mate, I'm sorry. Come on, Searight.'

'We can't leave him here.'

'Then we'll all die.'

We heard a shout. 'Anyone down here?' came the voice from the hatch.

'Aye!' shouted Swann.

'Get the hell out of there. She's going down any minute. Only one lifeboat left.'

Swann didn't need a second invitation. The ship suddenly lurched, the sound of screeching metal echoing through the accommodation as we were pushed back by a gush of water. Bouncing off the wall like a tide, the water was now at our chests. I saw Swann resurface from the water, shaking the filthy water from his hair.

'No, no,' cried Smithy, gripping my hand. A light above flickered on. His eyes glared at me, full of fear, his face black with dirt. Blood poured from his nose.

'Smithy, I can't... I can't.'

The light dimmed then went dark. Thank God, I thought. I couldn't have left him while I could see his eyes. I tried to pull my hand free but he wouldn't let go. Fear seized my chest. He meant me to die with him. 'Please, Smithy, let go.'

Swann had reached the rope. 'S'aright, Robert, you can't do anything for him,' he shouted back as a pair of hands reached down to help him up.

'Let go of me, Smithy. We tried, yeah?'

'You ain't leaving me.'

Swann was on the deck. Peering back down, he shouted my name again.

I'd never hit a man before, but with my right hand, I punched Smithy in the side of the face. It wasn't hard but, taken by surprise, he loosened his grip just enough. Wrenching my hand free, I fell again into the water. Buoyed by my lifejacket, I quickly found my feet. Unable to look back, I splashed through the water, climbing up the incline, pushing away wood and debris. 'Wait for me,' I shouted, desperate to get out.

'Don't leave me, you bastard, please… please, don't… don't…' Smithy's voice died away within his sobs. 'Don't leave me.'

I reached the rope, tears coursing down my cheeks. 'I'm sorry,' I muttered again and again. 'I'm sorry.' I pulled myself up on the rope, my training kicking in. Swann grabbed my wrists. 'Come on, mate, you can do it.' The ladder, though buckled, still provided support for my feet. With a final heave, Swann pulled me up out of the hatch onto the deck, now under water. He pushed me against the wall of the ship, as everywhere mules stampeded around us.

I could still hear Smithy's voice from below. 'You bastards, you…'

The mules, all of them panicked, ran into each other,

braying wildly, trampling over the dead bodies beneath their hooves.

'All the boats are gone,' shouted Swann, punching a mule away. 'We're gonna have to jump.'

'We need to get higher.'

Together, gripping onto the railings, we climbed our way up the ship as the bow sunk further into the sea. A mule, making a horrendous guttural noise, slid pass us, its ears pinned back. Others fell into the sea, their legs flailing almost comically in the air. We stepped over a sailor clutching onto his stump, his leg clean off at the knee, the other wrapped round the rails. Too much in pain, he didn't notice us as we jumped over him.

The ship seemed to be groaning as its metal strained under the pressure of breaking up. Further ahead, we could see the stern ablaze, black smoke blocking out the sun. The creaking noise of the ship intensified. It was time.

We stopped. Swann checked the fastenings on his lifejacket. I did the same. 'Bloody light's not working. Nor's yours.'

He was right; I hadn't noticed. The red lights attached on the lifejackets were notoriously unreliable.

Looking at the sea, I realised it was awash with mules – hundreds of them, swimming frantically in circles. Swann offered me his hand, as if he was inviting me to dance. Taking it, I almost laughed. We had no room for a run up. Slipping towards us along the deck, another couple of mules, making a frightful noise.

'Ready?'

I nodded.

Holding our noses, we climbed up the railing and jumped. The twenty feet felt like a thousand. I hit the water and the jolt of cold ripped through me like a sword of ice. Losing contact with Swann, I sunk further, the cold squeezing my insides. I kept falling, unable to do anything about it. I felt the pressure on my head and in my ears, within my lungs.

Finally, the lifejacket propelled me back up. I ascended at what felt like great speed, breaking the surface. I gulped in air, before being seized by a choking fit. I'd swallowed goodness knows how much oily water. All round me were mules and flotsam, chunks of wood and wreckage. I reached out for what looked like a door, pulling myself up on it. The waves rolled dramatically. Under a black sky, the ship made for a pitiful sight, bellowing smoke. The sea had already claimed two thirds of it; only the stern remained above sea level. I was still too close; I'd be sucked down as the ship went. Kicking my legs, I turned my door and swam with the current to get away. I cursed the failing lifejacket light. I heard a few shouts from somewhere, men crying for help, but couldn't tell whether the voices were far or near. I called out Swann's name. 'Over here,' came the reply, but from where, I had no idea. The number of mules seemed to be increasing – bumping into each other, frantically swimming in circles.

With a final, angry groan, like a wounded animal, and with much hissing of steam and air as the red hot vessel came in touch with the sea, the ship slipped beneath the waves. And then it was gone. And with it, my brother, my poor brother. May you rest in peace, Clarence, I said to myself, may you rest in peace. An eerie silence filled the air as the toiling sea settled and the bubbles disappeared. Without the presence of the ship, I felt more vulnerable and more keenly than ever the desperate situation I was in.

The evening sky seemed so vast and unending, the sea so unforgiving.

Someone somewhere shouted 'Sub'. Looking round, my heart lurched on seeing that the U-boat had emerged, a gigantic silver beast. A number of officers with binoculars appeared on the conning tower platform. Nearby, two men manned the machine gun, swinging it round to face us. Panic seized me – surely they wouldn't gun us down in the water? With a shouted order from the German captain, the machine guns let rip with a terrifying clatter. Inert, my eyes glazed over. I thought of my mother – losing both sons at sea. Bullets whistled all about, blood spurted, the air filled with the sound of agonized, high-pitched braying. The water round me swirled as mules, panicked by the noise, floundered in the water. And still the machine gun continued. Then it stopped as suddenly as it had started. The Germans retreated back inside the U-boat. Moments later, the submarine moved off, slowly gliding beneath the waves. And then it was gone, leaving us to our fate. All that remained was a chorus of whimpering as the last mules died.

I knew, as the others must have, that I wouldn't survive long in these waters. I had to find a lifeboat or a raft. The chances of being picked up here were so slim to be almost non-existent. The thought galvanized me into shouting out for help, hailing for all my worth. Nothing in return. Just the cries of men in the same predicament as me.

The minutes turned to an hour and more. Dead mules floated by. The waves settled. The smoke had finally cleared but night had fallen. The cries of help around me came less and less. I knew I was weakening; I had no more strength to shout for help. I could no longer feel my legs. I wanted to sleep, to slip away.

I don't know how long I floated on my wooden door but then came a cry that was music to my ears – men on a lifeboat calling out for survivors. 'Here, here!' I screamed back. The dark outline of the boat came into view. I waved and shouted, frantically kicking my legs to reach it.

'There's one!' said someone on the lifeboat. I was getting nearer but the effort was taking every ounce of my strength. The thought of being saved was enough to propel me towards them. Hands reached out for me. 'You swimming all the way home, mate? Come on, you're almost there. Keep going.'

A hand stretched down and clasped mine. A second hand took me by the wrist. I felt myself being dragged away from my door and hauled into the boat. It wasn't easy for them – my lifejacket and clothes were so greasy from all the oil on the water. Eventually, pulled onto the boat, I collapsed.

Oh, the joy of being on that boat. I thanked my rescuers but my eyes, clouded by seawater, were unable to focus. I reached over the side and vomited the oil and seawater out of my system. Someone patted me brusquely on the back. Numerous splinters from the wooden door pricked my fingers. My shoes and socks had gone – sucked off and washed away. But I didn't care, none of it mattered – I was out of the water; I'd been saved.

Of course, at that point, I wasn't to know that my ordeal had barely begun.

Chapter 5

The Boat: Day One

I woke up, my back stiff as hell. It took a moment before remembering where I was. I was sitting in a boat, my bare feet swishing in bilge water. The sea, vivid blue, was calm, the sun rising. In any other circumstances, one might describe it as idyllic. I stretched. I looked around at my fellow occupants in the boat – Swann, I was relieved to see, had also made it. He and I sat together at the back of the boat, blankets round our shoulders, Swann pulling on his beard. To my even greater delight, I spied a mop of blond hair and saw my friend, Owen Gardner. We acknowledged each other from opposite ends of the boat. There were six others, their lifejackets strewn around. The most senior, sitting at the bow of the boat, was Chief Officer Miles Hodgkin, a man in his late twenties but with the impression of someone three times his age. The others were calling him captain, having decided to unofficially promote him. With their backs to me, on either side of the boat, sat Seamen Edward Davison and Leo Arbatov, a

41

Russian by birth, each holding an oar. I noticed the swirl of hair round Davison's bald patch. One of the stewards, Charlie Palmer, was urinating over the side. Looking round, I noticed the boatswain, a chap called Harris Beckett, a short, muscular man with a thin moustache and a tattoo of a scantily-dressed, large-chested female on his right upper arm. He was, I noticed, eyeing me with almost a look of loathing. Averting my gaze, I wondered whether I had read his expression correctly and, if so, what had I done to earn such a look. Next to Beckett, his eyes cast down, was, I reckoned, the youngest man on board, a boy of no more than eighteen, John Clair – jet black hair, tall, lanky and awkward, as only teenagers can be. Clair leant against Beckett who, with a hefty shrug, pushed him off. Palmer, having relieved himself, was now scanning the waters with a pair of binoculars. 'Any more, Palmer?' asked Hodgkin.

'Don't look like it, Captain. I reckon they've all swam back to England by now.' Palmer had a way of speaking quickly, as if concerned he might forget what he wanted to say.

'Very funny, Palmer.'

On seeing me awake, Hodgkin bid me good morning. 'You managed to sleep the whole night through – rather impressive, I thought. So, I think you were the last, Searight, you and Swann.'

'So how many men went down?' asked Swann.

'Thirty-three,' said Hodgkin. 'Plus the two coolies.'

'May they rest in peace,' said Davison, crossing himself.

'Yes, indeed,' said Hodgkin.

'Thirty-five men and six hundred or so mules,' said Swann.

'Yes, Arbatov here made a point of freeing them, although to what purpose beats me.'

'Just seemed like the decent thing to do,' said Arbatov in his deep Russian voice.

'A lot of them were shot,' I told them.

'Shot?'

I related the tale of the Germans and their machine gun.

'No, that is terrible. Poor beasts,' said Arbatov, shaking his head.

'So the Krauts were being merciful then,' said Owen.

'Krauts – merciful? No, no, no,' said Arbatov, slicing the air with his hands. 'No such thing as a merciful German. No, they want target practice.'

'Well, their mercy didn't extend to picking us up,' I said. 'They simply left us to drown.'

Hodgkin scoffed. 'Thank your lucky stars, I'd say, Searight. You'd be a prisoner of war by now.'

'Yeah, but he'd be nice and cosy, wouldn't he, sir? said Palmer. '*Schön und gemütlich*,' he added in a shrill German accent.

'I say, you speak German, Palmer?'

'*Ein bisschen.*'

'What?'

'I said a little bit.'

'Hmm. Could prove handy that.'

'No, we speak with no German,' said Arbatov. 'We see a German, we kill him.'

'And with what, you stupid Russian git?' This Beckett, who until now, like John Clair, had said nothing. 'You'll bite them to death, will you?'

'I would die trying, Mr Beckett. And for your

information, I am not Russian. I am as English as you are.'

'With that accent, Comrade Arbatov? What sort of name is that? Anyways, I'm Welsh, me,' said Beckett, jabbing his chest with his thumb. 'And don't you be forgetting it.'

Hodgkin cleared his throat. 'Yes, thank you, Beckett. Calm down now.'

'What happened to the other lifeboats?' asked Swann.

'The two starboard ones copped it with the explosions,' said Hodgkin. 'The other one on port couldn't be freed in time – the davits had been wrenched. And this one… well, the mast is shattered.'

'So all we have are the oars?' I asked.

'Afraid so.'

'Too bad,' said Arbatov.

We fell silent for a while. I gazed round and a feeling of despair rose in my chest. Here we were, the nine of us in a tiny boat, some twenty-five feet long, eight feet at its widest, designed perhaps for twenty-five people, surrounded by sea. Sea, sea, sea, as far as the eye could see, and here we were in the middle of it, a speck, a tiny, insignificant little speck. The sun was rising and with it the heat. I closed my eyes and breathed heavily, trying to shake off the feeling of utter vulnerability.

My thoughts were interrupted by John Clair, rising clumsily to his feet. 'Are we almost there yet?' he asked, his voice as soft as a nervous child. He looked at us all, but without really seeing us.

'Get a grip, you silly beggar, said Beckett. 'Bloody sit down and stop leaning on me.'

Davison stretched out his hand. 'Leave him be, Beckett. You can see the poor boy's in a state of shock. He needs our help, not to be shouted at.' Davison, I knew, was a kind man. His cheeks always flushed, the end of his nose always red, men called him the Beacon behind his back. 'No, John, I'm afraid we're not almost there. But don't you worry, someone will come by shortly and pick us up, I'm sure.'

'I'm hungry, Ed. Really hungry.'

'I know, John. We all are.'

'Yeah, we're all hungry,' said Beckett. 'So, what about the rations now, Captain?' Turning to me and Swann, he said with a scowl, 'I suppose you two will be wanting your share.'

'Not surprising, is it, Beckett?' snapped Swann.

'OK, OK, enough now,' said Hodgkin. He stepped over a couple of benches and sat down. 'I've been giving this some thought. It's fair to say, gentlemen, we are in a tight spot–'

Beckett guffawed. 'You don't say.'

'Let the man finish,' said Palmer.

'Weren't you able to send an SOS from the ship?' asked Swann.

'Ha, no, 'fraid not. The radio was caught in the explosion. But don't worry, Swann, the captain sent a message beforehand, after we'd been spotted by the Condor, so Karachi will know we were in trouble and I'm sure they'll send something. We're in somewhat a precarious situation but it could be a lot worse.'

'Worse things happen at sea, sir.'

'Shut it, Palmer,' barked Beckett.

'Now, the natural instinct is to try for land – but we're a good nine hundred miles from India's southern tip, and even as fit men, that could take us over a month. And we simply do not have the rations to last us that long. Alternatively, we're on a well-used path here, and a convoy is bound to pass by eventually, that is if a search and rescue doesn't find us first. It's just a matter of how long. We put it to a vote last night, and we've decided to stay here in the vicinity of the sinking.'

'Don't we get a say?' asked Swann, jerking his thumb at me.

'We voted five to two, so it wouldn't have made any difference.'

'Something will come along soon, won't it, Captain?' asked Clair.

Hodgkin tried to smile. 'I've no doubt about it, John.'

Arbatov put his hand up. 'Can we have breakfast now?'

'Good idea,' said Palmer, rubbing his hands. 'Bacon and egg for me, Captain. Black pudding too, if you've got it.'

'And a strong cup of tea, no sugar,' added Owen.

'Yes, yes, very droll,' said Hodgkin. 'Right, these boats come with rations but they don't amount to much, I'm afraid. Some of it must be missing; I can't believe they'd supply so little. Anyway, I've taken stock, given that we now have two more men on board—'

'Lucky us,' said Beckett.

Swann glared at him but held his tongue.

'I've divided it up by seven days. We have, per person, per day...' He counted off the items on his fingers. 'A biscuit each, a couple of malted milk tablets, a tin of bully beef—'

'Each?' cried Swann.

'Ah, no such luck, Swann, between the nine of us. Also a mouthful of pemmican.'

'What's that when it's at home?' asked Palmer.

'Come on, Palmer, you know what pemmican is – it's dry meat paste, and very nutritious too, or so I'm told.'

'What sort of meat is it?' asked Owen.

'I don't know. Beef, I think.'

'Does that suit, Gardner?' asked Beckett. 'Because if you're not partial to beef–'

'He was only asking,' said Arbatov.

Hodgkin coughed. 'If I may continue. The real concern, of course, is water. We have six bottles of fresh water. If it's to last a whole week, we have to limit ourselves to one teaspoon in the morning and one at night, around dusk. That's about two ounces a day each. And no more.'

Swann groaned.

'Do we have a teaspoon?' I asked.

'We do indeed, Searight, and even a tin opener, would you believe? The navy authorities think of everything. We also have a basic medical kit and a flare gun with five flares. We even have a bucket.'

'To shit in?' asked Arbatov.

'I think it's more for bailing the water out.'

'Did they supply any fags?' asked Swann.

'I've got some fags,' said Palmer.

'You do?'

'Here…' He reached into his back pocket and produced a sodden pack of cigarettes.

'You bloody idiot. Why do keep them?'

'As a reminder of happier days, Swann. Happier days.'

'Tobacco is not a concern,' said Hodgkin. 'Water is my main concern.'

'No, wait, Captain,' said Clair. 'I've got my bottle. I

grabbed it at the last minute.'

'Good man,' said Davison.

Clair rummaged beneath the bench. 'It's here somewhere, I know it is. Here it is, here it is.' He held it up as if it was a trophy.

'Good lad,' said Hodgkin. 'Pass it here then.'

Clair's expression changed in an instant. 'No, it's mine,' he said, hugging the bottle to his chest.

'Hey, come on, boy,' growled Beckett. 'You pass that over.'

'No, you should have brought your own,' said Clair, turning away and hunching his body over the bottle.

Hodgkin stood up, causing the boat to sway a little. 'Now, you give that bottle to me, and that's an order, Seaman Clair.'

Davison patted the boy's arm. 'We're all in this together, John. If we're to survive, we have to share. You know that.'

'He's right,' said Palmer. 'We're all in the same boat.' He laughed at his own joke. 'In the same boat. Get it?'

'Shut up, Palmer,' said Swann.

Clair looked back at Davison from beneath his black fringe.

'Come on, John, pass me the bottle.'

Without taking his eyes off Davison, Clair passed him the bottle.

'Good lad. Now, let's just check to see if it's OK.' He unscrewed the lid and smelt its contents. 'Oh dear,' he said.

'What's the matter?' asked Owen.

Holding the bottle at an angle, he dipped his finger inside and sucked it. He shook his head. 'False hope, alas.

The sea's got in. It's salty.'

We all groaned. 'Idiot,' murmured Abatov.

'It wasn't his fault,' said Davison.

'No, it's fresh,' cried Clair. 'It's got to be. It's mine.'

'I'm sorry, John,' said Davison.

Clair gripped Davison's wrist. 'But we can still drink it, right, Ed? It'll still be OK.'

'You bloody fool,' barked Beckett. 'You drink seawater, you'll go mad.'

'If he's not already,' added Swann, tapping his temple.

Clair slumped.

'Well, back to where we were, gentlemen,' said Hodgkin. 'One teaspoon each by morning, one at dusk. And that's an order.' He sat back down. 'Lastly, I've devised a look-out rota. Two men at a time, one hour shifts. Gardner – it's you on the port and stern, and Searight, you can take your turn on the opposite side.'

Owen saluted. 'Aye, aye, Captain.'

'But first, let's have this morning's water ration.'

We formed an orderly queue with Swann and me, as the relative newcomers on board, at the back. Hodgkin gave us each a teaspoon of water, cupping a hand beneath the spoon, feeding it to us as if we were children. We all watched intently, making sure that no one got more than their fair share. It was only now I realised quite how thirsty I was. I swallowed slowly, enjoying the feeling of the water on the back of my throat. Hodgkin gave himself his share last.

I made my way to the front of the boat, swaying, stepping round the men. The boat had six benches and two more along the sides. Beneath the front bench, where Hodgkin took his place, was a little hold where he kept the rations and a box of first aid. As I passed, I noticed that Davison had his arm round Clair's shoulders. The boy was quietly crying on Davison's chest.

Chapter 6

The Boat: Day Two

I awoke on my second day on the boat some time around midday with the sun at its highest. It took me a few seconds to register. I was sitting on a bench, drifting in and out of sleep, wishing the sun would disappear, when I saw far away a dark shape on the horizon. Slowly, I rose to my feet, trying to work out whether I was imagining it or whether there really was a ship. 'I think… I can see a ship.'

The effect of my words was immediate. Everyone sprung up, shaking off their lethargy. 'Bleeding hell, he's right, there is as well,' said Palmer.

We all erupted into a state of excitement, shouting, waving our arms, rocking the boat. It was Beckett that told us to calm down. 'You fools, it won't see us from that distance. Or hear us'

'What direction is it going in?' asked Arbatov.

'Hard to tell from here,' said Davison.

'Impossible, I'd say,' said Swann. 'Too far to row

anyway.'

'Palmer,' shouted Hodgkin, 'pass me the flare gun.'

With his hands trembling, Hodgkin inserted a flare into the gun.

'Shouldn't we wait, Captain?' asked Owen. 'Until it gets closer.'

'And what if it's going the opposite direction, eh, Gardner? We can't afford to lose sight of her. Right, here goes.' The flare shot up, fizzing. We watched its trajectory intently as it arched into the sky. The red light it gave off seemed so inadequate against the vivid blue and in the full glare of the sun. We watched it as it descended, leaving a trail of smoke and light in its wake.

'They're never going to see that,' muttered Beckett.

'It only takes one man to be looking in the right direction,' said Davison. 'We just have to hope.'

'How many flares we got left now, Captain,' I asked.

'We've still got four. Still plenty.'

We all stood in silence, watching the ship, hoping, just hoping to God that it would give us a sign that it had seen us, that rescue would soon be upon us. The minutes ticked by. Nothing happened. Swann was the first to sit down.

'It hasn't seen us, has it, Captain?' said Owen.

'I fear not.'

'How about another flare?'

He shook his head. 'Too risky.'

'No, it might be our only chance,' said Swann. 'What's there to lose?'

'Quite a lot, I would've thought,' said Palmer.

'It's going away from us,' said Arbatov.

'I think you're right,' said Hodgkin.

'Shit, shit,' said Beckett.

One by one, we sat back down, each of us filled with utter disappointment. To think our salvation lay just a few miles from us, a ship full of healthy men with plenty to eat and drink, men able to turn in and sleep on a comfortable bunk. And none of them, not one of them, realised that within reach was a little boat with nine very desperate men.

Davison checked on John Clair. 'Was there a ship?' asked the boy.

'Yes, but it didn't see us, more's the pity.'

'There might be another.'

'Yes.' He patted Clair on the shoulder. 'That's right, John. There's bound to be. We just have to wait.'

*

'Are you married, Captain?' No one had spoken for hours. Davison's question came out of the blue.

'Yes, Ed, I'm married. Two years now. In fact, my wife is pregnant. Our first.'

'Congratulations, sir.'

Hodgkin laughed. 'Thank you, Ed. Yep, baby's due... well, any day now, I guess.' He sighed. 'It's killing me. Being stuck out here while on the other side of the world my child is being born. I'd promised her, my wife I mean, I'd get home as soon as I could. Doesn't look like I'm going to get home anytime soon, though, does it?'

'Course you will. Just think – going home to see your new-born baby. What are you hoping for? Boy or girl?'

'I don't mind really.' He tried to smile. 'I think a girl. If it's a boy, well, there's always the chance he might have to go fight, like we've all had to do. I wouldn't wish this on my worst enemy. A girl at least would be spared. I'd like to call her Alice.'

'Alice?' I sat up on hearing the familiar name. 'No, don't call her that.'

'Why not? It's a lovely name.'

'No, anything but that.'

'I'll call her what I like, thank you, Searight. It's none of your damn business.'

'Alice – that name belongs to someone else.'

Owen patted my arm. 'It's all right, Robert, calm down.'

'He can't call her that, Owen. It's not right.'

'It's just a name, Robert; just a name.'

Alice. Just a name, I repeated. Oh, Alice, where are you, my love? Where are you? I feel so empty without you. Come back to me; I miss you so much; so very much.

Davison cleared his throat. 'Well, whatever name you decide, Captain, I'm sure she'll be beautiful, and that you'll all be very happy.'

'And what about you, Ed; are you married?'

'Me? No, no, not me.'

'Not met the right woman yet?'

Davison guffawed. 'No, not that. I'm just not the marrying kind. In fact, I live with my mother. She's in her seventies. She's not a well woman. Losing her mind, the poor old thing. And then there's Sherlock, my dog, a cocker spaniel. My sister's staying with them while I'm away, looking after them both.'

'You're from the Lake District, aren't you?' asked Owen.

'Ah yes, indeed I am. The beautiful lakes.' He

scratched the swirl of his bald patch. 'I miss them, you know. Often, I take Sherlock for walks and I sit a while and admire the views. It's something I never tire of. I always feel humble – seeing God's work in all its splendour. My, what I wouldn't give to be back there now – perched on a hill, the blue sky above me, the hills rolling in the distance, the birds flying above me. Ha, I once tried to paint the view. Lugged an easel and paintbox all the way up. I had my picnic in my haversack, set everything up and started painting. Toiled all day while Sherlock dozed in the sun. It didn't work. I couldn't even begin to capture the beauty. Made me appreciate the work of men who can though; you know, real artists. I never tried again. I know my limitations.'

'You'll get back there one day, Ed; you and Sherlock.'

'I hope so, Owen; I do hope so.'

*

'My God, someone's in the water!'

I woke up from my daze to find Owen on his feet, pointing out to the sea, his hand shaking. We all clambered to our feet; only John Clair remained seated, hardly registering the commotion that had suddenly erupted around him.

'What? Where?' we all shouted. 'Where?'

'There, there. Can't you see?'

'Bloody hell,' said Palmer looking through the binoculars. 'There is, as well.'

It took me a few seconds longer but yes, about forty feet away from us, someone was in the water, lifelessly bobbing gently up and down with the waves. We all started screaming at the man.

'Is he alive?' asked Arbatov.

'I don't know,' said Hodgkin. 'Searight, Swann, man the oars.'

Swann and I did so, manoeuvring the oars into the rowlocks. Swann took the lead, circling the boat anti-clockwise while the men continued shouting.

Together, Swann and I began rowing towards the man in the sea. 'He's seen us,' said Davison, his cheeks redder than usual. 'He's alive!'

Harris Beckett pointed the way. 'More to the left,' he urged. 'That's it, that's it, straight ahead now.'

Soon we were upon him. 'Slow it up now,' ordered Hodgkin. 'Oars down.'

He was on our right; I could see him floating on a large slab of wood. On Hodgkin's orders, Owen and Arbatov jumped in the water. 'We've got you, son,' said Arbatov on reaching him. 'We've got you.'

Panicked, the man didn't want to let go off his float. Between them, Owen and Arbatov had to prise his fingers off the wood. 'It's OK,' said Owen, struggling in the water. 'You can let go now.' They dragged the man to the side of the boat as the plank of wood floated away. Helping hands pulled him up on board. 'Careful now,' urged Davison. His clothes had disintegrated into threads. He wore no shoes. His ankles had swollen and his legs were bleached white by the saltwater, while the top of his back and his shoulders were red raw from the sun.

They settled him at the bow, placing a blanket over him despite the heat of the day. I vaguely knew the man – he was a fireman from the *Academic*, a Spaniard called David Rodríguez Felipe. Most of the others knew him too, a short, tough bloke with piercing blue eyes, a veteran of the Spanish Civil War. We called him Pablo. Except for Hodgkin who insisted on calling him Señor Felipe. Clasping the blanket, he promptly vomited. Davison rubbed his back. The rest of us, except Clair, all settled in front of him in rows as if we were expecting him to perform something.

'*Agua*,' he croaked, shivering, wiping his mouth with the back of his hand. 'Water.'

'Yes, water,' said Hodgkin hesitantly. I knew what he was thinking, for I was thinking the same – we were going to have to make our meagre supply of water stretch even further. Hodgkin stepped behind Pablo and unlocked the locker. Sitting next to the Spaniard, he carefully poured water onto the spoon. 'Here we are,' he said. 'Take this.'

Pablo gulped the water then, with surprising strength, made to grab the bottle.

'No you don't,' screeched Hodgkin, yanking the bottle away from him. In doing so some of the water spilled. Beckett and Arbatov jumped to their feet, restraining the Spaniard.

'Water, more water,' croaked Pablo.

'You've had your share for today, mate,' said Beckett, holding him down firmly by the shoulders.

Hodgkin offered Pablo a biscuit. 'Eat it slowly,' he said, only to see the man swallow it down in one. More was offered – a spoonful of pemmican, a couple more of bully beef.

'More water.'

Hodgkin hesitated. 'OK, just a bit.'

'No,' said Beckett.

'Come on, Harris,' said Davison. 'He's been in the water for two days. He needs it more than us.'

'More than you perhaps.'

'Right,' said Hodgkin. 'Beckett, Arbatov, hold his arms down. Don't let him move.' And with that, Pablo got a second spoonful of water, while the rest of us looked on enviably.

Pablo sighed as if replete after a four-course meal. He leant against Hodgkin and closed his eyes.

*

'Feels horrible, doesn't it?' Owen, sitting next to me, was stroking his chin, feeling the start of his beard. 'Caked in salt and brine and God knows what. That saltwater's got into my skin. Bloody Pablo; I hope he appreciates it. Still, it's the least of our worries. And you, you don't smell so good, Robert.'

I laughed. 'And you do?'

'I used to love the smell of the sea. Not any more, I don't. Joanna was fond of going to the beach. Every weekend during the summer, we'd traipse down to the seaside with a picnic. She loved it. She told me it was because she'd never been to the beach as a kid. They lived too far away. She said she was already in her twenties when she first saw the sea. Imagine that? The cold water never bothered her a bit; she'd always go for a swim, whatever the weather. And we even went occasionally during the winter. She'd hike up her skirt and wade through the waves, not caring about the cold or how wet she got. I used to think her mad. Guess it was part of the attraction. She was an impulsive girl. If a thought came into her mind, she'd act on it. "I know,"

58

she'd say, "let's go to the pictures tonight." And off we'd go, all the way to Plymouth, not even knowing what we were about to see until we got there. Maybe, that's why the kids loved her. She was a good teacher.'

'Owen, stop talking about her in the past tense. You still wear the wedding ring I see.'

'Yeah. It'll soon be too big for any of my fingers. I'll have to wear it on my thumb.'

'You'll see her again one day. Soon.'

'You reckon so? I wish I shared your optimism. I wonder what she's doing now, right this minute?'

'Thinking of you, I'd imagine.'

'Yeah, maybe. Maybe. And what about you? Do you ever think of Alice?'

'Yes. Occasionally.' No, it was more than occasional. It was constant. At least Owen could picture where Joanna was, at home in the village, going about her chores, teaching at the school, thinking of her husband so far away, worrying about him, hoping for his safe return. I had no idea where Alice was, whether she had found herself a new man, a new job, a new life. A life without me. A life that had no place for me. I was no more than a memory to her. She had no idea where I was. If I were to die out here, would she ever know? No one would know how to contact her. She'd go through her life, perhaps once in a while thinking of me, perhaps wondering what I was up to, whether I also had married and settled down somewhere. She would never know I was dead, lost at sea, aged just twenty-three. Such a waste, people would say, his whole life still before him. But not Alice, the one person I would want to know. Oh, Alice, what could have been, what could have been.

Chapter 7

The Boat: Day Three

Pablo still hadn't woken up. Covered with a blanket, we took turns propping him up. Swann had already complained that our rations would have to be stretched even further. Someone, myself perhaps, should have told him not to be so harsh. No one did.

Harris Beckett, his eyes fixed faraway, was muttering to himself, winding himself up into a state of agitation.

'I'll bloody kill her next time I see her. Bloody kill her, I will. And him too, the bastard.'

'Something the matter, Harris?' asked Davison.

Beckett considered him for a while, perhaps wondering whether to say aloud what was on his mind.

Davison urged him. 'Sometimes it's good to talk about things. Get it out in the open.'

'Yeah,' said Palmer. 'Whatever it is, it won't go any further. Just us and the fish.' As always Palmer spoke quickly.

'Very funny, Palmer.'

'Ignore him, Harris.'

Beckett sighed, dropped his hand over the side, splashing his hand in the water. 'I was thinking back to a letter I got.'

'Go on.'

'Just before we embarked. It was from a mate of mine. You know, from back home. In Cardiff. A bloke I've known from a long way back, a fella by the name of Pryce.'

'And it was bad news, I guess.'

'You could say that. He told me… told me my missus was going on behind my back. You know, seeing someone else.'

'Oh dear. I'm sorry to hear that.'

'Not as much as I am. I know the bloke too, by sight, anyway. The butcher. Forget his name. Jones, I guess. Every other bugger on the street is called Jones. Ha, you can imagine the stick I got at school with a name like Beckett. Harris Beckett. People thought I was stuck up with a name like that. Anyhow, this butcher – old enough to be her father, he is. Fat and all. Well, perhaps not fat but portly all right. Can't imagine what she sees in him.'

Owen asked, 'Do you believe him, this Pryce?'

'He's got no reason to be fibbing, has he? Nothing in it for him. I suppose he thought he was doing right. But it's got to me, you know, right here.' He thumped himself on the chest. 'The thought of it. Makes me sick. We'd only been married the year before I was called away. As soon as all this was over, I was gonna go home and start up my carpentry again and make a real go of it. We were gonna have kids, you know, a proper little family, her and me.' He shook his head. 'Not any more.'

'You a carpenter then, Beckett?' asked Hodgkin.

'Yeah. My old man was. I took over when he retired few years back. I was going to write to her, ask her straight. Didn't get chance, did I? And now I'm stuck out here and it's all I can think about. It's not right, is it? The last letter I got from her, it was all sweetness and light. I read it so many times I memorized every word.'

'Did she mention the bombing?'

'She did that. They've had it hard; I know that. I prayed she be spared. Now, I reckon it'd serve her bloody right. I dream that a bomb lands fair and square on the butcher's and blows it to smithereens. That'd teach him to mess with other men's wives, the fat sod.'

'Is that your missus then?' asked Palmer. 'Her on your arm?'

Beckett glanced down at his tattoo as if he'd forgotten it was there.

'Yeah, right.'

'You weren't firm enough with her in the first place, if you ask me,' said Swann.

'I wasn't asking you, thanks all the same.'

'I ain't married, but if I was, I'd make sure she knew what was what.'

'Yes, thank you, Swann,' said Hodgkin. 'Not sure whether that's helping much.'

'I'm just saying, like, that's all.'

Beckett was on his feet. 'No, I don't know what you're saying except it sounds like a load of crap as usual.'

Rising to the challenge, Swann retorted, 'Well, perhaps this butcher's got something you ain't.'

'Meaning?'

Hodgkin tried to intervene. 'All right, all right, you two. Hold on there.'

'Meaning there's got be a reason.'

'Perhaps she's just lonely,' said Palmer. 'Either that or the butcher's tempting your missus with his extra pound of sausages.'

'Shut up, you idiot,' snapped Beckett.

'He may be right,' said Swann.

In a flash, Beckett was on him, a flurry of fists raining down on Swann. We all shouted, the boat rocking violently from side to side, as Swann managed to return a punch, catching Beckett fully on the chin. Hodgkin screamed for order while Arbatov dived in, prying the two men apart but not before Beckett landed a final punch in Swann's stomach, winding the man.

Beckett stood over Swann, snorting bull-like, his hands pinned down from behind by Arbatov.

'Finished now?' said Arbatov. 'Yes? All finished?'

Beckett nodded. 'Next time, Swann, I'll throw you overboard, got it?'

'That's enough now,' said Hodgkin, visibly shaking.

Stepping over the benches, Beckett made his way to the back of the boat where he sat down. Swann, gathering himself, sat down at the front.

'I expected better of you both,' said Hodgkin.

Leaning over to Owen, I whispered, 'That's the battle of the alpha males done then.'

He stifled a laugh. 'At least we know where we stand now.'

Puffing his chest out, Hodgkin continued, 'I'm half tempted to put you both on a charge of misconduct…'

He launched into a speech about the need for discipline, how we all needed to work together, peppered with words like duty, disgrace and British.

But no one was listening.

*

'Are you married?' I asked Palmer.

'What made you ask that all of a sudden? But yeah, I am as it happens. Just five months ago.'

'Congratulations.'

'Thanks.' He smiled a wistful smile. 'We were always going to get married, Betty and me. We've known each other since we were kids. Ah yeah, I'm a lucky man, Searight, married me childhood sweetheart. Well, no one else would have me. No, only kidding. She's good for me. I proposed last New Year's Eve. If truth be known, I had to have a skinful before I plucked up courage to ask. I thought she'd say yes but that just made it worse. What if I'd got it wrong? I got a ring, cheap one mind you, but it's the thought that counts, isn't it? Got down on my knee, the whole bit. "Betty," I said. "Will you do me the honour of being my wife?" I said it all proper. She called me a daft bugger.'

'But she said yes.'

'Yeah, she did all right.'

'Good for you.'

'Yeah.' He grinned to himself. 'What about you, Searight? Are you married?'

'Me? No.'

'It's great. I'd highly recommend it. Otherwise, who else will mend your socks? Only joking.' He punched me in the arm. 'Can't wait to have kids. We're going to have so many kids, I'm telling you. I've got all the names, up here in my head. The first one, if it's a boy, will be Adrian Charles Palmer. Great name, eh? Adrian was my grandfather, my dad's dad. The second one, if it's a girl will be called Anne Marie…' And so he continued, telling me all the names and middle names of all the children he planned to have with his Betty, and who they'd be named after, an uncle here, a sister-in-law there, reams of them. I stopped listening after a while and allowed Palmer to indulge in his fantasy, visualising this huge family of his.

A family that would never exist.

*

Our first days on the boat affected us all differently. Some felt certain we'd be picked up in no time; others, including myself, felt the perilousness of our situation, so far from land, so far from anything. Our biggest torment was the sun. Each day just became hotter and hotter. Some of the men jumped into the sea to cool off. Hodgkin advised them not to – it would drain their strength, he said, and if they swallowed any seawater, it would only make their thirst more intense. Worse still, he told them, we were in an area populated by sharks. We hadn't spied any yet but still, said Hodgkin, we had to be careful. 'Pablo didn't get eaten, and he was in the soup for two days,' remarked Palmer. Others, taking Hodgkin's advice, soaked their shirts in the water, placing them on their heads to help them cool down.

Pablo still slept for hours at an end, balanced on a bench, supported by one us, taking turns. He woke briefly and helped himself to numerous handfuls of seawater. We told him not, that it would make him feel worse, but either he didn't understand us or chose not to. He closed his eyes and promptly went back to sleep.

John Clair hardly said a word, sinking deeper and deeper into a state of lethargy. Edward Davison took it upon himself to look after the boy, offering words of encouragement. When, on the third day, Hodgkin declared it was time for our morning ration, Davison had to persuade Clair to get to his feet.

Afterwards, as we settled back down, I heard Clair say to Davison, almost in a whisper, 'I just want to go home, Ed.'

'I know, kid. We all do. And we will soon. I know it, I can feel it.'

'Can you? Can you, Ed?'

'Yes, have faith, John. Something will turn up.'

'I want my mum. She'd look after me. Like when I was small. A nice big dinner of mutton and spuds. Oh God, can you imagine that, Ed?'

'Shut up, Clair,' bellowed Beckett. 'You're making it worse for all of us.'

'Ignore him,' said Davison. 'Go on, mutton and spuds – delicious. And what about dessert?'

'You mean pudding? Mm, perhaps apple crumble. That'd be nice, eh?'

'Sounds lovely, John. Just lovely. What else would your mother do?'

'Early to bed with a cup of cocoa. She's always been good to me, my mum. It's not been easy for her, not after Dad died, and all that. Three boys to look after. Me and the twins. I never got cocoa after Dad died.'

'You have twin brothers?'

'Yeah. They're much younger than me though.

They're funny. Always getting into mischief. After Dad went, Mum said I had to be the man of the family now. I tried, Ed, really I tried. But it was difficult, you know? Expected to fix things, put things up, patch things up, and all that. I don't know how to fix things. I suppose that's why I joined the navy.'

'To escape?'

'No. I don't know. To be a man, I guess.' He lowered his voice, 'Like Beckett there. Or Swann. I like the sea; in fact, I love it.'

'Yes, well.'

'It's my birthday tomorrow.'

'Is it? That's great, John. How old will you be?'

'Nineteen.'

'Nineteen, eh? A lovely age. I'll be forty next week. Not exactly a joyful prospect.'

'I got a cake last year. Won't have one this year. I wish he hadn't died like that.'

'It must've been difficult for you, John.'

Owen and I looked at each other. Owen shook his head.

Palmer and Swann were on look-out. It was my turn next. God, my throat felt dry. I found myself chomping my mouth, masticating on nothing, trying to get some saliva going. The others were doing the same, constantly licking their lips, swallowing, trying to alleviate the thirst. Occasionally, we would talk – what we did before the war, what we'd do on being rescued, previous journeys, and stories that began with the words, 'I once heard about a ship…' But most of the time we sat in silence, cursing the sun, each man with his thoughts. God, I ached with hunger. My stomach groaned. Looking at

John Clair, I knew that the hardest battle would not be the hunger, or the thirst or even the sun, terrible though they were, but the mind. I had to maintain control of my sanity. If I lost my mind, then all would be lost.

Pablo finally woke up. He looked round him, absorbing his new reality. Hodgkin gave him his share of rations which, this time, he accepted more graciously. Scratching the sores on his torso, he told us his story. Following the sinking and finding himself in the sea, Pablo joined three others on the piece of flotsam we found him on. 'One of them,' he said, 'a steward has his arm ripped off.' He chopped at his arm to emphasize the point. 'He is in a hell of a state.' He swore in Spanish. 'That piece of wood isn't big enough to keep all of us afloat. They say I am last to arrive, I have to let go. I think, I'm not letting go.' He spoke quickly, becoming more excitable. 'We fight. The others – they know the steward is the weakest. They worry his bloody arm will invite the sharks, so they take my side and we kick him off. Kicked him off!' He paused, wringing his hands, his lips scowling.

'What happened to him?' asked Owen.

'What do you think?' said Beckett. 'He swam all the way back to Dover and is currently reading *The Times* in a gentleman's club in the Savoy.'

'Yeah, all right,' said Owen. 'Keep your hair on.'

'What came of the others?' asked Davison.

Pablo glared at him, his blue eyes vivid. 'They are weak. Weak. One by one, they slip off into the water. Puff! Gone. Just like that. This leaves only me. *Dios mío*. My God. Then, I think my time is up, I find you.'

'Well, we found you,' said Palmer. 'But let's not split

hairs.'

Pablo rose quickly to his feet. 'You say I'm lying. *Dios mío*, you call me a liar,' he said, jabbing himself in the chest.

'No, no, steady on, Pablo,' said Palmer, shuffling along his bench.

'Calm down, man,' said Beckett, gripping the Spaniard's arm.

Slowly, Pablo sat back down, pointing his finger threateningly at poor old Palmer.

I knew Pablo's background – he'd told it often enough. He'd fought on the Nationalists' side during the Spanish Civil War, then deserted. Fearing one side or the other might shoot him, he joined the Republicans. He didn't care which side won, he said, as long as he survived. He boasted that he served both sides, had fought in the war for its entire duration, and yet had never fired a single shot. Once Franco had taken power, he sought asylum in England, getting in by the mere fact that he had an English grandmother.

The day fell without further incident. The waves picked up, but nothing that concerned us. No one spoke. We sat in silence, the only sound being John's muffled sobbing and the occasional calls for his mother. It was, after a while, irritating. For sure, I felt sorry for the boy, but the constant crying began to tell on my nerves. I needed to keep my mental strength up and Clair's whimpering was rendering me miserable and was doing little for my resolve. Beckett also found the noise grating. 'Tell him to shut that noise up, would you?' he said a few times to Davison.

Ignoring Beckett, Davison tried to reassure Clair, and

the rest of us, with promises that we'd soon be picked up.

No one believed him.

Chapter 8

The Boat: Day Four

'John, wake up, wake up, kid.' I was woken up from my fitful sleep against Owen by Edward Davison's plaintive cries. The sun had not yet risen, the sky hung over us silvery blue. Davison was gently shaking the slumped figure of John Clair leaning heavily against him.

Hodgkin stepped over. 'What's the matter, Ed?' he asked.

'I think he's dead.'

Hodgkin lifted Clair's head. His eyes were still open but, dulled and vacant, it was obvious that the life had gone. Kneeling down, Hodgkin felt for the pulse. Gently dropping John's arm, he shook his head. 'Yes, I'm afraid so.'

We all sighed – a mixture of pity and relief. 'Poor boy,' said Owen. '*Dios mío*,' muttered Pablo.

'Nineteen years old today,' added Davison, shaking his head. 'No one even said happy birthday to him.' Carefully, he disentangled himself from the corpse and tried laying him on the bench, covering him with one of the blankets. But with the next wave, John's body fell off the bench, landing in the bilge water at the bottom of the boat with an undignified bump and a splash.

'You all right, Ed?' asked Owen.

'Yes, I'm fine. Thanks, Owen.'

'There's only one thing for it,' said Beckett.

Hodgkin cleared his throat. 'Edward, do you know any prayers appropriate for... you know?'

'Of course. But can't we wait a while? It seems a bit callous to... so quickly.'

'Hey, no,' said Arbatov. 'We do it now.'

'The Russian's right,' said Beckett. 'I'm not sharing a boat with a stiff.'

'Beckett, please,' said Davison. 'Have some respect.'

'I'm not Russian,' said Arbatov.

'No, of course not, Comrade Arbatov.'

'Enough now,' ordered Hodgkin. 'Come on, Edward. They're right; we have to do this now.'

Davison nodded his assent.

'He loved the sea,' said Palmer. 'He won't mind.'

'Swann, Arbatov, would you do the honours?' asked Hodgkin.

The two men stamped over and between them lifted Clair's body up. Hodgkin nodded at Davison.

Davison sighed. Putting his hands together in prayer, he began. 'Oh, Lord, we give unto you the soul of another of your flock, John Clair. May You receive him with Your blessing as we surrender his mortal remains to the mighty sea. Please, say with me, Our Father, which art in Heaven, Hallowed be Thy name...'

We joined Davison in reciting the Lord's Prayer, our

72

heads bowed, while Swann and Arbatov stood at the side of the boat, struggling to keep the corpse from sagging.

'… For ever and ever, Amen.' He made the sign of the cross.

Hodgkin nodded at Swann.

'Wait,' said Pablo. 'We keep the blanket, no?'

We all looked at Hodgkin. 'Well, yes, I suppose… it would be a waste. Edward, would you mind?'

'Well…'

'Sod that,' said Beckett. 'The gringo's right – why waste a good blanket?'

Leaning over, Davison removed the blanket, passing it back to me. Clair's eyes were still open. Davison stepped forward and with his fingers closed the boy's eyelids. 'OK,' he said.

Swann and Arbatov lifted the body over the side of the boat then, with a nod at each other, carefully dropped John Clair into the sea. Slowly, he floated away, rising up and down with the waves. Davison crossed himself again. Silently, we watched him for a long while.

It was Palmer who eventually broke the silence. 'Hey, why doesn't he sink?' he asked.

'He will,' said Swann. 'As soon as the air in his lungs is replaced with water.'

'Well, that's that,' said Beckett, rubbing his hands. 'Time for breakfast, methinks.'

We each took our portions. I tried to banish the thought that with Clair gone, we were back to our original rations. God, the thirst was getting worse. My stomach gnawed with hunger but the pain of it was dwarfed by the dehydration. Licking my lips, trying to force saliva, was getting more difficult. My every thought became obsessed by water. I'd look at the sea and imagine all that water to be fresh, dream of diving into it and resurfacing and being able to cup my hands and take in mouthful after mouthful of all that delicious, pure water. Swann had been the first to succumb. Declaring he could stand it no more, he scooped his hand into the water and gulped it down. Beckett called him a fool; Hodgkin told him he'd go mad. Swann tried to laugh it off.

Looking round at my companions, I realised just how much we had already changed. Each of us sported a beard or at least the start of one. Our skin was burning, turning a frightful red, parched and blistered all over, our eyes ghostly white. Owen, especially, with his blond hair, was suffering. Every man now had begun talking to himself. Pablo was the worst afflicted – muttering in Spanish, wringing his hands. Those who had tried cooling themselves down by placing their wet shirts on top of their heads were regretting it. The dripping seawater had caused hideous sores on their chests and down their backs, making their blisters worse and that much more painful.

Surely, I thought, it couldn't get any worse.

*

'What's that noise?' asked Swann.

We became aware of a deep rhythmic pulse, so low we could feel it in our stomachs. 'What is that?' I asked.

'Look everyone.' It was Hodgkin, standing, pointing starboard, and smiling.

'A ship?' asked Swann, scrabbling to his feet.

'Ships don't sound like that, Swann, but look…'

'Oh my, look at that,' said Davison. 'Now isn't that the most beautiful thing you've ever seen?'

He was right; it made for a jaw-dropping sight.

'*Ballena azul*,' said Pablo.

Half a mile hence, perhaps a little more, was a whale – a blue whale. 'Look at the size of it, it's as big as a ship,' said Owen. 'Must be seventy, eighty foot long. What a beauty.'

We watched open-mouthed as it arched in and out of the water, making its huge humming sound; every few seconds blowing vertical plumes of water some thirty foot into the air.

'Impressive,' murmured Arbatov.

'That's some fish,' said Palmer.

'For pity's sake,' said Beckett. 'Don't you know anything? That's no fish, that *fish* is a mammal.'

'Bloody hope it doesn't come too close. Can we kill it?' asked Palmer, speaking quickly.

'With what exactly?' said Beckett. 'Been hiding a harpoon on you?'

'No, but see those tins there,' said Palmer, pointing at the small pile of empty pemmican and bully beef tins. 'We could throw those tins at it.'

'Good idea, Palmer,' said Beckett. 'Off you go then. Good luck.'

'*Estúpido idiota*,' said Pablo. Stupid idiot.

Palmer laughed. 'I was joking, Pablo; just bloody joking.'

We watched as the whale swam away, fading into the distance, its plumes of water still visible.

'Come back,' I muttered. 'Don't go, don't leave us.'

'It's gone now, Searight,' said Hodgkin.

'Yes,' I sighed. 'It's gone.'

*

After almost four days in the boat, we'd taken the calm weather for granted. Each day, the sun had burned and sea had remained still, only occasionally building up to a gentle sway. But during the early evening of the fourth day, we all felt a distinct difference in the waves and the sight of white foam bubbling gently on the water's surface alerted us that the weather was about to change. The sea itself had darkened, turning grey, then a deeper grey by the minute. The gentle breeze soon became a growling wind. Pablo rose to his feet and pointed to the horizon. '*Dios nos ayude*, God help us,' he muttered. Following his pointing finger, we stood, agape, at what we saw – a huge, sprawling black cloud was making its way towards us, a swirling phantom of cumulus. 'Oh hell, brace yourself, boys,' said Palmer.

'Is that ration hold firmly locked?' Swann asked Hodgkin.

'Don't you concern yourself with that, Swann,' came the curt answer. 'Palmer, make sure those oars are secure. Get your lifejackets on.'

'God, it's coming on fast,' said Swann. 'It's going to hit us any minute.'

'It's a storm,' said Arbatov.

'State the bleeding obvious, comrade,' snarled Beckett.

The waves were rapidly becoming bigger, the foam resembling boiling water upon the marbled sea, the sky darker and more ominous by the moment as the storm rapidly blocked out the sun. We felt the first hint of rain.

I shivered – whether from fear of what we were about to experience or the sudden, noticeable drop in temperature, I wasn't sure. The wind howled; our little boat rose and fell as the spectral-like storm approached us. The smell of sea salt was suddenly more intense. 'Oh Lord, help us,' said Davison.

'I think that's what the Spaniard said,' said Palmer. 'Hey, anyone got a mackintosh they could spare? No? Oh well, I wanted a bath. Pass the soap, vicar.'

In an instant, the pitter-patter of rain became a deluge. Within seconds, we were all soaked, the rain piercing us like a thousand needle pricks, pounding our faces. I never knew until this moment rain could hurt. Our hair sagged with rain. Clenching my eyes shut, I turned my face upwards, opening my mouth but the joy of feeling fresh water on the back of my throat was short-lived. Hodgkin screamed at us to start bailing. Swann took the one bucket available to us, the rest used the empty bully beef tins, and together we tried fruitlessly to bail. We soon abandoned the attempt – swamped with water, there was nothing we could do. The sky turned black as the waves surged, throwing our boat up into the air as if it was a mere toy. We screamed, all of us desperately holding onto the side of the boat and the benches, our fingers biting into the wood. I knew we were now totally at the mercy of the storm and the sea. A bolt of lightning shot across the sky, momentarily illuminating us. A clap of thunder roared, shaking the world around us, causing us to cower. Our screams were lost to the storm. Palmer yelled something at me. Did he expect me to hear anything above the cacophony? His cheeks positively wobbled in the wind. The waves tossed and rumbled like so many fearsome beasts. A wave as solid as a cliff face, and just as large, crashed over us. Another, perhaps fifty, sixty feet, took us, carrying our boat higher and higher. We clung on for dear life; each man for himself. I knew the others were there, was aware of their presence, but paid them no heed, too wrapped up, as we all were, in trying to remain on the boat. My stomach flipped as we continued on this upward trajectory taking us all closer to heaven. I felt myself spinning until I could no longer tell what was up and what was down. Yet still I managed to hold on. Finally, at its crest, the wave left us suspended for an eternity as if nothing was beneath us, then, with a roar from Hell, we plummeted back down at a frightening speed, diving through the air as if in space, hitting what felt like the trough at neck-breaking velocity, only to swerve back up a moment later. Surely, our boat would break apart any second; how could its timbers survive such a battering? Death, I was certain, was but minutes or even a heartbeat away. How could we survive such a tempest? Wave upon wave took us on the watery rollercoaster. I could no longer see the horizon; instead we were surrounded by these mountains of water. I tried to keep my eyes open, being in the dark made things even worse, but the lashing rain and screeching wind was too much. Back to the bottom, into the whirlpool, I glanced up, and before us was a wall of vertical water, as solid as stone, down which, with unending fury, poured numerous waterfalls.

We'd found Hell, all right.

Chapter 9

The Boat: Day Five

The storm lasted most of the night. Sometimes the wind and the waves would subside, and we would all breathe a sigh of relief, only for it to start afresh minutes later. Finally, as the first streaks of pink sky emerged, it finished. No one spoke. We looked at each other with wide-eyed shock and exhaustion the like of which none of us had ever experienced before. We were all drenched and shivering. I sucked on my shirt, just for something to drink. There were seven of us. Two were missing but my thoughts were too jumbled to make out who. It was Hodgkin who first said it. 'Where's Palmer and Arbatov?' We all looked round the boat, as if we were expecting them to be hiding somewhere within it. Nor were they in the water, at least not as far as our eyes could see.

'We need to find them,' said Davison. His voice was cracked, like a man who'd smoked too many cigarettes in one sitting. The thought of embarking on a manhunt was abhorrent. I lacked the strength to lift an arm, let alone go rowing round looking for Palmer and Arbatov.

'We can't,' said Beckett, clearing his throat. 'The oars have gone.'

He was right – despite Palmer securing them, the oars were not there. The realisation induced within me mixed feelings. My immediate sense of relief that we need not expend any energy in a fruitless search gave way to the feeling that somehow we had lost a vital lifeline. Yes, we were far too far from land to contemplate rowing but the oars were there in case we needed them. The fact that we had lost Palmer and Arbatov concerned me very little. But without the oars, we really were at the mercy of the wind and current. As Swann so succinctly put it, 'That's us buggered then.'

'Poor Palmer,' said Davison. 'Poor Arbatov.'

We all half-heartedly nodded in agreement. Yes, Palmer's continual joking had been irritating but he'd been the only one amongst us that remained relatively upbeat. We would miss him – after a fashion.

'It's remarkable the storm didn't claim more of us,' said Davison.

'Must've been your prayers,' said Swann.

'You may mock. But I think you saw last night the full might of God's work.' The effort of speaking seemed to tire him still further.

'Leaving God to one side for a moment, can anyone else speak German?' asked Hodgkin. No answer. 'Pity.' He gazed up at the sky, at the encroaching dawn. 'Time for breakfast, I'd say. Let's hope everything's OK.'

The hold beneath the bow had held. 'Thank God for small mercies,' said Davison as Hodgkin reached in for our rations.

A scream took us all by surprise. There, standing at the stern of the boat, his back to us, Pablo was shouting at the sky; a torrent of Spanish words directed at God.

'Señor Felipe,' bellowed Hodgkin from the bow. 'Stop that noise at once.'

Pablo turned to face him, unsteady on his feet, his eyes rimmed red. 'You don't tell me what to do,' he growled, jabbing his finger from afar at Hodgkin.

A momentary flicker of fear flashed through Hodgkin's eyes. I, too, felt myself shuffle back along the bench. Regaining himself, Hodgkin said, 'I *can* tell you what to do. If we are to survive, we have to maintain discipline. This is the start of our fifth day and the discipline has been exemplary so far, as one would expect from British sailors.'

'Your *discipline*,' said Pablo, spitting out the word, 'means nothing to me.'

'I don't know what sort of army you fought with in Spain, Señor Felipe—'

Swann interrupted. 'He fought for whatever side would 'ave him, sir.'

'Questionable loyalty, if you ask me,' muttered Owen.

Pablo stepped over the benches, his bloodshot eyes fixed on Owen. Beckett blocked his way. 'You stay right there,' he said. The tattoo on his arm seemed to move as he flexed his biceps.

Pablo considered his options. He swayed, realising perhaps, just how tired he was. Heavily, he sat down.

'Well done, Beckett,' said Swann. 'Not bad for a Taff.'

'Look,' said Davison. 'Can we stop all this bickering and have our water? God, we need it.'

'Absolutely,' said Swann. 'After you, Captain.'

'I still can't get used to be called captain,' said Hodgkin.

'Water, damn it,' shouted Beckett.

'Oh, yes, of course.'

No one else spoke. We took our water and our milk tablets and our minute portions of pemmican. Owen and I sat together, as was now our routine, and leant against each other. 'You alright, Robert?'

I yawned. 'I think so. I'm done in. I could sleep for a week.'

'Yes, I know the feeling.'

The sun had risen above the horizon. Soon, we would be caught under its unrelenting glare. I felt myself dozing off. We all were. We'd given up on taking turns being the look-out. With heavy eyelids, I looked round at my companions, my fellow sufferers. Our clothes hung off us as rags; we'd all been burnt terribly by the sun; Owen's skin was now a mash of blisters. Our eyes, like the Spaniard's, had taken on a demonic red edge; our beards coated in brine. This was only our fifth day and yet it already felt as if I could not envisage another existence. The ship, and our life on it, seemed to belong to a different lifetime. I began to envy Clarence's early exit from this world. He, at least, had been spared this continual torment. The constant creaking of the boat's timbers slowly lulled me to sleep.

Opening my eyes momentarily, I caught sight of Swann cupping his hands and drinking more seawater. Having taken his fill, he glanced round and saw me watching him. He winked at me.

*

The scream awoke me with a start. My dazed mind jumped to several conclusions all at once – we were being attacked; we'd been spotted; the boat was sinking.

'Not again, Pablo,' groaned Beckett. 'Shut up, you daft Spaniard.'

Pablo was standing at the stern of the boat, screaming at nothing in particular, his arms wrapped round himself as if, despite the heat, he was cold. Beckett's words had the desired effect, and man ceased his wailing in an instant, but the way he glared at Beckett made me shrink.

'Uh oh,' muttered Owen next to me. 'This doesn't look good.'

The wind had picked up, the boat dipped up and down in the swell. Pablo stepped over the bench, approaching us. 'Those Germans – they win this war,' he shrieked. 'You wait and see. Just like Franco did in my country. *Hitler va a ganar esta guerra.* We fight to live but for what?' He threw his hands up in the air. 'So we can live in a German concentration camp all our lives? Spain, England. Fascists and Nazis everywhere. *Fascistas bastardos.* I tell you, I tell you now…'

Hodgkin rose to his feet. 'Enough of this defeatism–'

Pablo interrupted him, speaking quickly, alternating between English and Spanish, getting louder and more frantic by the moment.

'For Christ's sake, stop rocking the boat,' said Swann.

Pablo picked up the bucket and swinging it around, threw it into the sea. He laughed, a diabolic cackle resembling a pantomime dame. But no one laughed with him. Then, stopping abruptly, he yanked at his hair, screaming '*Jesús no puede salvarte ahora.* Jesus can't save you now.' With that, he positively flew across the length of the boat, launching himself at Swann. Catching Swann unawares, he punched him in the stomach. Swann fell back. The Spaniard dived on top of him, screeching, swearing, wrapping his hands around Swann's neck. Owen was the first to react; Hodgkin followed. Between them, they tried to yank Pablo away. We all gathered. Only Davison hung back. Pablo continued to struggle. Beckett swung his foot in, catching the Spaniard in the groin; Owen pulled his hair. I felt a surge of energy as I tried to help. Between us, we thought we'd succeeded, but still cursing, Pablo wriggled free and attacked Hodgkin, landing him a fist on his jaw. Hodgkin staggered back. 'Get him off the boat,' screamed Owen from behind us. Pablo waved his fists at all of us, daring anyone to try. 'You cowards, all English cowards,' he yelled.

Without stopping to think, I launched myself against him, rugby tackling him. My momentum carried us both off the boat and into the sea. Resurfacing, I heard the others cheer me on as if they were spectators at a fairground entertainment. I felt Pablo's hand on my head, pushing me down. I went under before having the chance to take in air. I could touch the boat; we were still so close to it. Struggling, I managed to free myself and resurface. Panic seized me, knowing I had no strength to fight. But then, something solid hit Pablo hard in the face. He fell back in the water, dazed, blood pouring from his forehead. 'Robert, get back,' shouted a voice from the boat. Outstretched hands reached out for me. Between them, they hauled me back into the boat. I fell in, landing next to Swann, propped against a bench, nursing his neck. He gave me the thumbs up.

'What hit him?' I croaked.

'I got him with the binoculars,' said Owen.

Trying to catch my breath, I watched as Hodgkin and Beckett kept Pablo away from the boat. The Spaniard managed to get his hand on the side only for Beckett to slash at his fingers with the jagged edge of an opened bully beef tin, causing a deep, ugly cut. Pablo screeched, falling back into the water. He didn't try again. The waves took him away from us, while all the time he maintained a string of abuses, shouting at us in English and Spanish, shaking his fist at us. We sat, too exhausted to speak, and watched Pablo as he drifted further and further away, still swearing, still shaking his fists, until soon he was no more than a dot bobbing in the water.

Then came the silence.

Chapter 10

The Boat: Day Six

'I can see a ship. I can see a bloody ship!' I was wide awake in an instant. My skin felt as if it was on fire; the saltwater eating into my sores. Harris Beckett was standing at the stern of the boat, his hand shielding his eyes, staring into the distance. We all scrambled to our feet, our hearts pounding with excitement and anticipation.

'Where?' cried Hodgkin. 'What ship?'

'There, over there. Can't you see it?'

We squinted and scanned the horizon, desperate to see the ship. 'I can't see anything,' I said.

'There's nowt there,' added Swann.

'Are you all blind? It's coming towards us. We're saved, for Christ's sake, we're saved!'

'You're seeing things,' said Owen. 'The sun's got to his head.'

'No, it hasn't. Here, this will attract them.'

'No,' screeched Hodgkin.

But it was too late. Beckett slammed a flare cartridge into its gun and fired. No one had even noticed he'd been holding it. We watched it as the flare fizzed and arched through the air. Its light was certainly impressive but too soon it fizzled out and fell.

'You fool,' said Hodgkin. 'There's no ship and now you've wasted a flare.'

'But… I swear…' Beckett's body sagged. Dropping the gun, he said, 'There was a ship; I saw it.'

We groaned with frustration. Davison put his hand on Beckett's shoulder. 'There was no ship, Harris.'

'I swear…'

'You were hallucinating, you fool,' said Swann.

'How many flares we got left now, Captain?' asked Owen.

'Only the three. Now listen, everyone… This is important.' One by one we sat down, still heavy with the disappointment. Hodgkin scooped up the flare gun. 'No one, and I mean no one, should fire a flare unless they have my explicit say-so. Is that understood?'

We all nodded.

No one spoke for a while. Each man sat with his own thoughts, coming to terms with the utter loss of hope. Owen and I, as per habit, sat together. Sitting on our hands, we leant into each other, trying to ease the discomfort of sitting with our bony buttocks against the hard wooden benches. The waves built up, and we had to hold on as we crashed up and down. Having survived the storm, I knew this was the least of our concerns. We had to wait until the waves had calmed down before Hodgkin would offer us our rations. We understood – nothing could be so crushing as seeing our precious teaspoon of water spilt.

Finally, after an hour or two, the waves calmed. 'I'm afraid, gents,' said Hodgkin as we gathered around him, 'that this is the last of our food. After this, there is no more. All gone.'

For a moment, I thought I was going to cry.

We waited in line, watching intently as Hodgkin used the teaspoon to measure out the minute squares of pemmican. Thank God Pablo had gone, I thought to myself, at least we only had to split it up between the six of us. Hodgkin, having divided up the last helping of pemmican, started handing them out.

'Hey, wait a minute,' said Beckett, pointing at Swann's portion. 'His is bigger.'

'No, it bloody isn't.'

'Yes, it is; it's much bigger.'

'Looks the same to me,' said Davison.

'Exactly,' said Swann.

'If it's the same, then swap,' said Beckett, offering his slice of pemmican in the palm of his hand.

'I'm not touching nothing that's been handled by a Taff.'

'Hey, that's enough now,' said Hodgkin.

Beckett's chapped lip curled up. He shuffled back to the stern which he'd claimed as his own, stepping over the benches, and sat down by himself.

I gazed longingly at my little slice of compressed meat. I tried to imagine it was so much more. Images of one of my mother's roast dinners floated into my mind. I could see the Sunday-best plates laden with thick slices of roast pork and crackling, a generous helping of steaming roast potatoes, nicely crisp, and the shiny bright orange of diced carrots. 'Gravy, Robert?' I wouldn't say no. Oh, the joy of such thick gravy, full of pork juice and fat. Mustn't forget the apple sauce. My mother always insisted Father said grace before dinner. A tedious tradition, I used to think. Perhaps this was now God's way of punishing me, for not having appreciated His plentiful offerings. I vowed if I ever escaped this boat I would never eat another meal without offering my thanks beforehand. I imagined taking my knife and fork and cutting into a succulent piece of pork, imagined the sensation of it on my tongue, relishing the different flavours in my mouth.

I placed the block of pemmican on my tongue. I couldn't decide what to do – whether to swallow it as one or nibble at it slowly. I opted for the latter. As I swallowed the last few crumbs, I experienced a rush of disappointment that it had gone all too quickly.

Next came the water. We had enough water for another three helpings each, said Hodgkin. After tomorrow morning, there'd be none left.

'We could drink our urine,' said Davison.

'Yeah, good idea, Ed,' said Beckett. 'But we've got nothing to piss out. When was the last time you had a piss?'

A thought occurred to me. 'Captain, shouldn't we have been in Karachi by now?'

'I don't know. What day is it?' Hodgkin considered this for a while, mentally counting the days off in his mind. 'By Jove, Searight, you may be right. If not today, then certainly tomorrow.'

'They'll be disappointed not to have their mules then,' said Swann.

'I wonder whether they're still searching for us?' asked Davison.

'Who knows,' said Owen. 'We could be within hours of being rescued.'

'They'll never find us,' said Beckett. 'They probably didn't send anyone in the first place. We're too low down on their list of importance.'

'They'll know which route we're on,' I said, realising immediately how naïve I sounded.

'Who knows how far we've drifted off course. And thanks to Gardner here, we don't have the binoculars to keep watch.'

'What happened to them?' asked Swann.

'Don't you remember? Gardner pelted Pablo with them.'

'We have to hope,' said Davison.

'Ed's right,' said Hodgkin. 'We can but hope.'

'And pray,' added Davison. 'We must always pray.' Closing his eyes, Davison put his hands together and started praying, beseeching God to help the naval authorities in Karachi in their search for us, asking Him to give us all the strength to survive. Together, we closed our eyes and bowed our heads. 'Dear God, we are entirely at Your mercy. We humbly pray that You may grant us a speedy deliverance from this most trying of circumstance.' Having said our Amen, Davison led us in a subdued rendition of *Amazing Grace*... 'Amazing grace, how sweet the sound that saved a wretch like me. I once was lost, but now am found, was blind but now I see...'

Exhausted, we settled back down. I noticed we'd fallen into this routine of having these brief conversations followed by long hours of silence. I closed my eyes, listening to the constant creaking of the boat, and dreamt of seaplanes taking off from Karachi with strong, reliable men, determined to find us, wherever we were.

*

I awoke to find myself bathed in sweat. The heat was like a presence – one was always aware of it, unable to escape it. The sun was burning us raw. Yet, the swell of the sea was still quite strong. On seeing me awake, Owen muttered, 'It's so bloody hot. I don't know how much more of this I can take.'

'Not much…' I found it difficult to speak. Reduced to a whisper, I tried again. 'Not much longer, you'll see. There'll be planes out there now, looking for us.'

'I wish I could believe you.'

'Think about Joanna; how happy she'll be when she sees you again.'

He tried to smile but his chapped lips were too painful. 'She's the only thing that keeps me going. Christ, I miss her so much. The first thing…'

The sound of a large splash took our attention.

'Swann,' cried Hodgkin. 'What do you think you're doing?'

'What's it look like?' shouted Swann from the water. 'Cooling off.'

We watched him, swimming round in circles, bobbing up and down with the waves. I wondered where he found the strength. Perhaps drinking seawater wasn't such a bad idea after all; he seemed no worse off for it. He dived under water, disappearing for a few seconds and then re-emerged, shaking the excess water from his hair.

'There might be sharks,' said Davison.

'Come in, it's lovely,' shouted Swann, as if he had gone in for a dip at the seaside. 'You'll feel better for it.'

'The man's an idiot,' said Beckett. 'When that salt dries off on his skin, he'll howl.'

I could only think of the present, and right now Swann seemed rejuvenated. I'd never been a good swimmer and those waves looked too strong for me but I envied his escape from the sun.

'Not so far, Swann,' yelled Hodgkin.

'What?'

'Oh, jeepers,' said Hodgkin under his breath. Summoning his voice, he called out, 'You're drifting away; come back in.'

'I'm fine.' We carried on watching him as he treaded water, occasionally laughing to himself. 'I think I'll catch meself a fish,' he called out, ducking again beneath the waves. This time he remained under for such a time we began to feel concerned. Stretching our necks like a row of meerkats, we waited anxiously for Swann to reappear. Finally, he did, laughing loudly. The relief of seeing Swann reappear was immediately erased by realising how far away he'd gone.

'Good God,' said Owen. 'He must be fifty or more feet away.'

A large wave washed over him, taking Swann from our view. When we saw him again, he was further away still. The expanse of water between him and us now seemed vast. Cupping his hands to his mouth, Hodgkin yelled out, 'For Pete's sake, Swann, get back here.'

Swann waved. 'Wait for me,' he yelled. He began

swimming, one arm after the other sweeping through the air with a strong, steady rhythm. He's a strong swimmer, I thought to myself; he'll make it back.

'Keep going,' shouted Owen.

He was making progress, I thought, but was it enough? We could see his face and his expression of determination. But he wasn't making up the distance; the waves were too strong.

'He's not going to make, is he?' said Owen.

We shouted at him, all of us urging him on.

I looked round the boat, as if I might find something that could help. There was nothing, not even a coil of rope. The oars had gone; we couldn't slow ourselves down. Slowly, Swann fell further back as his energy weakened. He kept swimming, pumping his arms and legs through the density of water. Another large wave briefly obscured our view of him. When we saw him again, he'd been pushed back further still. He began shouting through mouthfuls of water, waving his arms. 'Wait for me, wait for me.' His expression was now one of total hopelessness. He knew, as did we, that he wasn't going reach us. We watched in despair as the distance between us broadened. Davison knelt down to pray. The rest of us continued standing, our hands to our mouths, as Swann, like Pablo the day before, drifted further and further back. Ten, maybe fifteen, minutes passed before another large wave washed over him. This time, once the wave had disappeared, Swann was nowhere to be seen.

Chapter 11

The Boat: Day Seven

This morning we had our last teaspoon each of water. No one spoke as Hodgkin, adopting almost the role of priest, shared it out ever so carefully, ensuring not a drop was spilt. Our tongues had become so swollen that swallowing even this pitiful amount was difficult. I swilled it round my mouth, relishing the sensation; then felt it dribble down my throat. And then it was gone. The end of communion. I staggered back to my bench feeling bereft. The fact we'd always, until now, had another ration to look forward to, however minuscule, sustained us a little. Now, it was gone, every last drop of it, and the thought was unbearable. I looked at all the water surrounding us – it seemed so harmless, so tranquil, so tempting, but I'd seen, we'd all seen, the devastating effect it'd had on Pablo and Swann. What was it in the *Rime of the Ancient Mariner*? – Water, water everywhere and not a drop to drink. I trailed my hand over the side, simply to feel water against my skin but immediately the salt bit into the sores on the back of my hand and stung. I closed my eyes and fantasied about water. I saw myself standing under a waterfall, feeling it soak me to the skin with fresh, clear water. I felt it wash away all the grime from me, felt it cooling down my burning skin. I imagined absorbing it through every pore, allowing it to cleanse me from within.

I dreamt of Karachi. I'd never been to the place before. In fact, if truth be told, I wouldn't even be able to place it on a map. But in order to divert my thoughts away from water, I tried to visualize it. I saw trams making their way down long roads lined with palm trees. I saw grand houses fronted by wrought-iron fences topped with curlicue patterns. I saw men in turbans and women in saris. I dreamt of walking into a café and sitting outside under a parasol, being served sweet tea by an Indian waiter in a crisp white jacket. I light a cigarette and watch the plumes of smoke disappear into the hot Indian air. I sit alone; I have no need for company. All I need is my tea, a cigarette or two and maybe something sweet, perhaps a large slab of Madeira cake. I wonder whether they have Madeira cake in Karachi. Such simple pleasures but it's the simple pleasures that one misses most. Gentle music plays in the background, a string serenade perhaps. I buy an English newspaper – Plymouth Argyll have won the cup; England have beaten India by fifty runs; an inventor has come up with the means of turning salt water into fresh; the war is at an end. This time, unlike the last time, it really was the war to end all wars. Hitler has given himself up. The King has him locked up in the Tower of London. I longed also for a bed, a soft bed on which to lie out flat and sleep. The hard wooden benches were so painful on my scrawny buttocks and ribs. I longed for a ceiling above me; I was fed up with the night sky and its infinite stars. All that emptiness, all that nothingness, a constant reminder of my insignificance.

I dreamt of walking on the moor near the village. I tried to imagine the smell of bracken, the crunch of dried grass beneath my feet, of Angie chasing wasps. I dreamt of feeding a sugar lump to the old piebald horse that lived in a field next to the moor.

But, unable to hold onto them, the images faded. Instead, I thought of Bernard Swann. I hoped his end came quickly, that he didn't suffer for too long, but in truth I didn't feel anything for him. Or Pablo, or Charlie Palmer, Leo Arbatov or John Clair. Death no longer seemed to concern me now – I'd seen so much of it in the last few days. I felt as if my brother had been dead for years. My mind had shrivelled so much I lacked the capacity for grief or pity, each of them leaving just the faintest of somnolent traces on my mind. I grieved not for my brother or the others but for a cup of tea in a quaint Indian café. For a cigarette and a nice English newspaper.

*

Rain! It started off as little more than a pitter-patter but then, in no time, it became torrential. Suddenly re-energized, we positively danced while craning back our heads, savouring those first precious drops of rainwater. Owen hugged me. We had the rain without the storm. Thank goodness we hadn't thrown all the empty tins of pemmican and bully beef overboard. We lined them up and in no time they were half full. Five men; five tins. We gulped down the water. Too quickly perhaps, Hodgkin straightaway threw up. But it didn't diminish the elation he

96

felt, we all felt, at feeling the sensation of water in our bellies. Owen started singing *It Looks Like Rain In Cherry Blossom Lane*. Soon, we'd all joined in, crisscrossing our arms as if singing *Auld Lang Syne* on New Year's Eve. We'd regained our voices. After so long without speaking, how strange it was to talk let alone sing. Having sated our immediate thirst, we emptied the tins of water into the bottles, and every receptacle we could find. And still the rain fell in torrents, resembling a curtain, through which we could barely see a thing. Oh, the joy. We splashed our feet in the boat until a stab of fear struck me – what if this rain carried on and on? Eventually, the boat would fill up. There'd be no way we could bail at such a speed. We'd sink. The thought had not crossed the minds of the others. We'd be OK for a long while yet but now, having so happily welcomed the rain, I wished it to stop.

And then it did. As abruptly as it had arrived, the rain simply ceased as if God had turned off the tap. We remained on our feet, splashing in water, causing the boat to rock on the still sea, all happily drenched. Davison put the rain down to God, and with his arms outreached, proceeded to thank Him with lavish exaltations.

'Stop that,' yelled Beckett.

'Harris, what's the matter? Do you not believe the rain was God's doing?'

'No, I bloody don't.'

'Leave him be,' said Hodgkin.

'No. Anything good that happens is *God's work* but He doesn't take any of the blame for putting us in this shit in the first place.'

'I think you'll find, Harris, that that was the Germans.'

Beckett stepped closer to him. 'Yeah, but this God of

yours doesn't see fit for us to be rescued.'

'Fair point,' said Owen.

'No,' I said. 'If Ed needs his God, let him have it.'

'Yeah, but we don't want to hear it all the time,' said Beckett. 'Your God's happy enough to let us rot out here.'

'Everything has its purpose, God has His plan, and–'

'Stop, just bloody stop, won't you? I'm sick of it, you never used to be like this.'

'Perhaps that's the reason why we find ourselves here. Because we failed to believe…'

Despite Beckett's obvious anger, none of us expected it. He hit him so hard, Davison fell against the side of the boat, lost balance and with flailing arms toppled backwards overboard into the water.

'Christ, Beckett, what have you done?' I screamed.

'You idiot,' said Hodgkin.

Owen leant over the side. 'Ed, you OK? You OK?' Thankfully, Davison was still conscious, beating his arms in the water.

'He deserved it,' muttered Beckett. 'All that God stuff…' He shuffled back to the stern like a child who knows he's done wrong, while Davison flapped near the boat.

I joined Owen at the side of the boat. 'Your hand, Ed,' called Owen. 'Give me your hand.'

My heart stopped – there was something dark in the water. Something dark and not too far behind him, a sinister shadow moving at speed. 'Oh, God.' I knew with terrifying certainty what it was. 'Ed,' I yelled, the panic rising in my throat. Realising something was wrong, he turned round. He saw it too. Frantically, he tried to swim away but too late. His eyes ablaze with utter, gut-wrenching terror, he screamed as the shark emerged like a rocket from the water, its frightful triangular teeth exposed like rows upon rows of razors. The sea curdled as the beast lunged at Ed. We watched, our hands over our mouths, as the water turned red. The boat rocked; Ed's desperate shrieks filled the air. I saw the poor man hit the shark on its nose, fruitlessly trying to fend off this mountain of a fish. The shark had Ed by the leg, its teeth clasped vice-like onto his thigh, shaking him like a ragdoll. With his free leg, screaming frantically, he tried to kick at the shark. Unable to watch, I turned, pulling at my hair, hollering, Ed's terrified cries bouncing in my head. And then, abruptly, the screaming stopped, leaving only the sound of the bubbling water.

I turned. The water was still boiling, the redness seeping away, but Ed was gone. I saw a glimpse of the dark shadow sink into the sea. Owen vomited while I collapsed against a bench and sobbed uncontrollably.

*

I don't know how many hours passed but when I gazed over at the others, I found them, like me, all huddled up in balls in different parts of the boat.

When finally we mustered up the strength to gather, Hodgkin, Beckett, Owen and myself, Hodgkin suggested we pray. It was, he said, what Ed would have wished.

No one objected.

Chapter 12

The Boat: Day Eight

My parents have a larder. That's where I see myself now. It's big, as big as a modest living room; grey slate floors, a huge white cupboard – one half of which is full of tins and packet food. Perhaps not now, not with the war on, but when I was a boy, my mother stored enough food to sink a battleship. Perhaps that's not the best analogy to use given my circumstances. The other half is stacked high with plates and bowls and cups and saucers and serving platters and dishes and baking trays and a weighing machine and a myriad other things useful in the kitchen. More than we could ever need. My mother can't bear to throw anything away; my father puts it down to her threadbare life as a child. The larder walls are thick, the windows small, covered with thick curtains permanently drawn. Even in the height of summer, this place remains cool. At the near end, next to the door leading to the kitchen, a huge table made of thick wood. More food. A tray of jams, another of pickles and condiments. Wire mesh domes cover the cheese board, the remains of last night's roast beef supper and suet pudding. A dish of leftover vegetables sits covered by a tea towel. There are the bread bins and bottles of milk, a fruit bowl and even a bowl of nuts. Father believes nuts are a vital aid to healthy bowel movements. There's a large tin full of little homemade cakes. I stand in the middle of this gastronomic heaven and spin round, breathing in the mixture of intoxicating smells: meat, bread, sweet – all mixed into one glorious symphony of food. My mouth salivates. How long now is it to dinner? I'd never appreciated my mother's larder before – it was just there. By God, I do now. But I've yet to mention the centrepiece of this fabulous place. At the far end of the larder, cemented into the ceiling are a couple of hooks. And hanging by a piece of string wrapped round its feet from one of those hooks is a dead pheasant. It's a male with its dazzling feathers of speckled golden brown, its turquoise neck and its red face. It's a beautiful bird – even in death, even hanging upside down stripped of its dignity in my mother's larder. Beneath it, a newspaper – just in case, my mother says, it drips blood. It won't drip blood now, I think, it's too dead. If asked, my father will claim to have shot it. He has a shotgun, never used as far as I know, which he keeps hidden away in the scullery. But, in truth, Mum bought the bird in the market at the nearby village.

So, back to the table with its bounty of food. What to eat first? I reach for an apple. But as I grab for it, it disappears. I must have imagined it. A slice of bread. Yet, it too vanishes at the point I almost touch it. No, this cannot be true. Perhaps a chunk of beef. God, yes, that'd be nice. But no, no, it's gone. Strange. Everything's disappearing before my eyes. Soon the larder is bare – all gone, nothing on the table; nothing in the cupboards, just the plates, endless empty plates. I'm so hungry, so thirsty.

*

'I can hear something.' Owen's voice, as with the rest of us, had become little more than a growl.

I tried to speak but my swollen tongue seemed to fill my entire mouth. 'What?' I croaked.

'L-listen.' His breath smells like death, his voice like that of a ghost.

Beckett struggled to his feet. 'He's right. Look, it's a plane, a bloody plane.'

'Get the flares, Gardner' ordered Hodgkin.

'Is it one of ours?' I asked.

'Does it matter?' said Beckett. 'It could be a Martian for all I care.'

'It's a long way off,' I said. 'It's flying away from us.'

'Still worth a shot.' With trembling hands, Hodgkin inserted a flare into the gun.

'Are you sure, Captain?' asked Owen.

'It's worth a try.'

Hodgkin fired it into the sky. 'Surely, they'll see it.'

We watched as the flare descended, knowing that the plane hadn't seen it.

'Do another,' said Beckett.

'No,' I said. 'We've only got the two left.'

'Searight's right; it'd be a waste.' Hodgkin, his eyes still cast towards the sky, didn't see Beckett approach him until he had snatched the flare gun from his hand.

'No, Beckett, what do you think you're doing?'

'You sent it in the wrong direction,' said Beckett.

'Don't do it,' I said, wanting to do something to stop him but lacking the strength to reach him.

'Put that down, Beckett,' said Hodgkin. 'That's an order.'

Stepping away from Hodgkin, Beckett slotted in another flare. Hodgkin reached him just as Beckett was about to fire. He grabbed for Beckett's tattooed arm, pulling it down at the point Beckett pulled the trigger. The flare shot straight into the water.

We all stood, slumped, lost for words. Looking up to the sky, I saw the aeroplane grow smaller and more distant.

'You bastard,' snarled Beckett.

'Don't you speak—'

'Do we think I give a fig for your authority? You're weak, *Captain*; always have been. Weak and useless.'

Hodgkin didn't seem to have it within him to respond.

'So now thanks to that little adventure, we've only got the one flare left,' I said. 'Well done, Beckett.'

'And you can shut it, Searight.'

I did. Not because Beckett told me to; I just didn't have anything else to say, too wrapped up in another disappointment. No one spoke another word for hours.

*

'We've got company, boys.' The voice belonged to Beckett.

On opening my eyes, I noticed that the boat was moving unusually fast – a wind had blown up and was pushing us on – to where, of course, we had no idea. Beckett was right – mostly to our starboard side we were being overtaken by huge numbers of flying fish. What a sight – silvery blue things with their enormous wing-like fins skimming across the water. There seemed to be an unending number of them and rapidly they came nearer and nearer to the boat. I knew we were all thinking the same – how to catch one. Then, as if to answer our question, one flew straight into the boat, landing at Beckett's feet at the stern. Beckett lunged and caught it. It slipped out of his hands. Before it had chance to move again, Beckett stamped on its head, killing it. A moment later, he'd picked it up and with his teeth tore into its flesh. Then, finding a lid from a discarded tin of bully beef, he used its jagged edge to cut away its head.

'Hey, stop,' shouted Hodgkin. 'We have to share. Beckett, stop, that's an order.'

But Beckett, having given up on trying to remove the head, had no intention of sharing the fish with us. Grunting loudly, his head shaking as he bit large chunks, he devoured it all with astonishing speed. Afterwards, he stood panting, catching his breath, his lips red and glistening, blood and gunk dribbling down his chin onto his chest. He smiled a manic grin at us, his eyes those of a wild beast. Whatever was left of the fish, and there wasn't much, he threw back into the sea. With his soiled fingernails, he picked at his teeth.

'You selfish bastard,' said Owen.

'Right, that's it,' said Hodgkin. 'I'm now officially putting you on a charge of indiscipline. When we get back to port, you will be–'

'I don't give a fuck what you do,' growled Beckett,

speaking slowly. 'You're all dead anyway.' He lumbered to the stern and, sitting down, leant over the side of the boat and vomited. He leant back, clutching his neck and groaned. Hodgkin, Owen Gardner and I sat at the bow, wanting to keep as much distance between us and Beckett as possible. It worried me the extent of animosity Beckett had for Hodgkin. Somehow, I knew our 'captain' needed protecting.

Meanwhile, the flying fish had gone.

*

I don't know how long I'd fallen asleep but when I opened my eyes, it was night-time. A half-moon brightened the world, casting what in any other circumstance might be considered a beautiful glow. Piled on the bench opposite mine a bunch of bananas had appeared. I counted them – six yellow bananas, as yellow as yellow can be. I didn't question where they'd come from; all that mattered was that they were there. With a thumping heart, I glanced at the others, making sure they were still asleep. I had no intention of sharing. All I had to do was reach out for them. I began to weep, so thankful for this deliverance. Owen woke up. 'You OK, Robert?'

I had to tell him. 'Look,' I said, pointing at the bananas.

His eyes followed my finger. 'What are you pointing at?'

'Bananas,' I whispered, winking at him.

'Where?'

'There,' I said impatiently. How could he not see them?

'I don't see no bananas.'

Your loss, I thought. Summoning my strength, I stretched out my hand, shaking with anticipation. But they'd gone. As soon as I'd reached for them, they'd gone. 'Hey? Where did they go?'

'The bananas?'

'You took them, didn't you? You took my bananas.'

He shook his head in a pitying way.

'Give them back. Give them back, you swine. They were given to me. What have you done with them?'

'Robert, calm down, mate. I didn't take them.'

'So where have they gone? They were... they were right there.' I began to cry again.

'There were no bananas, Robert.'

'But they were just there. Six bananas, I counted them, and they were mine. Mine.'

My voice woke Hodgkin and Beckett up.

'What's up with him?' asked Beckett.

'He's hallucinating.'

Hallucinating. As soon as he'd said the word, I knew it to be true. I put my face into my hands and sobbed.

'I just want her to come back,' I said.

'I know, Robert. I know.'

'Where did she go? Where did she go, Owen? Why did she leave me? I thought... I thought she loved me. She said she loved me. We should have been married. She was my future. I thought I was hers. Why did she leave me? I just want to see her again – just one more time before... before...'

Chapter 13

The Boat: Day Nine

'Today's the day,' said Hodgkin. 'My daughter's been born.'

'Received a telegram, have you?' snarled Beckett.

'No, I feel it. I can feel it in my bones. I have a child – a girl.' Hodgkin rose shakily to his feet. 'Alice. She's called Alice.'

'Congratulations, Captain.'

'Thank you, boys. What day is it?'

'I don't know,' said Owen. 'June tenth, eleventh?'

'I thought it was the twelfth,' I said.

'It doesn't matter,' said Hodgkin. 'All I know is that she's been born. I am a father.'

'Immaculate conception, was it?' said Beckett.

'Shut up, Beckett,' said Owen.

Hodgkin sat back down muttering, 'I am a father, I am a father.'

'Just imagine,' I said, 'imagine holding her in your arms, your Alice.'

'Yes, what I'd give to do that now. Sorry you don't like the name, Searight.'

'It's OK, sir. It's a lovely name.'

'I want to go home. I want to see my daughter. Oh, for Christ's sake, when are we going to get out of this? I need to get home, I need to see her, my daughter, my new daughter…'

'It's OK, sir, we'll get you home soon,' I said.

'And exactly how you're going to do that, then, eh, laddie?' scoffed Beckett.

Hodgkin shook his head. 'I wish I could believe you, Searight. Beckett's right, damn him.'

'Damning me, are you, Captain? I'll see you dead first.'

'Hey, Beckett,' said Owen. 'Leave him be. You can see the state he's in.'

'Yeah, leading by example – as always.'

Hodgkin had gone in on himself. 'I want to see my daughter,' he said quietly.

*

Another hour or more passed. Owen and I leant against each other, back to back. Swivelling round, he said quietly, 'Hodgkin's in a bad way, mate.'

'I know.'

'I'm not… I'm not too good myself.' His breathing, I noticed, had become laboured. 'I can't carry on, Robert. I can't do this any more. Hodgkin's right – we're not getting out of this.'

'Hang on, Owen. We've seen a ship and a plane. Something else will turn up; it's bound to.'

He shook his head. 'I don't care. I'm all done in.

*

I look at the water, all that water, unending, stretching as far as the eye can see. It's perfectly still and blue, reflecting the sun. As much as I hate it and resent it, it looks quite dazzling in its beauty. I feel increasingly drawn to it. How simple it would be to surrender myself to it; to slip under the waves and feel its coolness embrace me. I want to be as one with the sea in all its infiniteness. I am dying, I know I am, and it's an ugly, sordid death – burnt, skeletal, puss-ridden, fetid and painful. I want an easy death and the sea beseeches me, promising just that – an escape from all this indignity. My skin feels as if it's on constant fire, ulcerated sores punctuate my body made worse each day by the sun. My beard is foul to the touch – brittle and filthy; and my fingernails have shrunk and turned black. My arms and legs feel constantly numb, our clothes disintegrating. Indeed, Beckett had jettisoned his clothes in a fit of fury, throwing them into the ocean. How much easier to succumb to the ocean, to allow it to strip away the pain, to take me whole. Oh, to end this misery, this non-life. The thought of descending slowly into those calm, soothing waters and lying forever asleep on the seabed tempts me. How much nicer a watery grave than this living grave on this wretched creaking boat, baked by the sun, watching my body disintegrate before me.

Alice. I think of you. I want my last thoughts to be of you, the great, unfulfilled love of my life. I want to die with your name on my lips, your image embedded on my mind. If only you knew. If only you knew how much I miss you. I can hear your voice with its lilting West

Country burr, I can see your eyes, those emerald eyes; I can smell you, that smell of freshness as if the moorland air has blown through you. Alice, if only you knew…

*

I had my eyes half-open when I saw the naked Beckett rise to his feet at the far end of the boat. By the position of the sun, I guessed it to be mid-afternoon. Owen and Hodgkin were asleep, Owen next to me, as was our habit, and Hodgkin in the middle, his back to Beckett. Like a drunkard, Beckett staggered about a bit, causing the boat to sway. I spied the reflection of the sun on a piece of metal in his hand. Something felt wrong. He stepped over the benches coming towards us, grunting. I tried to stir but, too weak, felt unable to move.

Now, standing behind him, Beckett's shadow fell across the sleeping Hodgkin. With deft movements, he yanked up Hodgkin's head by the hair. Hodgkin's eyes sprung open. He screamed as Beckett drew the tin lid across his throat. Owen and I sprang to our feet, too shocked, too frightened, to intervene. Hodgkin fell forward, choking, his hands at his neck. Beckett grunted, threatening us with his weapon which, I noticed, he had filed down to resemble a knife. Hodgkin, lying at the bottom of the boat, started convulsing violently, emitting pitiful gurgling noises. His bloodied hand fell against a bench. Beckett attacked again. Pulling Hodgkin up, he straddled him from behind and again, with the sound of sharpened tin against flesh and sinew, cut at his throat. Blood gushed everywhere in torrents. Satisfied, Beckett stepped back. Hodgkin, still gurgling, slumped forwards. To our shame, Owen and I, clutching each other like

110

petrified school kids, left Beckett to it. We watched in horror as Beckett twisted Hodgkin over onto his back. Now silent, almost dead, Hodgkin's throat was a mess of blood and gaping flesh. His body twitched as Beckett, tensing his muscles, drew his blade deeply down Hodgkin's chest, not once but twice, close together in parallel lines. Beckett yelled like a man from the Stone Age, then plunged his hand into Hodgkin's bloodied chest between the two slashes. Owen began sobbing as we watched Beckett pull out Hodgkin's heart, stretching it until the strands of flesh ripped. With it dripping in blood, Beckett sunk his teeth into the still beating, glistening organ, ripping it apart like a frenzied dog. With his mouth and hands and chest coated with Hodgkin's blood, he held up the heart to us, grunting, offering us a bite. Absurdly, we both politely said no.

Trembling, Owen and I watched Beckett but had to turn our heads as he devoured another of Hodgkin's organs. Then, seemingly satisfied, he lugged Hodgkin overboard. Hodgkin's corpse floated on the water when, alerted by the smell of blood, a white shark appeared. I lowered my eyes, unable to watch as the shark, with its huge mouth, pulled Hodgkin down.

Beckett screamed at the gods as if the devil had seized him, beating his chest. He paced up and down at his end of the boat, this naked beast of a man, as frightening and unpredictable as the wildest of animals. Finally, he slumped to the bottom of the boat, leaning against a bench, and closed his eyes. Sleep finally took hold.

Owen and I couldn't take our eyes off him. For what seemed like hours we stared at this man-cum-devil, too shocked to move or speak, too numb to comprehend what we had just witnessed. It was me who spoke first. 'You know,' I said in a whisper, 'we're going to have to kill him. He's done it once, he'll do it again. It's him or us.'

'I know.'

'We have to do it now, while he's asleep.'

'How?'

'I don't know.' I looked round the boat, hoping to find something we could use. 'I don't know.'

'We could take his knife off him.'

'Too risky; he might wake up.'

'He must've spent ages sharpening that thing. He must have used another tin lid to get it to such a fine point.'

'There's got to be something else. I know, we'll simply throw him overboard.'

'There's no way I could lift him.'

'No, you're right.'

Without taking his eyes off Beckett, Owen put his hand on my arm. 'I know what we can do.'

'What?'

'The rowlocks.'

'Good God, yes.'

'Do you want to do it?'

'No.'

'Nor do I.'

'Listen, Owen, there're two of them. We'll both do it. OK?'

'Yes, OK.'

'We have to do it now. If we stop to think about it, we'll never do it.'

The boat creaked as always. Beckett, his stomach full,

was still fast asleep, snoring. I knew full well that even an earthquake wouldn't wake him now. Nonetheless, Owen and I crept across the boat, like a couple of pantomime baddies, looking ridiculous. I found one rowlock, Owen the other. I weighed it up and down in my hand. It was hefty enough; it would have to do; it was the only thing we had. I felt terrified – this was no less than murder. I had to look upon Beckett as a rabid dog that had to be put down. We had no choice.

Bench by bench, we inched across the boat, closer to the sleeping Beckett, stepping round the pools of Hodgkin's blood. Inadvertently, I kicked an empty tin. We froze, waiting for Beckett to open his eyes. He didn't stir. Taking deep breaths, we moved closer. Now, we were upon him. His arms lay limp, his right hand closed over his blade, his legs beneath one bench, his head thrown back over another. The stench was foul. God, he looked more beast than human, his mouth and chin coated with dried blood, human blood congealed in his beard and his chest hair, on his hands up to his wrists. The big-bosomed, winking woman on his tattoo seemed to be mocking us.

'OK?' I mouthed.

Despite the uncertainty in his eyes, Owen nodded.

It was now or never. I gazed heavenwards. Please, God, forgive me for what I am about to do. I raised the rowlock high above my head. I thought of Hodgkin's baby girl, the daughter he would never see, the little girl denied her father. Do this for them. He deserves to die. Kill the bastard; kill the murderer, death to the cannibal in our midst.

Tightening my grip on the rowlock, the small but

solid lump of metal, I held my breath. Then, tensing every wasted muscle in my body, I screeched as I brought down my arm. The rowlock smashed into Beckett's forehead. Beckett screamed, cut short by another blow as Owen brought down his rowlock, smashing Beckett's nose, causing an eruption of blood. Screaming again, Beckett covered his face with his hands as alternately Owen and I pummelled him again and again. Beckett twisted to his side, involuntarily kicking his legs frantically. My mind empty, we smashed him in the side then the back of his head, grunting as we rained our lumps of metal on him. One after the after, in perfect rhythm, we hit him and hit him and hit him until finally… finally, he lay dead, his face and head a mess of blood, matted hair and broken bone.

Feeling faint, I tried to catch my breath. The bloodied rowlock slipped out of my hand, landing on the bottom of the boat with a thud. I stepped away from Beckett's body, over one bench and another before falling to my knees. I looked again at the heavens. White clouds moved slowly across the sky, too thin to block out the sun. Murder is a noisy business. Now that it was finished, the sound of silence seemed louder than ever, only the sound of my rapid breaths and that damn creak-creaking of the boat.

I closed my eyes, and felt the world spin ever faster around me. I felt myself fall into somewhere deep and black and blacker still. I couldn't stop, the momentum carried me further and further down, as if falling into Hell itself.

Chapter 14

The Boat: Final Days

Another morning dawned. The sun had yet to make its appearance. The silvery sky loomed above us, the stars slowly fading away one by one as if God was creeping around turning them off one at a time. A gentle rain fell. Owen was already awake, lying on the bottom of the boat. 'We have to eat him,' he said.

'No.'

'It's our only chance.'

I shook my head. 'I can't allow it.'

He glared at me. 'You can't allow it. Since when… We eat him or we die.'

'I'd rather die.'

'You can't mean that.'

I tried to pull myself up to a more comfortable position but the effort was too much. 'I do. I'm sorry.'

He began whimpering.

'You eat him if you want,' I said.

'You make it sound so easy. I can't if you can't.'

'Why not?'

'I just can't.'

After an hour or more, we'd gathered enough rainwater in our tins to have a few sips of fresh water. We managed to stagger across the boat and with great effort, dumped Beckett's naked body overboard. With Beckett gone, we stumbled back to the bow, away from all the blood and mess in the stern, and lay down. We'd used up the last drops of rainwater, and had not had anything to eat for days. We spoke not another word for hours to come.

Night came and with it the brightest of moons, illuminating the sky and bringing out the stars in all their glory. Such beauty and how I hated it. Owen muttered something.

'What did you say,' I croaked.

'I want to be as far away from here as possible. I want to be up there – on the moon.'

We fell asleep again. Another day came and went and then another night. We never moved. On that second night, a brisk wind blew up. A few more drops of rain fell but not in enough quantity to make any difference. I drifted in and out of consciousness. Each time I opened my eyes it was with the hope I'd find myself dead. Each time I was to be disappointed. In the few moments I was capable of coherent thought, it astonished me how much punishment the human body can take.

*

The following morning, I felt my arm being gently shaken. I opened my eyes. On seeing me awake, Owen pulled his wedding ring off his thumb. He passed it to me. I shook my head. I didn't want to take it; if I took the ring it meant he was accepting defeat. He nudged me on the arm and proffered it again. Still I refused. He opened his mouth and tried to speak. Eventually he managed to force out the word 'Joanna'. His breath came heavily. The effort of saying his wife's name had cost him. So, I took the ring, placed it also on my thumb, scraping the brittle skin as I eased it on. Even there I feared it would slip off. Owen blinked at me, a thank you. I shook my head at him, telling him he couldn't give up. But he'd already closed his eyes.

Owen never opened his eyes again. He died some point that morning, quietly slipping into eternity while lying next to me.

I lay there in a state of shock. Owen's death had been the most predictable but his departure left me feeling dazed and vulnerable. I realised then that he'd been right – we should have eaten Beckett. Owen would still be alive.

Ten men had at some point been on this boat. Now I was the only one. John Clair had been the first to die. It seemed a lifetime ago. I wouldn't survive for much longer; I knew that. I just hoped death, if it was to come, would come for me sooner rather than later. But whereas in the previous day or so I would have welcomed death, now I wanted to live. The reason for my new desire for life was that simple band of gold on my thumb. I had to live in order to deliver it to Joanna, as Owen wanted, and to tell her his story, to tell her his last word was her name.

I knew I should heave Owen overboard, to allow him the dignity of a watery grave but I couldn't do it, I had not the strength even to stand up, let alone lift a dead weight. And so we continued to lay together – Owen Gardner and me, both as still as the other. My mind at least had become more active. Owen's ring had re-galvanized my brain. I stared at the ring and willed a ship, a plane, anything, to appear. Something had to appear. For the sake of this ring I had to be saved.

*

I lay in the bottom of my boat in my silent world, silent save for the constant creaking. One day, I thought, someone would find us, and what a gruesome find it would be – two skeletons in a boat. At one point, during the night, a thunderstorm brewed up. Rain lashed down, piercing me. I opened my mouth and drank the rainwater. Streaks of lightning shot across the sky as the waves swelled. My empty stomach lurched as the boat rose and fell with the waves. If this continued to build up, I thought, then I was done for; there'd be no way I could cling on as I did the last time. But the storm proved relatively benign. The intensity of the rain refreshed me, both inside and out, and gave me a degree of renewed strength. I held up a tin and each time it filled up, I poured the water into a bottle. By the time, the rain finally eased off, I reckoned I had enough water for a number of days. All I needed now was for a flying fish to land at my feet. The storm had worked itself out by the time dawn broke and I drifted back to sleep.

*

What made me open my eyes at that precise moment, I will never know. It was still a mere dot in the distance, too far away to hear its engine, but I could see the sun reflecting off its metallic body. Although I could see it with my eyes it took a while before it registered in my brain. And when, finally it did, my heart pounded into life.

Staggering to my feet, I felt thankful to have had my fill of water. Without it, I don't think I could have moved. Now I could hear the deep groan of its engine, it was getting closer. I found Hodgkin's flare gun in the hold at the bow and the last remaining flare. Slotting in the flare, my hands began shaking uncontrollably. I had but the one flare and it had to count. My life depended on it. If they didn't see it, I was finished. It was certainly heading in my direction but perhaps slightly to the side. I could see it clearly now – it was an RAF Liberator presumably patrolling the ocean looking for U-boats. Surely, it would see the flare. But I had to fire now, it seemed to be rapidly veering away. I lifted my arm, pleaded to God, and pulled the trigger. The flare whooshed into the sky with its red light burning. And that was it – my last flare, my last throw of the dice. I waited, praying that I had done enough. The seconds ticked by – it hadn't seen me, it was flying on; it had gone past me. But then… wait, I think it was turning. Yes, it was turning, turning back towards me. The plane swooped down to less than two hundred feet, so low I could see the men in the cockpit. I waved at them, positively jumping up and down. The plane roared over me, dipping its wing. Praise be – I was saved. I was saved! The pilots circled round and this time, as it flew straight above me, they dropped a bag into the sea where it landed with a mighty splash with remarkable precision – within an arm's length of the boat. My whole body trembled with anticipation as I reached out, stretching for all my worth, and managed to pinch the canvas bag enough to pull it towards me. I heaved it into the boat crying with gratitude. I watched the plane disappear. It was a heart-wrenching sight but I knew I was safe now. They'd report back my position and something else would be along shortly to pick me up. I waved it goodbye. All I had to do was wait – and eat my provisions. I sat in the middle of the boat – away from the bloodied end and away from Owen at the other. With trembling fingers, I untied the knot on the bag and removed the flotation collar. Like a child on Christmas morning, I pulled everything out one by one. There were five 3½ ounce tins of beef pemmican, each with its own ring pull, bars of chocolate, biscuits, boiled sweets and bottles of water. They'd also included a pack of cigarettes but no matches, a new flare gun and a number of flares, and a basic first aid kit. No Christmas had ever been as joyful as this moment as I surveyed what was in front of me. Having had no food for so long, I now felt strangely anxious at having this bounty land at my feet. I couldn't open the tin of pemmican – I wasn't strong enough; perhaps I would be after a bit of chocolate and a few biscuits. With difficulty, I tried instead to coordinate my fingers to unwrap the first bar of chocolate. The smell! My insides jumped a somersault at the rich intensity of it. Lifting the chocolate to my mouth, I nibbled the smallest corner, allowing it to melt on my swollen tongue. My whole body sagged with relief. And then I swallowed, feeling the chocolate cascade down my throat like liquid gold in a furnace. I had never tasted anything like it in all my life.

I told myself to ration out my provisions for a few days at least – I knew it could take a while before anything appeared to rescue me. But, unable to restrain myself, I ate everything, bar the sweets, over the course of the day, washed down with the water. Afterwards, as evening began to fall, I felt bloated and drunk and very, very happy. My stomach hurt and I feared I would puke it all up again. But I managed not to.

Revitalized, I decided it was now time to take leave of Owen. He was stiff to the touch. How ugly we look in death. But it mattered not to him now. I grunted and groaned as I dragged him to the side of the boat. Having swung his legs over, which remained suspended in the air, I hoisted the rest of him up and over, and watched as he sunk into the water with a splash. 'Goodbye, old mate. You saved me. Thank you for everything.' I played with the ring on my thumb. 'I'll make sure she gets it.'

Returning to the centre section of the boat, I lay down, popped a boiled sweet into my mouth and, closing my eyes, starting dreaming about Alice. But no, I thought, as I rolled the sweet round in my mouth, that was too painful. So instead I dreamt about Angie. The thought of my little Jack Russell dog caused me to smile, cracking my lips, for the first time in weeks.

Chapter 15

Taking his glasses off, Major Bryant considered me, rubbing the distinctly red bridge on his nose. To his left Private Jones finished writing up the last few words and to his right Doctor Karr took a sip of water only to spill some of it on his pristine white coat. The fan spun above us. Outside, an old bent man in baggy grey clothes was escorting a mule and cart, the cart laden with bananas. Two boys speeded past either side on bicycles, both blowing whistles, causing the mule to momentarily rear its head.

'Interesting,' said the major. 'Like I said earlier, there were forty-two of you on the ship, plus the two coolies, ten on the boat. And you were the only one to survive.'

'Sir.'

'So, within twenty-fours of being spotted by the Liberator, you were picked up by...' He consulted his notes. 'By a Norwegian tanker.'

'Yes.'

Doctor Karr cleared his throat. 'What a relief that

must've been. They looked after you well?'

'Very well. I had a wash, cleaned my blackened teeth, got a new set of clothes and slept in their infirmary where I was set up with a drip and my skin covered in various creams. They fed me soup, and allowed me to sleep. And boy, did I sleep.'

The doctor laughed. 'I bet.'

'Altogether, a harrowing experience, Searight.'

'Yes, sir.'

'Those U-boats are lethal and they're run by very experienced men. The ones we're seeing at the moment are, according to our sources, armed with six 21-inch torpedo tubes and can carry twenty-two torpedoes. You bump into one of those and, as you found out to your cost, there's likely to be only one outcome. Shame about the mules. They would have proved useful. You still have Gardner's ring?'

'Yes.'

'It's quite a list, isn't it?' He picked up his sheet of paper on which he'd written all the names of the men on the boat. 'To recap – John Clair went mad and died, David Rodríguez Felipe was pushed overboard, Charlie Palmer and Leo Arbatov were lost to the storm, Bernard Swann went for a swim, Edward Davison was taken by a shark, Miles Hodgkin, your senior officer, was killed by Harris Beckett, while Beckett himself was killed, in self-defence it has to be emphasised, by you and Owen Gardner, while Gardner just died from, well, let's say starvation.' He paused, casting his eyes over the list of names. 'It reads like something Agatha Christie would've written. What's the name of that book, Private Jones? You've read it.'

'*And Then There Were None.*'

123

'Ah, yes, thank you. *And Then There Were None*. Or, in your case, Searight, And Then There Was One.'

I felt myself shrink under his scrutinizing gaze.

Clearing his throat, he continued. 'Now, the ship went down on June the second. We know because that's when we lost all radio contact with the *Academic*. We would have sent a rescue but I'm afraid we had an even bigger crisis nearby. And according to Captain Egeland from the Norwegian tanker, you were picked up on the fourteenth of June, ten days ago. So, I make that a total of thirteen days you were adrift.'

'Yes, sir.'

'Yet, according to my notes, the food, pitiful as it was, ran out on the sixth day.' Turning to his left, he asked, 'Is that what you've got, Jones?'

Sophie Jones flipped through her notes, quickly turning back the pages of her spiral bound notebook. 'Yes, that's correct, sir. Day six.'

'That means, Searight, you went seven days without a bite to eat. Not a – single – bite – to – eat,' he said, accentuating each word. 'Is that correct?'

I nodded.

'What?'

'I said yes sir, that's correct.'

'And you didn't exactly have much to eat on the first six days. It's remarkable given your circumstances – the salt water, the heat, the sun, et cetera, et cetera, that you managed to survive at all.'

'Miraculous, I'd say,' said the doctor.

'Yes, exactly, thank you, Doctor Karr.'

Karr addressed me. 'You told me, Robert, you didn't know how heavy you were to begin with. But we

124

reckoned,' he continued, turning to the major, 'assuming an average weight for a man of Robert's size and age, that he lost about thirty pounds during the ordeal.'

'Mm. Two and a bit stones. Could have been worse, I suppose. You're one very lucky man, Searight.'

'I appreciate that, sir. I thought I was going to die,' I said, rather too loudly. Private Jones looked up from her notebook, her eyebrows raised. 'At various stages, like I told you, I *wanted* to die. It couldn't have been any worse.'

'Yes, all right, Searight,' said Bryant, palms face up. 'I'm sorry. I'm not trying to imply anything. I just want to make sure we have the story as straight as possible. After all, it's now my unpleasant duty to write to each of the next of kin and inform them that their son or husband, whoever, is dead. Although I have absolutely no details for the Spaniard or the Indian chaps. Concerning the other eight men on the boat, I shall keep it vague. No one needs to know the details. You got everything, Jones? Good. Well, thank you, Searight. You've been very thorough. I apologise if this has been difficult for you but it's done now. We've detained you long enough. Unless there's anything else you want to add, you're free to go.'

'No, sir, I can't think of anything else. Nothing that springs to mind.' I stood up, self-consciously straightening my jacket and patting my pockets. 'Thank you, sir.' I nodded my thanks to Doctor Karr and Private Jones. They both half smiled back at me. I glanced up at the portrait of the king.

Removing his glasses, Bryant said, 'I understand you'll be heading back to England in a couple of weeks. Once home, you'll have twenty-eight days' leave. Something to look forward to, I would've thought.'

Yes, I thought, it was. Very much so. After all, I had to see someone about a ring.

Part Two

A Village in Devon, Southern England,
August 1944

Chapter 16

Unsurprisingly, the morning after my welcome home do at the White Ship, I woke up with a sore head. I opened my eyes to find Angie lying at the foot of the bed. She squirmed up, her short tail wagging, and licked my face. Exactly the same routine as before. Funny how dogs never forget. I wondered whether she'd done the same during her extended stay with Jenkins. I rather hoped not.

The memories of the party the night before came back to me – Gregory playing the piano and Mr Jenkins, the headmaster, mentioning a football match and saying Owen's wife had left the village: *She just upped and left one day,* he'd said. *Didn't even have the decency to hand in her notice. The house is empty.* I remembered how Abigail, Parker's daughter, had grown and her mother, June, escorting me home.

Stumbling downstairs, I looked through Mr Hamilton's cache of groceries, half of which he'd placed in the fridge. There was bacon, bread, tomatoes, eggs, tea, milk and sugar. Perfect – apart from the bacon.

I liked the kitchen. Being small it maintained the heat during the winter, yet, with thick walls, remained cool during summer. It had a bulky dresser decorated with cake tins I never used, a large sink, and dominated by a large green stove. I half expected to see Clarence. I almost called out to him to ask whether he fancied a cup of tea. Poor old Clarence. I had to face my parents some point.

Feeling revived after a hefty breakfast, I ambled across the village square to the public telephone box. I rang my parents. My mother answered – she always did. She screeched on hearing my voice, berated me for not telling her I was coming home and told me she hadn't stopped crying since she'd received the telegram about Clarence. I listened, twisting the phone wire round my fingers. The pips went; I had no more change. She told me to come round for lunch today. I couldn't face it and managed to postpone it twenty-four hours. It was a date, she said as the line went dead.

Returning home, I dug out my old bicycle from the shed at the back of the house, put Angie in the little basket at the front, and cycled the steep hill up to the moor gate. Leaving the bike at the gate, Angie and I went for a bracing walk. The sun peeked out from behind a pure white cloud; the grass was as green as it could be. My word, it was good to breathe in the moor air, to feel its grass beneath my feet, to watch Angie running round in circles, randomly sniffing at things. I'd been looking forward to this for weeks. Often, on the boat, I would dream of walking on the moor, brushing my hand against the bracken, of breathing in the pure moorland air. I dreamt of walking along the granite wall that ran along the path, of going up to the field with the piebald horse. She was still there. She came trotting up to me, shaking her head, as if she recognised me. I held out my palm with a sugar lump and laughed at the feeling of her bristly lips on my skin as she scooped up the lump. Lurking behind me, Angie growled at her.

I picked up a stick and threw it for Angie. She ignored it entirely, too busy with her own business. I walked up the hill, not too far, and on reaching a familiar spot, a small mound of stones, I sat down and admired the view. Angie trotted up and sat beside me, panting. There, in the distance, was the town of Brent-in-the-Moor with its church spire clear to the eye. If one squints, one can follow the route of the railway line. Sure enough, a train passed, billowing steam, barely audible from this distance. I traced its course as it disappeared and re-appeared from the trees in the valley, across a viaduct and through Brent. Beyond the village, it turned a corner and faded out of view, its steam the only evidence that it had passed. It had a long journey ahead of it – all the way to London, some two hundred miles or more.

I closed my eyes and revelled in the utter silence. I had longed for this stillness. We spent long periods on the boat in silence but it wasn't the same. The sense of anxiety never left one; the sound of the sea and the boat was always there, menacing even when calm. But this, this was heaven. I felt myself relax as I breathed in the freshness of the air. The navy had granted me four weeks' leave in order to recuperate, to use their word. I planned to do absolutely nothing, except perhaps paint the fence in front of the house, and enjoy these weeks of peace. I deserved it.

The only sound was that of Angie's jaws snapping shut as she tried, unsuccessfully, to catch a wasp. 'You silly thing,' I said, patting her on the back. I waved at an elderly couple walking further down the hill, their Golden Labrador bounding up the hill to greet Angie. They waved back. Angie had no interest and growled at the dog. The man called his dog back.

Walking home, I wondered how I would find Joanna. Surely, she must have left a forwarding address, otherwise how would Owen, had he survived, have found her?

I cycled back down the hill into the village, perhaps too fast as Angie, in her basket perched above the front wheel, looked somewhat worried, her ears flapping in the wind. I slowed down as I entered the village square. I spied Abigail and a boy of about eighteen loitering inside the bus shelter, Abigail sitting on the bench while the boy hovered over her in what, to my eyes, appeared a rather intimidating stance. I guessed this must have been Dan. I jumped off the bike and pushed it. He was a big chap, strong-looking with thick arms, thick black hair, wearing a red-checked shirt. They did not give the impression of being love's young dream. Indeed, Abigail seemed to be crying. 'You wouldn't speak like that if Dad was around,' I heard her say. Of course, I thought, her father – Pete Parker, due back on leave any day.

'Yeah, but he isn't, is he?'

On seeing me, Dan stepped back, muttered something and left. I noticed he walked with a limp.

'You OK?' I asked her, pausing at the bus shelter.

'Yeah,' she said with a petulant shrug of the shoulders.

Sensing it wise not to push her, I remounted and cycled away.

I cycled over to Joanna's cottage. She lived on the outskirts of the village; a quarter of a mile past the village

132

shop. The house did indeed look deserted. The garden gate had become unhinged and I had to lift it in order to push it open. The small area of grass either side of the path was overgrown with brambles and stinging nettles, but the house itself looked in good nick – the window sills looked freshly painted, although the flower pots next to the front door were in poor health. Placing Angie on the ground, she skipped round my feet as I knocked on the door despite knowing it was pointless. Sure enough, no answer. Raising the flap, I peered through the letterbox into the darkened interior; I peeked through windows but the curtains were drawn at each one. Pushing open the garden gate, I went through to the back garden. Still no sign of life. On the trellis table was a cup; a patch of mould had grown inside. The branches of an apple tree pushed against the panes of an upstairs window. The back door was locked. I wondered whether I should return with the ring in an envelope and push it through the letterbox, but I had the feeling she had gone for good.

From Joanna's, I cycled the short distance to June's house.

She opened her door and seemed pleased to see me. 'Good night last night, weren't it? Have you recovered?' she asked, leaning against the doorframe, accentuating the shape of her hip.

I laughed. 'I came to apologise–'

'Don't be silly; we all have one too many every now and then.'

'It was more than the one.'

'Well, Robert, if anyone deserves it, it's you after all you've been through.'

'Well, I just wanted to say thank you for looking after

me and getting me home in one piece.'

'Robert, I was wondering…' She glanced back indoors, as if making sure she wouldn't be overheard. 'Would you like to come over for dinner? Perhaps on Wednesday?'

'Erm, well, yes, that'd be lovely. Thank you.'

'Shall we say seven o'clock?'

'Sure. It's a date.'

Another date.

*

Returning home, I stopped off at the shop. Outside, in front of its large windows, shaded by a red and white stripped tarpaulin, a small display of vegetables fresh and, mostly, not so fresh. Inside, Mrs Hamilton, her hair in curlers, was serving a young woman whose son lurked near the door. Upon the counter was a display of cereal packets, alongside a set of scales. A ladder rested against the stacks of shelves. Having made her purchases, including a wax bag of assorted sweets, the woman walked out but not the boy. I realised then they weren't together. A freckly chap, about eight or nine, he wore long grey shorts and an oversized herring-bone jacket that looked as if it belonged to an adult. The poor boy; one could tell at a glance he was a loner.

'Are you wanting anything, William?' asked Mrs Hamilton.

The boy shook his head. With hands in pocket, he sauntered out and left, the shop bell tinkling in his wake.

I thanked Mrs Hamilton for the groceries and paid my bill. 'So, do you know, Mrs Hamilton, what happened to Joanna?'

'Who?'

'The German woman? Owen's wife.' She knew full well who I meant.

'Oh, her,' she said as if she'd just swallowed something unpleasant. 'No idea. One day she was here, the next she was gone.'

'And you have no idea where she went?'

'No, none at all.'

Mr Hamilton appeared from the back, wearing his long brown apron, his grey hair slicked back. Pushing aside a bead curtain, he took his place beside his wife behind the counter. 'Hello, Robert. You're asking about Joanna, I hear.'

His wife tidied a display of chocolate bars. 'I hadn't realised we'd sold so many of these,' she said to herself.

'Yes. I've just been to her cottage.'

'You won't find her there.'

'No forwarding address?'

'No. She left… how should I say it, in somewhat of a hurry.'

'Did she? Why was that?'

He shrugged his shoulders. 'Now, is there anything else we can help you with?'

'What? Well, yes, as I'm here, I could do with a couple tins of dog meat.'

*

Back at home, I had a visitor – my friend Gregory, a short man with round spectacles and a wild sweep of blond hair, wisps of which lay on the collar of his jacket.

Sitting at the kitchen table, he accepted my offer of tea and asked me, stuttering, whether I was pleased to be back.

'Of course.'

135

'It m-must have been awful out there.' Angie sniffed his shoes.

'Yes.'

'You don't want t-to t-talk about it. I understand.'

'Yeah, I don't want to appear rude but…'

'You're not ready.'

I nodded. 'Here, your tea. Angie, get away.' I sat down opposite him.

'S-she's alright,' he said, stroking her.

'How's it going with you, Gregory? Still teaching kids the piano?'

'Yeah. It's bloody painful, t-to be honest. The mothers all think their kids are mini-M-Mozarts yet most of them don't know the difference between a qu-quaver and a crochet h-however many times I tell them. But it p-pays my way so I mustn't complain. I've got one girl, though, well, a woman.'

'Go on.'

'S-she's called, called, she's called R-R-Rebecca.'

I knew by the way he had such difficulty saying her name that this Rebecca had taken my friend's fancy.

'Nice, is she?' I asked.

'Yes, well, you c-could say that.' He sipped his tea.

'Pretty?'

'S-she's very good on the p-piano. Well, m-maybe not so good.'

'Yes, of course. Sorry, old man.' Angie sauntered back to her dog basket next to the stove and, after much scratching and rummaging, settled down.

'So, how m-much leave you've got?'

'Four weeks. Time, they said, to help me get over the ordeal.'

'Is that enough?'

'They could give me four years and it still wouldn't be enough.' I swept some breakfast crumbs off the table. 'Tell me, do you know what happened to Joanna?'

'Owen's wife? No but I know p-people didn't l-like her.'

'What do you mean? She was fine the last time I saw here.'

'I don't know. Suddenly people t-took against her b-because of her accent. German.'

'Yes, I know that.' We watched Angie lick the crumbs from the floor. 'I hear June's husband is back soon.'

'N-not for long, I h-hope, the low life. June is a nice w-woman; she'd be better off without h-him. L-listen, do you fancy c-coming out fox hunting with me?'

'Fox hunting?'

'My d-dad's lent me his hunting gun and lamp. There's a fox who keeps terrorizing my c-chickens. The b-bugger even managed to kill a couple. I don't k-know how. He breaks into the p-pen.'

'Perhaps the slats are too wide apart.'

'Perhaps. Listen to this...' Placing two fingers in his mouth, he proceeded to make a strange high-pitched mewing noise. The effect on Angie, dozing in her basket, was electric. She sprung up, her ears alert, her tail erect, and darted manically round the kitchen, yelping, her nose to the ground. I laughed – what was she doing, the silly thing?

'What in the Dickens was that?' I asked once Gregory had finished.

'It's good, isn't it?' he said, grinning. 'My dad t-taught me – it sounds like a wounded rabbit.'

'Ha! I've never heard a wounded rabbit but I'm impressed.'

'Well, it certainly f-fooled Angie. Look at her.' The dog was still in a state of high excitement, following her nose, the fur on her back standing on end, sniffing out the source of the noise.

'Angie, calm down, there're no rabbits here. Can you fire a gun?'

'Of course. Well, I haven't tried for years but when I was a k-kid, I did. T-the night after t-tomorrow, after dark. F-fancy it, then?'

'Yeah, why not?'

After Gregory had gone, Angie continued prowling round, sniffing every conceivable place.

Poor Gregory. He was obviously smitten with this Rebecca. I'd never heard him mention a girl before and I knew full well that he'd never had a girlfriend; aged twenty-three, the man was still a virgin. I wondered what she was like, whether there was any chance that she might like her piano tutor.

It was time, I decided, for a spot of lunch. Oh, the joy – of being able to decide to eat, and to decide what to eat, and to eat from a plate at a table with a knife and fork. It's amazing how one longed for these little things when they are out of reach and denied to one.

So, I wondered, what could have happened to Joanna? Why did she leave? She had a job, a home and a supportive community around her, or so I thought. What had made her up and disappear, apparently, from what I could tell, rather suddenly?

I went to bed early but couldn't sleep – too many memories. I had lived – they had not. I should have died alongside them; I had no right to have survived. I felt as if I had been handed a second chance and that, as a result, I should make the most of the rest of my life, as if I should venture out into the world and explore all its delights from one continent to another. But, if truth be known, I was a little scared by the prospect – the world out there seemed a frightening place. I simply wanted to hunker down and hide away from everyone and everything.

Chapter 17

I paused at the garden gate, my hand on its latch. I had spent many an hour on the boat remembering my childhood home, enjoying bouts of nostalgia which could keep my mind occupied for hours on end. Oftentimes, I honestly believed I'd never see the place again. But now that I was here I was surprised by how little emotion I felt. I'd expected to be overwhelmed by relief, by my childhood memories, and especially by the anticipation of seeing my parents again. I felt none of these things. Indeed, I felt gripped by an obscure sense of dread. Having seen the house, satisfied it was still there as I had remembered, and safe in the knowledge that my parents would be inside, I had to fight the urge to turn tail and flee. The house was certainly handsome – red-bricked, tall chimneys, arched windows with leaded grilles, trails of ivy. It had character but I couldn't decide what – by day it resembled a vicarage but by night it had a more Gothic feel, where one might spy a young girl in a white nightdress peering anxiously out of the window. It reflected my father perfectly – solidly middle class, grand in an understated way and proudly old-fashioned, sure of its place in the world. But it was my mother who took the greatest pride in her home. 'A million miles,' she would say, 'from the damp-ridden outhouse that was my home on the west coast of Ireland.' My mother had put great effort in distancing herself from her humble origins, embracing the life of the wife of a middle-ranking, besuited governmental bureaucrat, a 'bourgeois pen-pusher,' as my father once described himself in a rare moment of self-deprecation. Occasionally, if she was particularly tired or if one listened carefully, one could detect the hint of an Irish accent. It was a fine house to grow up in – Clarence and I had the woodland behind all to ourselves, perfect for tree houses, swings and hide and seek, and a stream that masqueraded as a river. Rare was the day, whatever the season, that my mother didn't exclaim at our dirty knees. The house had always seemed big but surely now, without two boys running amok, it was too big for our genteel parents. But it was theirs, it was paid for, and I knew the upheaval of moving would be too insurmountable a prospect to even contemplate. As children, we had an elderly couple who lived in and, between them, did everything – cooked, cleaned, washed, stitched and mended. But on my father's retirement, they too finally took retirement. 'We can cope on our own now,' declared my father, and promptly left everything to my mother.

Finally, I pushed open the gate and, closing it behind me, stepped onto the gravelled path. The lawn either side of the path leading to the porch was, as always, finely manicured and the honeysuckle bush as resplendent as ever. My father had always insisted on an impeccably-clean garden, especially the front, exposed as it was to the visitors he never received, and employed a gardener all year round to see to it.

Halfway up the path, I saw the flutter of a downstairs curtain and, seconds later, the front door opening. 'Robert!' screeched my mother, waving at me from the porch. She'd dressed up for me – a long blue skirt, a dark green blouse with a matching necklace. 'It's really you. Praise be! Robert, let me take a look at you. Oh, my dear boy. Come here and give your mother a hug.'

'Hello, Mum.' We embraced. Her skin, which had always defied the years, still looked smooth, her hair as long as ever, carefully plaited.

'Oh, Robert, I can't tell you… we thought we'd lost both of you. It's been so… just so difficult.'

'I can imagine. I'm sorry.'

'What are you apologizing for?'

'It's OK, Mum. Don't cry now, don't cry.'

She thumped me playfully on the chest. 'You almost die in the middle of the ocean and you tell me not to cry. Robbie, I've cried so much in the last weeks I could have made my own ocean.'

'How's Father?' I'd always called my father 'father' while calling my mother 'mum'. Habits die hard.

'Looking forward to seeing you. We weren't sure what time to expect you. He's in the drawing room having his mid-morning nap. Come, let's go in; I'll make you a cup of tea.'

Inside, we sat down at the kitchen table. I used to love the kitchen as a child, spending hours at the huge old table, drawing and writing stories. It was high-ceilinged with heavy beams decorated with brass plaques; the fireplace

142

was so big that as kids, during the summer when it remained unlit, Clarence and I used to hide behind the stove. During the winter, the heat it gave off was wonderfully intense and comforting.

'Can you come also for lunch on Friday?'

'Yes, guess so. My time is my own for now.'

'Good. I've invited your Uncle Guy and Aunt Jo. They can't wait to see you.'

'Yeah, that'd be great.'

'Robert, I know…' She scooped up a tea towel. Twisting it in her hand, she continued. 'I know you have a tale to tell, about your experiences and everything, but…'

'Don't worry, Mum, I won't tell it.'

'Oh but, Robert, you're probably dying to–'

'No. I had to tell it often enough to the debriefing chaps. I don't need to tell it again.'

'It must have been awful, I know, but I can't face it, Robert. I'm not strong enough to hear what ordeals my poor boys underwent. I want to believe that Clarence died without pain, that he quietly slipped away but I'm not naïve; I know he would have suffered.'

I nodded.

'Did he mention me?' she asked, her voice barely a whisper.

'Of course. You were never far from our thoughts.'

She bit her knuckle and almost staggering took a seat at the kitchen table beside me. Taking my hand, she whispered, 'I know the two of you didn't always get on but he was a good boy; you both were. I was awfully proud of you both, you know that, don't you, Robert?'

I patted her hand, forcing a smile. 'Of course I do.'

'You were such lovely boys, always so considerate.

Different though, both so different.' She smiled, her eyes faraway. 'Robert, I don't know what day he died on. What day did Clarence die?'

'June the second.'

'June the second,' she repeated slowly, as if mulling the date round her mind. 'June the second, 1944. Thank you.'

'Father's napping still?'

'Yes. Poor Lawrence.' She picked up the saltcellar, turning it around in the palm of her hand, eyeing it as if seeing it for the first time. I remembered it. It'd been there for as long as I could remember. In fact, looking round, there was nothing in the kitchen that was new. Nothing had changed – the clock on the wall decorated with a hen, the ceiling hooks on which hung various kitchen utensils, the portrait of the king, and a souvenir coronation cup and saucer. My Irish mother had always embraced the Royal Family with a passion. 'It's been difficult for him too, of course. He sleeps a lot now. Always early to bed. He used to be such a night owl.'

'Has he talked about it?'

She shook her head. 'I wish he had.' She looked at me, her eyes filled with wistfulness. 'You know your father – never been a talker. But this, what happened to Clarence, has driven him into a corner so dark, so far away, I've lost him altogether.'

'I'm sorry.'

Placing the saltcellar neatly beside the pepper pot, she continued. 'He doesn't think that perhaps I need to talk, that holding this sadness inside me, never being able to give voice to it, is torture for me. What can I do?'

'Your sister? Uncle Guy? They don't live that far.'

Sighing, she let her head fall back. 'I know. But it's not

144

the same. Grief – it doesn't announce its arrival. I'll be hanging out the washing when suddenly it creeps up on me and takes my breath away. I find myself in floods of tears while a pile of wet underwear fall at my feet. That's when I need my husband but no…' Fishing out a handkerchief from her skirt pocket, she wrapped it round her forefinger until it resembled a bandage, unaware, I think, of what she was doing. 'I've known grief like this before.'

'Uncle Jack?'

'Jack Searight. Killed at seventeen. Still a boy. Just a boy…'

'Are you OK, Mum?'

'What? Yes, yes. I'm sorry. It was all a long time ago. Robert, please go see your father now.'

'Of course. Perhaps then you could make that tea.'

She laughed. 'Oh my goodness. What a mother I am. Silly me. You go now.'

*

I found my father, as mother had said, in the drawing room. The curtains were drawn but a crack illuminated the familiar room. I caught a shadow of my reflection in the huge gilt-edged mirror above the mantelpiece. The ornate clock flanked by cupids which my father always loved and my mother found overly ostentatious, showed a few minutes to eleven o'clock. Father, his legs crossed, in his corduroy trousers and V-necked jumper, was sprawled in the armchair, his glasses resting on a newspaper open face downwards on his lap. Next to him, on the small rounded table, a cup and saucer, a few crumbs of a biscuit or two, his pipe resting in an ashtray. He looked older than I

145

remembered – his face heavily lined, his beard almost grey. I realised I felt the familiar twinge of anxiety – that old feeling I had so frequently as a child, the sense of having done something wrong, but having no idea what it was, the fearful anticipation of being berated. Everything about the room was how I remembered it, a pair of prints depicting finely-dressed Japanese ladies, the bookshelves, a bonsai tree, the standard lamp.

My presence was enough to stir my father. He opened his eyes and seeing a figure before him, squinted. 'Clarence? Clarence, is that you?'

This wasn't a good start, I thought. 'No, Father, it's me, Robert.'

He sat up, fumbling for his glasses, his hands trembling. 'No, it can't be,' he said with a nervous laugh. 'Don't be daft.'

I waited as he put his glasses on. On seeing me, his hand clutched his heart. 'Oh, God, I thought...' he said breathlessly. 'Oh my, it's you. Oh, my Lord.' Sitting forward, he clasped his temples. The newspaper slid off his lap. He muttered my brother's name numerous times.

I stood, as nervous as a child before his headmaster, wondering whether to apologise, when I realised my mother had joined me.

'Lawrence, it's Robert.'

He looked up at us, a fury within his eyes. 'I can bloody well see who it is. It's Robert. Welcome back,' he said in a tone that implied he didn't mean it. 'Welcome back. You survived. I thought you were...'

'I know.'

'But Clarence didn't survive, did he? No, you survived – he didn't.'

146

'And you know that, Lawrence.'

'I hoped... Aren't those his clothes? I recognise that jacket.'

'My clothes are too–'

He sprung up from his chair. 'What are you doing wearing his clothes? The boy's dead and you're–'

'Lawrence, stop this. Stop this now.'

He scooped up the newspaper off the floor. 'I wish to be left alone.'

'Aren't you going to welcome your son home?'

Leaning against the mantelpiece, his back to us, he said, 'I've said it, haven't I? I'll hang out some bunting later. Now, leave. Please.'

My mother pulled an apologetic face. 'Come,' she said, taking my hand. 'We'd better leave.'

'He's been terribly upset by Clarence's death. He doesn't mean to take it out on you.' We were back in the kitchen, a lukewarm cup of tea on the table. I sat down heavily.

'Mum, you've forgotten the sugar.'

'Silly me. I should have remembered.'

'The wrong son died.'

'No, Robert, don't you be saying that; it's not true. It's just...'

'Yes? Go on, what?'

'Give it time, that's all I can say. Give it time.'

Chapter 18

It was a fine day, sunny with a slight, pleasant breeze. I'd made a list of all the things I needed for my larder and with Angie at my feet returned from the shop with a number of heavy bags having spent far too much. I saw a group of children playing around the bus shelter, many on their bikes. Among them, sitting by himself on the bench within the shelter, was the small boy I'd seen previously at the shop, William, still wearing his herring-bone jacket. It occurred to me that several of them might have been taught by Joanna.

'Hello there,' I called out to a couple of girls playing tag.

'Hello,' said one, a girl of about ten with neat ponytails.

'Did you girls know Mrs Gardner at school? Was she your teacher?'

'Yeah but she's gone now.'

'Do you know where she's gone?'

The girl and her friend both shrugged their shoulders. 'We're going to have a new teacher,' said the other.

'Not Mrs Gardner then?'

'Uh-ah.'

'And what about you,' I said, approaching the bus shelter. 'It's William, isn't it? Did you know Mrs Gardner?'

He looked at me sullenly from beneath his fringe but said nothing.

'Was she your teacher?'

Nothing, not even a nod of the head. I thought it best not to pursue it.

*

That night, Gregory and I went foxhunting. I went to his house, a little bungalow, not unlike mine: low ceilings, stone floors and dark rugs, old wooden furniture. He showed me the hunting gun, laying it on his kitchen table. Although old, almost antique, it was still an impressive piece of equipment. 'So this is your father's? Are you sure you want to use it?'

'No but my c-chickens. The b-bugger tried to take another last night. I rushed out and scared him off. Big b-brute.'

'And you know how to fire this thing?'

'Yeah, b-but I was r-rather hoping you'd do it.'

'Me?'

'You're in the m-military.'

'No, Gregory, you know full well – the merchant navy doesn't count.'

'Still.'

'Have you warned your neighbours?'

'Oh yes.'

'And you got the lamp? Good, let's go then, get it over and done with.'

We set up in his backyard, the lamp at the ready, Gregory holding the gun. It was gone midnight. Every few minutes, he'd make the noise of the wounded rabbit, surprisingly loud at this quiet hour. The chickens clucked within their pen. An hour passed, perhaps more, and still we waited. The night, thankfully, was warm but very dark; no moon to see by. I looked up at the stars. Were they really the same stars I stared at for hours at a time far, far away? The deep dark sky and the silence reminded me too much of the boat. I shuddered at the memory.

'Have you seen Rebecca today?'

'No. Shush.'

'Perhaps he can smell us,' I whispered.

'P-perhaps but he won't be able to resist hunting out a wounded prey.' With that, he resumed his whistling. How Angie would have loved this.

I heard something – a rustle near the fence at the back of Gregory's yard. I gripped his arm. He nodded and produced another whistle. More noise – something was definitely there. Gregory took the gun and nestled its butt into his shoulder. I rested my finger above the lamp's 'on' switch, ready for Gregory's order.

'N-n-now,' he managed to whisper.

I flicked the switch and the yard was suddenly thrust into a sheer white light, brighter than day. And there, its eyes caught in its beam, just a few feet away, was the fox. The deafening crack of the gun rattled the silence of the night. The fox seemed to fly across the yard in a ball of fur and blood. Gregory screamed. The chickens erupted into a flurry of agitation and noise. Dogs all round the village, or so it seemed, started barking. Unlocking the gun, Gregory rushed over. I joined him, kneeling over the shattered body. The fox was dead, his torso a mess of blood.

'Wow, a direct hit, Gregory.'

'Yes,' he said, but there was no hint of triumph in his voice. Shaking his head, he added, 'Poor beast. I'm sorry.'

'It had to be done. It was him or your chickens.'

'I feel s-sick.'

I patted him on his shoulder. He was distressed, regretting taking the life of such a fine creature. 'Come on, let's go back in. I'll come by in the morning and clear him out, if you want.'

He nodded. I helped him up. Removing his glasses, he wiped his eyes.

'Are you OK, Gregory?'

'I will n-never in my life ever kill another living an-animal.'

*

I left Gregory preparing to go to bed, still upset. I stumbled home in the dark, passing through the village centre with the church spire silhouetted against the black sky. Passing various front gardens, the air smelt deliciously of night stock. I heard whispered voices coming from within the bus shelter. Immediately, I recognised Abigail's plaintive tones. 'No, Dan – my dad will kill me.'

'And how's he bloody going find out?'

'Mum will know and she'll tell him.' She was crying.

'For fuck's sake, how will she know?'

'She just will.'

I cleared my throat.

'Who's that?' said Dan. 'Oh, it's you,' he said on seeing me. 'Our very own war hero.'

'All right, Dan.'

'You spying on us?'

'I was just passing.'

'At this time of night?'

'Yes, at this time of night.'

He considered me for a few seconds. 'Sod this, I'm off. You coming, Ab?'

'No,' she said, unseen by me inside the shelter.

'I'll take you home,' he said.

'I'll go by myself.'

'No.' He made to snatch her hand.

'Get off me.'

'She said no,' I said, hoping I sounded authoritative enough.

'You what?' said Dan, squaring up to me.

Now, a few months back, before the sea had taken its toll on me, I would have felt strong enough to hold my ground. Not so much now. Nonetheless, I had to see this through. 'Go home, Dan. I'll walk Abigail home.'

He held out his hand for her. She shook her head. He considered his options for a few moments. How could he back down without losing face?

'I'll see she gets back OK,' I added, hoping to make it easier on him.

'Right. OK. I'll see you later then, Ab. But this ain't finished, right?'

'Just go, Dan.'

He shot me a filthy look before limping off into the night.

'Come,' I said to her.

She emerged from the shelter, clutching her handbag to her chest, looking round as if making sure Dan had gone. Her hair was dishevelled, her make-up smudged. She wore a flowing floral dress but her white blouse, I noticed, was torn. 'I'm alright,' she said. 'I can walk by myself.'

'No, I said I'd take you, and I will.'

We walked slowly, Abigail wrapping her arms round herself.

'Are you cold?'

'No.'

'Do you want to tell me what that was about?'

'No.'

I wondered how to frame the next question. 'Is everything OK, Abigail? Did Dan hurt you in any way?'

'No, of course not.'

We walked the rest of the way in silence, Abigail's eyes fixed on the road in front of her.

A car passed us by, its headlamps momentarily catching us in its light. Who it was, what sort of car, I couldn't tell – it was too dark to see.

We arrived at her home. 'Here we are,' I said, pointing out the obvious. She retrieved a key from her handbag and, without a word, without looking back at me, walked up to her door and went inside. On closing the door, I heard shouts from within – June had been waiting up for her and was understandably cross that her daughter had returned so late.

Chapter 19

The following morning, a lovely day, I decided to make a start on sanding the fence. I was hunting round for some sandpaper under the stairs when Angie jumped up and started barking. There was someone at the door. It was Abigail, looking breathless and in a state of some anxiety. I invited her in while Angie ran round her in circles. She took a seat in my kitchen, her knees clasped together and, turning down my offer of tea, stroked the dog. 'Get down, Angie,' I said.

'She's all right.'

Tonight, I was due to have dinner with her mother. 'So what brings you here in such a hurry?' I asked while drying a cup and saucer that didn't need drying.

'Last night – I don't want you to tell my mum.'

'I had been thinking about it.'

She looked at me with fright written all over her face. 'No, you can't.'

'So tell me what happened then?'

She was wearing her yellow dress with small red spots.

Pulling her dress over her knee, she crossed and uncrossed her legs. 'Dan, he – he wants to… you know.'

'I see. But… you don't.'

'No. I'm not…'

'You're not ready yet.'

'Yes, that's it. I'm not ready yet. Anyway, it's not as if we're engaged or anything.'

I took a seat and sat opposite her. 'Abigail, did Dan… did he, how shall I say this, did he force himself on you?'

She pulled on a loose strand of her hair. Sucking it, she shook her head.

'So why are you crying, Abigail? I noticed last night your blouse was torn.'

'He… he tried to. I had to…'

'Go on.'

She scanned the kitchen, her eyes wide with apprehension. 'I had to push him off. He's strong though. It was difficult. It was… it weren't nice.'

'Did he hurt you?'

She shook her head again, staring now at Angie lying at my feet.

'You have to finish with him.'

'No,' she cried. 'I can't.'

'Why not?'

'I…'

'Yes? You can tell me.'

'I love him.'

'Oh.'

'But I'm only sixteen. He's nineteen though, so he reckons we should… you know. Mum doesn't like him, thinks he's rough. He is, I suppose. And if she tells Dad, he'll kill him, I know he will. She tells him everything I do and he gets… Dad gets angry.' She looked up at me. 'Please, don't tell my mum.'

I felt the need to rest my hand on her shoulder, to reassure her. Here was a young, attractive girl on the verge of womanhood but still, in essence, a small girl. It was the small girl that now sat in front of me sucking on her hair. I couldn't help but feel pity for her. 'OK, I won't tell your mother.'

'You promise?'

'I promise.'

She sighed with relief. 'Thank you. Thank you.'

Abigail's visit disturbed me. I'd promised her but already I was regretting it. Her mother had a right to know; Abigail had to be protected. Yet, a promise is a promise, even one made in haste. My enthusiasm for sanding the fence had evaporated. I decided I'd go visit Gregory. That, I thought, would cheer me up.

*

I wanted to see whether Gregory had recovered from his bout of fox killing. Along the way, I stopped off at the shop. Despite having bought so much recently, I'd forgotten a few essentials. I was just dismounting my bike when I saw the boy, William, charging out of the shop with Mr Hamilton in his wake. 'Oi, you boy, come back here, you little bugger!'

The boy didn't stop, running down the road and around the corner.

'Are you OK, Mr Hamilton?'

'Oh, Robert. Did you see that?' He had a couple of sausages in his hand. 'That little scamp. I just caught him shoplifting.'

'I'll chase after him.'

'No, no, don't worry; I'll get him. Would you believe it? Does he not think I don't know who he is or where he lives? Anyway, what can I get you? Have you found your teacher yet?'

'Joanna? Unfortunately, no.'

The sudden appearance of June in front of me took me by surprise. Hamilton returned inside. 'Robert, can I have a word? Have you seen Abigail?'

What could I say? I said no, the lie, so easily said, piercing me from within.

'She said you walked her home last night.'

'Did she? Well, yes, last night I saw her.'

'Was she OK? Was she upset?'

'She – she didn't say much. It was late. I think she was tired.'

'Was Dan with her?'

'Not when I saw her.'

She considered my answers for a few moments, her eyes boring into me. 'Why?' I asked. 'Is something wrong?'

'No. Perhaps. I don't know. Listen, Robert, about tonight.'

'Dinner? I'm looking forward to it. Do you want me to bring anything?'

'No, I think… What I mean to say is that… Look, I don't think it'd be a good idea.'

'Oh.'

'Look, I'm worried about Abbie, and Pete's back in a few days. You know what village gossip is like; it might starts tongues wagging. I'm… I'm sorry.'

*

Standing outside Gregory's door, I could hear the piano coming from inside. Someone was practising their scales – and not very successfully. I wondered whether I should return later but the thought occurred to me it might be this Rebecca, and the temptation of seeing the object of Gregory's desires was too much to resist. I knocked. The piano stopped but there was some delay until Gregory finally answered the door.

'Am I disturbing you?' I asked.

'W-well, we're just s-starting a lesson but y-you can come in if you want.'

He led me through to his living room where, sitting at the keyboard, was an attractive dark-haired woman perhaps in her early thirties in a fetching light green dress and a red jacket. 'T-this is R-Rebecca. Rebecca, this is m-my f-friend, R-Robert.'

'Nice to meet you,' she said, offering her hand. 'I've heard a lot about you. You must be pleased to be home.'

'Yes, I am.'

'W-well, I, I mean, we n-need to c-carry on.'

'Yes, don't let me disturb you. In fact, I'll come back later. I only wanted to...' I hesitated, somehow I felt Gregory wouldn't want me to mention the dead fox in front of his pupil.

'I've d-done it,' he said, reading my mind. 'T-thanks anyway.'

'Excellent. I'll… leave you to it.'

'Bye bye, Robert,' said Rebecca, smiling brightly. 'Nice to meet you.'

'And you.'

I did wonder, as I left, whether Gregory's stutter was more pronounced in front of her.

Dressed in my pyjamas, I was cleaning my teeth, when, near midnight, I heard the urgent rap on my front door. Angie, lying on my bed, leapt off and charged downstairs, barking frantically. Who on earth could that be at this time, I wondered, concerned. I knew that whoever it was, this didn't bode well. With a heavy heart, I unlocked the door and pulled it open.

'You bastard,' yelled June, marching in uninvited.

I stepped back. 'What?' With Angie yelping at our feet, she pummelled me on the chest with her fists. 'June, stop, stop; what's the matter?'

'I trusted you, you bastard.' I caught her fists. 'It was you; she told me; she told me everything.'

'What? Who?'

I let her go. Her eyes were red. Speaking through clenched teeth, she spat out her accusation, 'Don't pretend you don't know. Proud of yourself, are you?'

'June, please, calm down. Get down, Angie,' I said, pushing her away with my foot. 'Is this about Abigail?'

'Oh, so you admit it. How could you, I trusted you, how… She's just a child.' She collapsed in tears.

'And she told you it was me? It wasn't me, June. I swear to you, I did not touch her.'

'No?' she screeched. 'She told me it was. Should I not believe my own daughter? I should tell the police, but no, I don't want to upset Abbie any further.' She wiped her eyes with the back of her hand. 'But you listen to me, if you've not left this place by the time Pete returns, he will kill you with his bare hands.'

'June–'

She put up her hand. 'Don't. I don't want to hear it, you pathetic excuse of a man. He'll kill you, I swear it. That German whore got what she deserved and you will too.'

'But, June...'

Throwing me a hateful look, she sniffed, turned and left. With my heart thumping, I watched her stride away into the night.

Gently, I closed the door. Feeling weak, I climbed back up the stairs and got into bed. Angie leapt up and snuggled down. Promise or no promise, Abigail had to tell the truth. I told myself I had nothing to worry about. We would soon have it cleared up. The thought didn't console me.

I turned off the light.

It was only after a few minutes, as I played the conversation back in my head, I wondered who on earth was the German whore?

Chapter 20

The following morning, I had an early visitor. 'I've j-just been to the shop,' said Gregory. 'What have you d-done, Robert?'

'What do you mean?'

'Everyone's t-talking about you. Something t-to d-do with that girl. Her mother's accusing you of all s-sorts of things. Said you–'

'Well, it's not true,' I said brusquely. He stroked the dog, refusing to meet my eye. 'Gregory, for Pete's sake, you don't believe them, do you?'

'They s-say you ravaged her. T-that she came home w-with her blouse all r-r-ripped.'

'Yeah, that's true. But it wasn't me who did it to her.'

'S-someone saw you.'

'Who?'

'The b-blacksmith, Mr Pearce. H-he was driving by. He s-saw you, Robert, you and her.'

'So that makes me guilty then, does it?'

'I don't know.'

'I was about to have some breakfast. Do you want some?'

'No. What h-happened then?'

I sat down. Angie put her paws on my knee. I beckoned her onto my lap. 'Good dog. Are you a good girl? Yes? Look, Gregory, she came to see me yesterday. Begged me not to tell her mother that that boyfriend of hers tried to...'

'R-ravage her?'

'Yes. I suppose her mother tried to force it out of her, so she panicked and told her it was me.'

'W-why would s-she do that?'

'She's trying to protect Dan. She's terrified that her father finds out.'

'I d-don't blame her. The s-sod. It wasn't you then?'

'Gregory, look at me. No, I would never do something like that. She's sixteen, for God's sake.'

He puffed out his cheeks. 'OK, I b-believe you. I t-think I'll have some of that breakfast now.'

I laughed. 'Good man. One huge greasy breakfast without meat coming up. Then you can tell me all about Rebecca.'

*

Later in the morning, Gregory and I ventured out. With Angie on a lead, we wandered over to the shop. Unusually, it was full. Both Mr and Mrs Hamilton were busy serving customers. Old Bill Fraser was there, as was Mrs James, a kindly woman in her forties, a widow since the Great War, and a couple of others.

'That'll be nine pence, please, Mrs Courtauld,' I heard Mr Hamilton say from behind the counter. 'Oh, Lord, look what the cat's dragged in.'

I almost stepped back as a bank of eyes turned to look at me. Mrs James, holding a can of tinned milk, sniffed; Fraser scowled at me.

'We don't need your custom, thank you very much, Mr Searight. Good day.'

I felt myself standing there, absorbing his words. Wasn't I still the same man, the man who, just days earlier, had been feted and welcomed back into the bosom of the community? And now, here I was, not only accused but judged guilty. Their eyes bore into me and I knew they were seeing me as if for the first time, gone was the man deserving of sympathy, replaced by a monster that had defiled not only the girl but each and all of them. I became aware that Gregory, just behind me, was trying to speak but his stutter was getting the better of him.

'You need to say something, Gregory?' asked Mr Hamilton.

'R-R-Robert didn't d-do… do it.'

'What didn't he do, Gregory?'

'He's sticking up for him. They as bad as each other,' said Mrs Hamilton.

'That poor girl,' added Mrs James.

'Come on,' I said to Gregory. 'Let's go.'

But then, just as I turned to leave, the shop door opened, the shop bell tinkled, and standing there like a cat caught in the headlights was Abigail. No one spoke.

Eventually, Mr Hamilton made his way to her. 'Come in, Abigail. These gentlemen, so-called, are just leaving.'

With the shopkeeper guiding her in, she sidled in, her eyes wide with fright, as if fearful I might pounce on her.

'T-t-tell them the t-truth. It's n-not fair. It's… it's…'

Poor Gregory, his face turned red, unable to finish his sentence.

'Get out,' growled Hamilton. 'Both of you.'

But it was Abigail who fled first.

*

'I d-don't understand,' said Gregory, once we were safely away from the shop. 'Why – why didn't you s-say s-something?'

'Because they won't believe me. It has to come from Abigail.'

'She won't say anything now. It's t-too late.' I knew he wanted to say more but it was just too much effort for him. He'd been shaken by being labelled with me.

'No, she'll say it eventually. She won't be able to maintain the lie forever.'

'Well, I just h-hope she – she says it b-before P-Parker returns. For your sake, R-Robert.'

I tried to smile. 'Yes, I know. So do I.'

*

My ordeals for the day were not over. Near bedtime, I'd settled down in my living room, listening to the radio, with Angie dozing on my lap, a standard lamp behind my armchair. An almighty crash of breaking glass made us jump. I sprang out of my seat, my heart thumping. Angie tumbled to the floor. Righting herself, she yelped manically. The window was smashed. What on earth caused that? And then I saw it – a brick on the floor, lying amongst the shards of shattered glass, a sheet of paper wrapped around it, secured by an elastic band. 'It's alright, Angie, it's alright. Good girl.' The fur on her back stood

164

on end, a run of white spikes. I untied the elastic band, my heart still beating too fast. There was but the one word written in large looping letters on the sheet of paper – 'Pervert'. I simply stood there, peering at the word. I felt shocked. Who would do such a thing? The irony began to take hold – that I had survived so much, survived the impossible, and yet, here I was, in my own home, feeling distinctly unsafe.

Chapter 21

I woke up with a heavy heart. I checked the pads of Angie's paws for any shards of glass while I considered my position – labelled as a rapist, branded a pervert. The whole village knew and I'd been condemned in the eyes of each and every one of them. Only Gregory knew of my innocence – he and Abigail and, of course, Dan. I wondered who in the village could fix my window, or whether I'd have to go further afield.

Locking Angie up in the kitchen, I swept up the broken glass in the living room. The night before, I'd stuck up on an old sack I found in the shed. It wasn't big enough but desperate to go to bed, I didn't care. The light of the day filtered in, either side of the sack. Having ensured I hadn't missed any bits of glass, I allowed Angie back in, who sniffed round, darting from one side of the room to the other, her tail wagging. I smiled. What a tonic that little dog was. I needed breakfast but I had no appetite. I told myself the piece of paper was nothing to worry about, yet I was worried. That someone out there should think so poorly of me worried me a lot.

Today, being Friday, I returned to my parents for lunch with my Uncle Guy and my mother's sister, Aunt Josephine. I was happy to leave the village behind for a few hours.

Letting myself in, I found my mother in the kitchen. The place smelt of cooking – a joint of beef was in the oven. My mother, always a resourceful woman, had, she said, called in a few favours with the village butcher. Having kissed her hello, I asked whether Guy and Jo had arrived

'Not yet, but they'll be here soon. Your father's in the dining room laying the table. Lunch is all but ready. Just waiting for the potatoes.'

Various pans simmered on the stove. I lifted the lid of one and breathed in the nauseous aroma of beef gravy.

'Mum, I hate to tell you this but I've turned vegetarian.'

'Veggie-what? What on earth is that?'

'Someone who doesn't eat meat.'

'Doesn't eat meat? That's… I don't know. How utterly strange. Why on earth wouldn't you eat meat?'

'It's a long story.'

'Well, you'll just have to have the vegetables then. Luckily the soup is vegetable.

We heard a car draw up and park outside the front gate. 'They're here,' announced my mother.

We met them at the front door – my Uncle Guy and Aunt Josephine. 'Hello,' they waved, smiles upon their faces. How dapper they looked – my aunt in a knee-length floral skirt and a light green cardigan; my uncle in a tweed jacket and trilby, a pin in his tie, his shoes polished. No one would know by looking at him that he had lost a leg.

167

Josephine kissed me on the cheek. Guy tipped his hat and offered his hand, then, with abandon, threw his arms round me. 'Robert, good to see you. So sorry about your brother.'

'Thank you.'

'How are you?' asked Josephine. 'We were so worried about you, weren't we, Guy?'

My mother led us all into the kitchen. 'A round of tea is in order, don't you think?'

'Hang the tea,' said Uncle Guy. 'Jo – let's get that bottle open!'

'Champagne?' exclaimed my mother as her sister fished a large green bottle from her handbag. 'Oh, Guy, it's far too early.'

'Too early my invisible foot. Robert is back safe and well. If that's not cause for celebration, I don't know what is. Where's Lawrence?'

'I'm here,' said my father, entering the kitchen. He looked tense, his jaw twitching beneath his beard. 'Welcome,' he said in a hollow voice.

Josephine kissed him on his cheek; Guy shook his hand. 'Thank you, cousin,' he said.

'Guy, save the champagne for dinner.'

Later, we sat down to eat in the dining room, a room we rarely used, save for occasions such as Christmas and days like today. Father, probably on Mum's instructions, had laid a white tablecloth over the oval table and produced their best cutlery and crockery. With so many framed prints on the wall, the room felt like a small art gallery – rural landscapes featuring windswept moors with threatening clouds, plus another of a Nelson-era galleon upon the high seas, its sails buffeted by the winds, a flash of lightning. The image of the dark, menacing waves caused me to shudder. But I noticed something was missing – Father's framed display of his war medals. Indeed, on looking more closely, I spied the shadow on the wallpaper where, until recently, they'd been. Why had he removed them, I wondered? Or perhaps Mum had. I was about to ask but something, I don't know what, held me back.

'Come, you sit here, Robert, next to your uncle,' said my mother, patting the back of a chair. 'That's it.'

'Well, what a fine spread, Mary,' said my aunt. 'You're doing us proud.'

'You wouldn't think there was a war on,' said Guy.

'I batted my pretty Irish eyelashes at the butcher.'

Josephine laughed. 'I do that all the time. It never fails to work, does it?'

The dining room had a chandelier, the French windows framed by heavy velvety drapes, a potted plant and candles on the dresser. Everything minutely arranged over the years by my mother.

My father started, as always, with a prayer. We sat with our heads bowed as he thanked God for my safe return, and remembered Clarence, that he may rest forever in peace, that we should all meet again one day under His presence.

'Amen.' He tucked his napkin into his collar, a lifelong habit I always found slightly irritating.

'Right,' said Guy, a little hastily perhaps, 'let's crack open the champagne.'

My father stiffened. 'I really don't–'

'Lawrence,' snapped my mother.

His left eye twitched. 'Yes, fine. Good idea.'

Uncle Guy's toast was muted – to sons and nephews present and departed. A half-hearted clink of glasses.

The soup was, if truth be told, a little bland and I noticed Uncle Guy pep it with doses of salt.

'Robert's a vegetable person now,' declared my mother.

I explained.

My uncle was as perplexed as my mother. 'They say Hitler's a vegetable man.'

'Vegetarian.'

'Whatever you call it. So,' he said, leaning towards me, 'what do you think of this attempt on Hitler's life?'

My parents and my aunt were discussing, loudly, the cost of living.

'He was exceedingly lucky,' I said.

'Yes, wasn't he just? Doesn't change anything though. He must know the war's as good as lost.'

'He's not going to give in until Germany lies in ruins.'

'The man's a lunatic and the quicker we put him back down the hole he came from, the better. So how are you, Robert? You look remarkably well – considering.'

'The merchant navy's been good to me. Given me lots of time to recuperate.'

'Yes, well, what with Clarence, the poor boy, I know the feeling now. I've had my whole life to recuperate,' he said, patting his knee.

'You were out on the Western Front, weren't you?'

'Yes. Another man-made Hell. But we never learn. Pass the salt, would you? Lovely soup, Mary,' he said, raising his voice. 'Thank you.'

'You don't think it's a little watery?'

'No, not at all. Delicious.'

'We used to have this sort of soup back home, didn't

we, Mary?' said Josephine.

My father laughed. 'Back in the mother country, eh? I thought you only ate potatoes,' he said, mimicking the Irish accent.

'I think we've heard that joke often enough over the years, thank you, Lawrence.'

The lunch, at least the vegetable and potato part, was very nice. I realised it'd been some time since I ate so well and years since I had had any champagne. My father was telling Mary and Josephine about his desire to keep chickens or buy a dog – he couldn't decide which. Feeling slightly lightheaded, I leant towards Guy and asked him about his wound. I felt, somehow, that through my own ordeal, I had earned the right to ask such a direct question.

'Maybe I'll tell you about it one day,' he said quietly. 'I'll tell you also about the ship I was on that went down. You and I, we have much in common. Do you remember, as a kid you used to call me Uncle Hobbly?'

I laughed. 'I used to think what fun it must be to have a false leg. My mother mentioned you had a brother – Jack. I never knew until a couple years ago I had another uncle.'

He stabbed at half a boiled potato with his fork. 'A lot went on during the war, involving all of us,' he said, waving his knife at his wife and my parents. 'Jack wasn't as lucky. He was killed in action. Eleventh November 1917.'

'Is there a gravestone?'

'Sadly not.'

'An inscription somewhere?'

He hesitated. 'No.'

I knew I couldn't ask any more.

'We were like you and Clarence – brothers off to war. He was a good lad.' He paused, concentrating on his food.

'There's not a day when I don't…'

'Not a day when you don't what, Guy?' asked my mother, chirpily.

Guy laid his knife and fork neatly on his plate. 'I was saying to Robert there's not a day goes by when I don't think about Jack.'

My mother's smile froze on her lips. Josephine bowed her head. My father, helping himself to extra gravy, broke the silence. 'Yes,' he said, in a booming voice. 'Well, I know the feeling now. Of course, Mary, you had a thing for Jack, didn't you?' With a snarl, he added, 'And, while we're on the subject—'

'Enough, Lawrence. Please.'

'It all turned out for the best in the end,' said Josephine breezily.

'Not for Jack, it didn't,' said Guy.

'No, of course… I didn't mean…'

'It doesn't matter.'

'I'm not sure my wife would agree with you, Jo.'

'Lawrence, please,' said my mother quietly, her eyes downwards. 'Stop this.'

'Yes, well.' He took a mouthful of food while, I noticed, everyone else seemed to have lost their appetites. Josephine sipped her champagne. 'I didn't mind,' said Lawrence, swallowing, 'being third choice. It didn't matter to me. There was Clarence. Not any more.'

My mother's jaw clenched. 'You still have Robert, Lawrence dear.'

My father looked at me and I knew what I had said earlier was utterly true – the wrong son had died. 'Quite, we still have Robert.'

'Yes,' said Guy, squeezing my wrist. 'And for that we

have to be thankful.'

'Thank you, Uncle Guy.'

'Uncle Hobbly to you.'

'Well,' said Josephine, her face flushed. 'Anyone for more champagne?'

*

I was part of a close-knit family – two sisters had married two cousins. But obviously, my other uncle, Jack, had had an influence. And tensions I never knew about until now simmered under the surface. My father had said he was the third choice, that my mother had had a 'thing' about Jack.

After lunch, we walked off our food, as my father put it, by embarking on a gentle stroll down the lanes, enjoying the afternoon sun. Uncle Guy and Aunt Josephine, holding hands, walked ahead, talking to Father who seemed to be waving his arms about. A couple of swallows whizzed past, butterflies danced and the hedges hummed with the sound of bumble bees. My mother slid her arm round mine and apologized for my father. 'Don't be angry with him, Robert,' she said. 'Your father has never been one to express his feelings so that when he finally does, as he did today, he gets it all mixed up and says… well, as you heard, he says all the wrong things. He's still in shock – we all are, but your father… I cried and cried over Clarence, I still do, but I also know how thankful I am that we still have you. But it was as if it took me time to realise it at first. I was too consumed by grief to appreciate that we almost lost both of you. Your father hasn't got to that second stage yet. He'll get there.'

'Will he?'

'Yes. I promise you, he will.'

'It's obvious Clarence was the favourite. Not just now but when I think back over the years, he always was.'

'No, that's not true, Robert.'

'Oh, Mum, come now, of course it is. I don't mind, I really don't, but did he have to make it so obvious?'

I felt her tighten her grip on my arm. 'Maybe you're right. Maybe… Maybe it was because he saw in Clarence a reflection of himself. Whereas you, you're more like me. You're like an Irishman with an English accent.'

'Should I be taking that as a compliment?'

'But of course.'

An elderly farmer with bowed legs accompanied by two sheep dogs passed us. 'How do,' he said to each of us in turn. 'Lovely day again.'

'What are you two gossiping about?' said Guy, waiting for us.

'My mother thinks I'm a true Irishman.'

'Robert, I didn't take it that far.'

'Ha, but she's probably right. You've not been to the Emerald Isle, have you, Robert?'

'No.'

'You should.'

'One day, I will.'

'Where Mary and Jo come from, out on the west coast, it's quite a heaven on earth.'

'A blustery one, mind you,' said my mother.

'This is true. Now, Robert, how about meeting me for a coffee in town next week?' He was, he said, meeting a friend – half business, half pleasure. He suggested we meet afterwards in a café he knew on Argyll Street.

'Lovely,' I said. 'I look forward to it.'

Chapter 22

I needed to go out to find a glazier but kept finding excuses to delay my re-appearance in the outside world. I couldn't quite face it. Then, to worry me more, came a knock at the door. It was still only eight. Standing at the door, I found June; her daughter a good few feet behind.

'Hello, Robert,' she said. 'We need to speak to you.'

I showed them through to the living room. 'It's dark in here,' said June as she took a seat. 'Oh, what happened to your window?'

'Here.' I showed her the sheet of paper.

'Look at this,' she said, thrusting it at Abigail. 'Proud of yourself?' Abigail averted her eyes. 'My daughter has something to say to you.'

'Oh?'

We both looked at her as she visibly seemed to shrink in front of us.

'I'm sorry,' she muttered, her eyes still cast down.

'Louder,' said June.

'I said it, didn't I? I'm sorry.'

June rolled her eyes. 'Go on, why are you sorry, hey?'

Abigail swallowed. I felt pity for her but knew it wasn't my place to intervene. 'I'm sorry I told everyone you tried to hurt me.'

'I'm… well.' I wasn't sure what to say. Yes, I felt pity for her but she had to know what torment she'd put me through.

'We're both very sorry, Robert. Abigail told me the truth this morning. Of course it wasn't you who assaulted her. You're not that sort. I know that.'

'It's OK.'

'It's just… when she first told me I was so shocked and angry, I didn't stop to question it. If you could ever forgive us both.'

'Of course.' Turning to Abigail, I added, 'I understand why you did it, Abigail, and I suppose you could never have imagined how people would react, but as you can see from my window, they reacted rather harshly.'

'We'll pay for it,' said June. 'Send us the bill.'

'No, that won't be–'

'I insist. It's the least we can do.' She got to her feet, brushing away an invisible speck of dirt from her coat. 'We'll leave you to it. There's someone else we need to go see. Isn't there, Miss?'

The girl nodded.

'That young thug has a lot to answer for. I still haven't decided whether to tell Pete. He's back this afternoon some time. It'd be for the best if he didn't know but if he finds out from someone else, there'll be hell to pay.' She looked at her daughter, shaking her head. 'You silly, silly girl.' They got up to leave, Abigail beating a hasty retreat outside. June offered me her hand. 'I regret cancelling our dinner date now.'

'Not to worry.' Frankly, I was relieved.

'Yes, well. Thank you, Robert, and again – many apologies.'

I tried my best to smile.

*

I had to go see Gregory straightaway – he seemed more shaken up by this affair than myself. I found him leafing through sheets of piano music, expecting Rebecca at any moment.

'Well, that's f-fantastic news,' he said, once I told him. 'I hope they were both suitably c-contrite.'

I laughed. How pompous he could sound. 'Yes, they were suitably contrite.'

'What's s-so funny?'

'Nothing. Nothing at all. What's that smell?'

'Smell? What s-smell?'

'I don't know, like a cross between vanilla and something musky. Is it your aftershave?'

He looked embarrassed, as if I had just discovered a dirty secret. 'M-maybe,' he muttered, concentrating on a piece of music.

'It's nice,' I said, feebly. I guessed it was for Rebecca's benefit.

'You don't think it's too overpowering?'

'No, no, not at all,' I lied.

A figure passed the window. 'H-here she is,' said Gregory.

'In that case, I'd better go,' I said, rising to my feet.

Rebecca and I passed at the front door. 'Oh, hello,' she said, holding my gaze. 'How are you, Robert?'

'Yes, fine, thanks.' Why, I wondered, did she render me so nervous?

'You're leaving already? Don't go on my account.'

'H-he's just leaving, aren't y-you, R-Robert?'

'Yes. Absolutely.'

I returned home via the shop. I had no need for anything; I popped in merely to gloat, I have to confess, because they would have heard by now. This time, it was empty, just Mr Hamilton wearing his apron, behind the counter, re-arranging his display of chocolate bars.

'Ah, Robert,' he said on seeing me. 'You OK? Erm, Mrs Parker was here earlier. She, er, told us it wasn't you who... you know.'

'Yes.'

'Oh dear. I think I owe you an apology, Robert. We all do. Of course, you wouldn't do something like that; not a man like you. I am sorry.'

'Yes, no one stopped to question it; that's what I find so upsetting. Everyone just assumed. Someone threw a brick through my window the other night.'

'No. Hooligans.' He shook his head. 'Listen, care for some soup?'

'No, I'm fine, thanks.'

'No, I insist. It's a new brand. Mushroom. A gift by way of an apology; a peace offering, if you like.' He held out a tin for me.

I took it. 'OK, thank you.'

'You know Parker comes back today? Not exactly a joyful prospect. The man was a one-man crime wave. Let's hope the army's instilled some decency into him.'

'Yes. Thanks again for the soup.'

*

It was a pleasant day – a good day, I thought, to sand the fence after my last aborted attempt. I'd been putting it off too long; I still felt physically weak. I wondered whether I'd ever be strong again. Hamilton's mushroom soup, his peace offering, was indeed very pleasant. Having rummaged around in the garden shed, I found some sandpaper. I'd been working for about twenty minutes, with Angie sunning herself, when I became aware that I was being watched. Looking up, I saw the boy, William. He was on his bicycle with a bag swung round his back, and had stopped nearby to watch me with an inquisitiveness that, had he been an adult, would have been deemed quite improper.

'You OK there?" I called out.

He didn't answer. His eyes narrowed as he looked around, staring off into the distance. Eventually, he placed a foot on a pedal and cycled slowly off. Why, I don't know, but I rushed through the house, into the yard at the back, and grabbed my bicycle. Calling Angie back in, I locked her inside the house, and sped off in the direction the boy went. Seeing him in the distance passing by the church and through the square, I slowed down – I didn't want to catch up with him. Standing up on his pedals, he speeded up as he cycled along a lane leading out of the village. I kept up, staying behind by a couple hundred yards. He didn't look behind. He kept going – a good mile or so. Eventually, he veered right and disappeared from view. I heard the sound of an engine approaching. Catching up, I saw that he'd turned up a path evidently used by tractors, given the strip of long grass separated by two muddy tracks. After a few yards, it swung right,

179

presumably leading to a field. I was about to follow, when the car came into view, an old black Austin. It beeped its horn on seeing me. I didn't recognise the driver, a young chap wearing a cap, but there, in the passenger seat, I saw Pete Parker with his jet-black hair, his heavy eyebrows, wearing a khaki shirt. He gave me the thumbs up. The car stopped, and Parker, leaning over the driver, shouted through the open window. 'I heard you were dead, mate?'

I shrugged my shoulders, forcing out a feeble laugh. 'You heard wrong.'

'So I see. What are you doing out here, then?'

Why had his question unnerved me? Because, I suppose, following a small boy on his bike felt wrong. 'I was just on my way back,' I said.

'Right.' He considered me for a few seconds. 'See you later then.'

The driver grinned at me. Parker said something to him, and he laughed. The driver revved the engine and off they went, leaving a trail of dust in their wake.

*

I'd eaten lunch and fed the dog. Turning on the radio, I settled back in my settee to listen to an afternoon play, when I heard another knock on the door. Angie leapt from my lap, barking. It was Parker.

He'd changed and was wearing a checked shirt and a pair of black trousers. 'I understand my family owe you an apology.'

'It's nothing,' I said. 'Your wife came to see me earlier today.'

'Are you going to invite me in?' he said, peering over my shoulder into the house.

'Sorry, yes, come in.' I showed him through to the living room where he plonked himself in my settee. So much for the radio play. 'Can I get you anything? Cup of tea?'

'Got any beer?'

'No. Sorry.'

'I'm alright then.' He took in his surroundings, appraising my meagre room and its paintings. 'What happened to your window?'

'Long story.'

'Like that, is it?' He crossed his legs. 'How's your dad?'

'My dad?'

'Send him my regards. Not that he'll thank you for it. Your old man and me, well, we didn't see eye to eye. Remember that time he came to visit you and your brother in his car? I only wanted a quick look inside. God, man, you'd think I was trying to steal the crown jewels. Your dad, he thought I was, I don't know, from the wrong side of the tracks, let's say.'

'I wouldn't say that.'

He raised an eyebrow. 'No? I reckon he did. Thought I was a bit rough.' He cleared his throat. 'Rather be a bit rough than go round as if I had a spoon stuck up my arse. No offence. You're not like that.'

'Thanks.'

'Pleasure. So, yeah, about Abbie. She's a wayward one, that one. Always had a will of her own. Girls, eh? They grow up so fast these days; think she knows it all. When I left two years ago, she was still daddy's girl, now look at her. I'm no longer the top dog. She's discovered boys. What can a father do? But she's still young and there're not too many boys around, what with the war. So, she hangs round with a reprobate that even the army wouldn't touch with a bargepole. Colour blind, he reckons. No brain, I reckon; nothing between the ears. He'll have even less when I catch up with him.'

'I thought it was because of his limp.'

'Well, there's that too. I reckon he and your mate, Greggers, are in competition to be crowned the village idiot. Now, he's another who's escaped doing his bit.'

'Not his fault, surely?'

'There's always a job to be had if he put his mind to it. You and me, we do our bit, don't we? Risking life and limb for king and country, while Greggers puts on his stutter and hunkers down here, all nice and safe. I mean, shit, how does a stutter stop you from firing a rifle?'

'It's not so much his—'

'So, have you seen him?'

'Gregory?'

'No, this… this Dan bloke.'

I shook my head.

'No, no one has. He's gone to ground. Don't blame him. I'll root him out, don't you worry. Anyways, it wasn't right of Abbie to go telling all and sundry it were you, and I'm sorry for that.'

'It's fine but thank you all the same.' I couldn't help but wonder how he took the news, whether Abigail escaped with no more than a shouting down. I hoped so.

'So, I heard you had a tough time of it. Lost at sea, I hear.'

'Yeah. It wasn't easy.'

'I bet.' He considered me a few moments. I think the mere fact that I had suffered had perhaps boosted me in his estimations.

'You were in Italy, I hear,' I said, wanting to divert the conversation away from me.

'Yeah. Bloody tough, I tell you. Lost some good mates and all. Finally managed to get meself some leave. 'Bout bloody time too.'

'Good to be back?'

'Thought it would be but... you know, now I'm here, I'm already looking forward to going back and being with the boys. That's the thing about the army – you make some bloody good mates. Not like the retards here. Hey, I see I've got back in time for the football tomorrow. I hear you're not playing. What's wrong with you?'

'Doctor's orders,' I lied.

'Right. So instead we've got Greggers in defence. I reckon your dog here could make a better go of it. Now, listen, come down the pub tonight, the Ship.' He winked at me. 'I'm having a little welcome home party.'

'Oh, I'm not sure if–'

'Come on, man. I got Greggers to play the piano for me. I'll stand you a drink. Least I could do for you after that... *misunderstanding*.' He pronounced the word slowly.

'Well, yes, OK then. I will. Thank you very much.'

'Ah, that's a pleasure,' he said, stretching his arms behind his head. 'We'll be there from about eight. Should be a laugh.'

*

The hubbub of animated conversations could be heard halfway down the street as I approached the pub. The place was packed, smoke everywhere despite the windows being open. The 'Welcome home' banner with its two exclamation marks had been put back up. I spotted, or rather heard Parker, in the middle of a group of men, laughing while holding his glass up. He saw me and shouted at the young lad behind the bar, telling him to get me a pint and put it on his tab. I mouthed a thank you and sauntered over to the bar where the lad poured me my drink. Further along, old Bill Fraser propped up the bar, smoking his pipe. He saluted on seeing me.

Hearing my name, I saw Gregory and Rebecca sitting with Jenkins, the headmaster, and Mrs James, in the corner of the pub.

'This is the quietest spot in the whole place,' said Jenkins as I perched on a stool next to him. 'A bit more raucous than your do. I'll not be staying long.'

'Are you making a speech?'

'No, thank God.'

'Are you playing the piano?' I asked Gregory.

'I-I'm t-trying t-t-to get Re-Rebecca to play.'

'No way,' she screeched. 'Not in front of all these people.'

'Hello, Mrs James,' I said.

'Hello, Robert.' She tried to smile. 'Erm, Robert, I'm sorry… you know, about the other day and all that.'

'It's all right. The whole village has been apologising to me.'

'Should think so too,' said Jenkins. 'Disgraceful business. No disrespect, Mrs James.'

'None taken,' she said.

'So, Gregory,' said Jenkins. 'Are you all ready for the football tomorrow?'

'No.'

Jenkins slapped his knee. 'Don't look so glum; it'll be fine.'

'All in a good cause,' said Mrs James.'

'Absolutely.'

'R-Robert, d-do you…' Poor Gregory, he couldn't speak. We all waited, embarrassed for him, hoping he'd be able to finish his sentence. Rebecca twisted the stem of her wine glass. He leant back, defeated by his own disability. The air hung awkwardly in silence as elsewhere, around us, shouted conversations only highlighted our discomfort.

Eventually, Rebecca broke the silence by asking me about Angie. Her parents had had a Jack Russell, she told me, and we launched into a conversation about dogs and horses. She was to be the new teacher, starting in September; a replacement for Joanna. Jenkins and Gregory spoke about music but I had the feeling that Gregory was keeping his eye on me.

Parker approached us, already swaying slightly. 'All right, folks? What's the matter with you all? Cheer up; it's a party not a bloody funeral,' he said, waving about a tankard of beer. 'Good turnout, isn't it? So, how about tinkling the ivories for us, eh, Greggers?'

Gregory muttered something.

'What did you say? Go on, give us a tune. Let's do it now. I'll buy you another drink.' Gregory tried to say something, to protest. Ignoring him, Parker turned his back. Raising his glass, he shouted, 'OK, everyone, bit of shush please. Hey, shut up, will you?' Quickly, the pub turned quiet. 'Silence in court.' Having gotten everyone's attention, he continued. 'Ladies and gents, boys and girls, it's the moment you've all been waiting for. Put your hands together for our very own tunesmith, the master of the ivories, Mister G-G-Gregory…'

His friends laughed and cheered raucously as Gregory,

his face like stone, took his drink and, with a nod to Rebecca, made his way to the piano. People shouted out their requests, bombarding Gregory with the names of various songs. Resting his glass on the top of the piano, he launched into a rendition of *It's a Long Way to Tipperary*. People applauded and started to join in. Parker and a couple of his mates danced a jig in the middle of the pub while, at the far end, his wife and daughter watched with rather appalled expressions.

Jenkins leant over towards me. 'He didn't have to mock him like that.'

'No, that was nasty.'

'And calling him Greggers – very disrespectful, I thought.'

'He's good though, isn't he?' said Rebecca. 'He's a good teacher as well. Very patient.'

'He's a good man.'

We sat and listened for a while and watched the men dance and the women clap in time with Gregory's playing. Rebecca jiggled in her chair, tapping the rhythm on her knee.

'Mr Jenkins, what do you know about a boy called William?'

'William?'

'The one in baggy shorts and a jacket.'

'Oh yes, William. Quiet boy, intelligent, a little strange maybe. But then, he's had a difficult time, poor lad. His father was killed last year in North Africa. It's affected him, of course.'

'Does he have friends?'

'Not at school he doesn't. The other kids don't know how to talk to him. Rita, his mother, is nice enough. Can't be easy for her.'

After a few more minutes, during which Gregory continued his playing, Jenkins announced he had had enough and was off home. Having watched him leave with, on my part, a degree of envy, Rebecca asked me whether I saw much of my parents. We resumed our earlier conversation, talking about my life as a merchant seaman and hers as a teacher, when Gregory's recital came to an end. He received a boisterous cheer for his efforts and, as he came back to us, Parker slapped him on the back and thrust another pint of beer in his hand.

Gregory came to join us. 'You two s-still t-talking, I see,' he said to us, clearly disgruntled.

'Yes, we were just—'

'I don't n-need to know.'

'You all right, Gregory?' I asked.

He gulped his drink. Placing the glass on the table, he announced he too was off. And with that, he was gone, the beer still swirling in its glass.

'Is he OK, do you think?' asked Rebecca.

'Yeah, he's just a bit grumpy. He doesn't like being treated like a performing monkey.'

'No, don't suppose he does.'

'He'll get over it.'

Chapter 23

Today is Sunday. Today would have been my first wedding anniversary. One year of marriage. All the more reason not to go to church. But still I plan to go. I dress slowly, imagining I am dressing on the morning of my wedding. I put on my suit, a drab brown affair that used to belong to Clarence. A year ago, it would have been a morning suit with tails, top hat, the works. Mum and Father would have arrived in their finery, my mother wearing something green, as she always did on special occasions. Special occasions always brought the Irish out in her, hence the green, a nod to home. I put on my tie – plain, dark red. A year ago, it would have been a bowtie. I put on my ordinary brown loafers; a year ago it would have been a pair of shiny black leather shoes. I brush my hair. A year ago, I would have added a bit of pomade – Brylcreem. I remembered the advert, promising glossier hair. A year ago, instead of getting married to the woman I loved, I went to visit my parents, needing to escape the village and all the sympathetic faces. My mother fretted, wanting to make sure I was all right. As if I'd be all right. I sat in the kitchen, my mother making me cups of tea, unsure of what to say, offering to take me out for lunch. At least she tried. My father's only effort was to say 'plenty more fish in the sea'. My mother shooed him out of the kitchen. I didn't see him for the rest of the day.

The first time I met the woman who almost became my wife was at the cinema in Plymouth in April of 1943. Plymouth had been badly hit by the Blitz a couple years back. Damaged and ruined buildings still lay all about, piles of rubble, massive craters, everywhere devastation. Charles Church near the city centre had been reduced to a skeleton, destroyed by German incendiary bombs in 1941. All but one of the city's cinemas had been destroyed and, two years later, were still out of operation. One cinema, however, the Forum, although damaged had survived. The buildings either side were still being patched up having fallen victim to the bombs. And it was there, at the Forum, that I'd been to see *Gone With the Wind* with Owen and a couple of pals from work. Afterwards, I waited for them in the foyer while they collected their coats. I saw a cinema ticket on the floor behind a blonde girl in a knee-length coat talking to a couple of friends. Picking it up, I asked her whether it was hers.

'Why yes, it is. Thank you.'

'Did you enjoy the film?' I asked, wondering why I had.

'Oh my, it was heavenly.'

'"Frankly, my dear…"'

She completed the quote and we laughed. Stepping away from the companions, she waxed lyrical about Vivien Leigh. 'Isn't she beautiful?'

'I prefer a blonde,' I said, pointedly, trying to imitate

Clark Gable's voice.

'Oh, you do, do you?' she said, flicking her hair with a rakish smile.

She wore a lime green blouse with large buttons, a string of pearls, and a small red bow in her hair, its colour matching that of her lipstick. Her face, so pale, radiated kindness and fun, her eyes, vibrant green, drew me in. I thought her the most beautiful person I'd ever seen. Yet, her beauty, far from inhibiting me, brought out the best in me. My pals reappeared. I was about to introduce her when she was called away by her friends. 'Well, it was lovely to meet you,' she said, offering me her hand. Before I had chance to respond, she'd been whisked away out into the street.

'You old dog, Searight,' said Owen. 'Can't leave you for a minute.'

'Did you catch her name?' asked my other friend, a chap called Peters.

'No.'

'Or her number?'

I shook my head.

'Then you're a bloody fool,' said Owen. 'Go catch her up. They won't have got far.'

'I'm not sure–'

'Go, man; just go.'

So I did. Pushing past people leaving the cinema, I barged out into the warm spring night. Looking left and right, I saw them turn the corner into Albion Road. Running, jumping over a pile of masonry, I caught them up. 'Excuse me, excuse me.' I bumped into someone, a dark figure in a coat. 'Hey, watch where you're going, can't you?'

'I'm sorry. Excuse me.'

They turned. The girl stepped towards me. 'Did I drop something else?' she said with a playful smile.

'No, I just… I mean…'

'Yes?'

One of her friends behind giggled.

'You lot go ahead,' she said to them over her shoulder. 'I'll catch you up in a minute.' We looked at each other, unaware of people passing, of a car beeping its horn, of someone laughing on the other side of the street. She smiled. 'My name is Alice and the answer is yes.'

*

I had a terrible case of first date nerves. I scrubbed myself clean, donned my best suit and tried on various ties trying to decide which looked the most suitable – nothing too showy but which still had a bit of colour. I settled for plain blue. I slicked back my hair and splashed myself with liberal amounts of aftershave. All the while being watched by Angie, sitting comfortably on my bed. It was a Saturday night. I came downstairs to find Clarence sitting in the living room with a glass of beer, sucking on a cigarette, reading the paper. 'You're going to great effort for this new girl. I hope she appreciates it – that is if you don't knock her out first with that perfume. Is she worth it?'

'I'll say.'

'So who is she? Will I approve?'

'Don't know much about her, to be honest, and as to whether you'd approve or not…'

He put his hand up. 'I know, I know, you couldn't give a fig what I think…'

'Right, how do I look?'

'Like a spiv.'

'What? Do I? Heck…'

'Good God, I wish I'd never said it. No, really, you look fine. Quite the gentleman around town. Now get out of here. Go forth and sweep this young belle off her feet. And don't let her get you drunk.'

I waited for her outside the theatre. On seeing her walking towards me, this blonde siren, looking divine in a dark blue jacket over a mauve dress, I felt almost weak.

The play by Terence Rattigan, although good, was poorly acted. Afterwards, we went to a restaurant on Union Street where we ordered a beef pie and giggled and mocked the awful acting.

'I'm so sorry about the play,' I said once we'd ordered.

'Don't be silly; it's hardly your fault.'

'The local rag gave it a good review.'

'Shows how much they know. Anyway, it's the company that counts. Don't you think?'

I laughed.

And so we had a pleasant evening – eating, drinking too much wine and finding out about each other. She lived not so far from me, a village about eight miles hence, and, from what I could tell, came from a well-to-do family, her father being the local estate agent with a large remit of properties at any given time. He had given her a car for her most recent birthday – a brand new Ford Anglia. Indeed, she said, she'd parked it just up the road. 'I'll give you a lift home tonight, if that would please sir.'

'That would very much. But can you drive after so much wine? I don't have a car but when I drive my dad's old banger, I find alcohol makes me go blurry and I usually end up in the hedge.'

'Oh, Robert, you sound like my father. I find I drive better after a few glasses.'

And so, once we'd eaten and I'd paid the bill, Alice took me home driving at an alarming speed through Plymouth and out into the Devon lanes. In no time, I was home. Deposited outside my door, feeling rather nauseous, I wondered whether I should invite her in. Somehow, I couldn't face subjecting her to Clarence's scrutiny or the inevitable comments afterwards – comments like *What does a girl like that see in you?* or *She seems far too good for the likes of you.* 'I guess you'll be wanting to head home,' I said, 'but if you want to…'

'No, awfully sweet of you but you're right – I ought to get home. I may be a big girl now but Daddy will still be waiting up for me, the old sausage.'

'Yes, of course. Well, anytime… I mean, if you'd like…'

'Another time? Would love to.' She planted a kiss on my cheek. I watched her drive off, a cigarette between her lips, careering round the corner, and disappearing into the night.

'My God,' I muttered to myself. 'What a girl.'

I found Clarence still up, still in the armchair, a book face down on his lap, the empty beer glass at his feet. I wondered whether he'd moved at all during the time I was out. The only difference was now he was wearing a pair of slippers.

'What are you reading?' I asked.

'Never mind about that? Where's the girl?'

'She went home.'

'She went home? You are a gentleman. So, tell me all. What she like?'

193

'She's lovely,' I said, exaggerating a yawn. 'I'm really tired.'

'Is that it? Lovely?'

'Lovely and unconventional.'

'Lovely and unconventional? Oh Lord, I don't like the sound of that one bit.'

*

I woke the following day, a fine spring Sunday morning, and positively leapt out of bed. I felt different somehow. I looked the same; the world outside looked the same, yet everything was different. Wanting to avoid my brother, I scoffed down an early breakfast, listening to but not absorbing the news on the radio, and gulped down my tea. Feeling in need of exercise, I decided to take Angie for a walk on the moor. Outside, the church bells rang for early matins, a service I left for those more pious and appreciative than myself. Waving hello to various people, I cycled briskly through the village and out onto the track that led up to the moor gate. Although sunny, the air had a cold pinch to it – summer was still a long way off. The moor smelt fresh, the grass still damp with dew. The shadow of a cloud drifted across the beacon. A flock of starlings skimmed past, a stray sheep kept a worried eye on Angie who, unusually, too enamoured with other olfactory delights, failed to spot it. Yes, I thought, Alice was certainly unconventional – she smoked, she drank, she drove, she made jokes, she turned up at dates without a chaperon. My father would be scandalized; he'd be appalled that I should make the acquaintance of such a woman. There are unspoken rules and civilised people, people of a certain class, should know how to abide by them. Alice seemed to delight in doing all the things that 'nice girls' shouldn't do. I laughed aloud, feeling absurdly proud of her, my 'lovely and unconventional' companion. It was then, at that moment, with Angie yelping at some unseen foe, that I realised why I felt so different – I was in love.

*

The first time I took Alice home to meet my parents wasn't exactly an unqualified success. I'd already met her parents. Her father, a short, rather plump man, shook my hands with both of his, and peered at me over his half-moon spectacles while puffing on his pipe, producing clouds of thick blue smoke. I took her over to my parents one Sunday morning for lunch. Clarence had come too, arriving separately – it was the first time the two of them had met. 'So, you're the girl that's got my brother all hot under the collar,' he said, as we gathered in my parents' hallway.

'I have that effect on men,' she said as quick as a flash.

Clarence laughed but I could tell that my father hovering in the background was less than impressed by her response.

'It's lovely to meet you,' said my mother.

'And you, Mrs Searight.'

'Oh, please, call me Mary. And this is my husband, Lawrence…'

With introductions over, we adjourned to the drawing room where my father offered aperitifs before moving to the dining room for a lunch of roast rabbit. Clarence, rejecting my father's offer of wine, helped himself to a bottle of beer. Although she tried to hide it, I noticed

Alice, sitting between us, place her hand over her nose.

'Are you all right?' I asked her in a whisper.

'I hate the smell of beer. Can we swap places?'

'Is it something I said?' asked Clarence.

'No, no,' I said quickly. 'Alice's got the sun on her back.'

Poor Alice – throughout lunch she endured my father's interrogation – where do you live; what do you do; what do your parents do? He wasn't impressed by what he would have considered her frivolous lifestyle – a bit of work in her father's office every now and then, she said, driving round Devon lanes too fast; shopping, going to the pictures, nothing too strenuous. If Alice could sense my father's disapproval, she certainly made no attempt to tone herself down. But I could tell Father was rather more impressed with her father's estate agency – an occupation that made money and carried prestige, things my father looked favourably on.

Noticing his framed display of medals on the war, Alice asked, 'You fought in the war, Lawrence?'

My father bristled – my mother may have given her permission to use her first name but he certainly hadn't. 'Yes. Nothing too heroic but I was there.'

'My father was too – Gallipoli. Where were you?'

'Yes, where were you, Father?' echoed Clarence. 'You never talk about it.'

'Alice,' said my mother, 'more potatoes?'

'It's not something one talks about.'

'Or more carrots, perhaps?'

'Did you see the whites of the enemy's eyes?' asked Clarence.

'Or fired a gun?' I added. 'Uncle Guy undoubtedly did.'

'Of course,' said my mother. 'Guy lost a leg.'

'I have an uncle,' said Alice quietly. 'But he didn't fight. He didn't do anything. He was old enough. Asthma, he says. Asthma, my eye.' She stabbed a carrot.

A few moments of awkward silence hung in the air.

'Yes, well...' said Clarence. 'Go on then, Father, do tell.'

'Boys,' said my mother. 'Leave your father be.'

'But you've never mentioned it,' I said.

'You will one day, won't you, Father?' asked Clarence. 'You know, before it's too late. Perhaps you could write it down.'

'That a good idea,' said Alice. 'Like a memoir. I should ask my dad to do the same.'

'Look, I'd really rather not talk about this any more, if you don't mind.'

'Quite right, Lawrence,' said my mother. 'Now, there's more of everything if anyone wants seconds.'

'Wouldn't mind a top-up of your fine wine,' said Alice. 'If I may?'

Clarence and I exchanged glances – Father wouldn't like that.

Afterwards, as Alice drove Clarence and me home, I apologised for my father's barrage of questions.

'Don't be silly. Your father's lovely. They both are.'

'Lovely?' said Clarence from the back. 'I've never heard him described as that before.'

*

The nation may still have been at war but my life had changed entirely for different reasons. I was in love – utterly and totally in love. We went for day trips out to the seaside, took Angie for walks on the moor, dined in Plymouth, a city under blackout, went to the theatre and the pictures. We were in love, and that was all that mattered.

Chapter 24

The church, for the size of the village, is ridiculously large. Thus although most of the villagers were attending the Sunday morning service, the place still seemed half empty. The church, I knew of old, was perpetually cold, with its thick sandstone walls discoloured in several areas by dark green patches of damp. The smell of damp hung in the air. If drabness had a smell, then this was it. I sat towards the back, hoping that by my mere presence and participation, I could reconnect to a faith I had long since lost, if indeed I ever possessed it in the first instance. Reverend Pritchard led the service, his white cassock perhaps not as white as it once was. He delivered his sermon without much enthusiasm, as if his own words bored him. I tried to concentrate but instead remembered how Davison had led the prayers on the boat. There, with our lives in the hands of an unseen force, it felt real. Here, in this cosy if claustrophobic village, with half the congregation drifting off and the other half preoccupied by their own thoughts, Reverend Pritchard's words felt almost irrelevant. The whole ceremony felt little more than a charade – the vicar feeling obliged to preach, his congregation, their attendance more an act of routine than an act of faith, obliged to play their part by being present.

Dotted round the church were the familiar faces – Mrs James sharing a pew with Mr Fraser but seated at the far ends. Mr Jenkins sat near the front together with his wife who, a sufferer of arthritis, rarely left her home. Jenkins had read the lesson with considerably more gusto than Reverend Pritchard delivered his sermon. A couple of rows in front of me sat June and Abigail, but not Pete Parker, June wearing a fetching dark blue hat with a peacock feather, Abigail sitting with her shoulders hunched. Behind them, to the right, I noticed William sitting with his mother, her arm draped over his shoulder. The boy sat with an air of impassivity, neither animated nor bored by the service and its rousing hymns.

It was the hymns that I enjoyed the most. My singing voice, though far from awful, was not, I knew, particularly good, but it didn't stop me from adding my voice and singing with enthusiasm. The church possessed a choir consisting solely of middle-aged women who, in such a large space as this, had difficulty making themselves heard above the organ. The organist, playing twice every Sunday, was Gregory. Listening to my friend play made me appreciate just how versatile he was – from jaunty pub singalongs to Sunday service favourites and a bit of Chopin in-between, his repertoire was impressive. The creative tragedy for Gregory was that no one truly appreciated him and he lacked the conviction in his own talent to move to somewhere that had an audience with more refined musical tastes. I took communion, grateful to receive from the vicar the small, squared-shaped piece of dry bread and a sip of sweet wine. It was not so much the religious symbolism that comforted me, but the sense of community. I was back, having been presumed dead, and, but for the misunderstanding with Abigail, felt eternally grateful to be here, in this oversized and impressive church and its congregation.

After less than an hour, and finishing with a muted rendition of *Immortal, Invisible, God Only Wise*, the service came to an end. Reverend Pritchard led the choir down the aisle and into a room round the back of the nave, only to reappear moments later at the church door. I remained in my pew while others made their exits, shaking hands with the vicar. I admired the large stained-glass window behind the altar, a triptych depicting Christ on the cross in its middle panel, a lamb at his feet, its primary colours heightened by the piercing rays of sun. Jesus looked suitably mournful, his eyes cast down, resigned to his fate. The image had a soothing effect on me, perhaps God Himself had, after all, allowed me to survive for a purpose. It was up to me now to find that purpose, to give my life meaning. Yet the doubts nagged at me still, the questions I knew would forever remain unanswered – why did I, and I alone, survive? Why had God deemed my life alone worthy of saving? Had not the others been deserving of a future life? Charlie Palmer, with his new bride waiting for him at home and all the children he planned to have, a whole family that never saw the light of day; Ed Davison yearning for the beauty of the Lakes and home, dead a week before his dreaded fortieth birthday; Hodgkin with the child he had yet to see and never would; John Clair dead on his nineteenth birthday. Had one made a list of the men ordered by a sort of worthiness, then surely I would have been at the bottom of it. No one depended on me, my mere existence did not impact on any other human being. Yet it was me who lived.

Rita, William's mother, I noticed, was talking to a couple of other women, the three of them huddled together, whispering, halfway down the side aisle. Gregory was still playing the organ, a rousing tune to accompany the worshippers as they exited the church. William was left alone, still in the pew, sitting on his hands, with his oversized shorts and socks rolled up above his knees. He made a forlorn figure. I tried to catch his eye but he seemed lost in his own misery, somehow.

'Hello, William. Are you OK there?'

He looked at me, eyeing me from head to foot. He nodded, then looked away.

As I left, I shook Reverend Pritchard's hand. Standing at the church entrance, he squinted against the sun as he asked how I was. 'I trust you're settling back in after your ordeals?'

'Yes, although I feel as if I'm still trying to find my land legs.'

'I can imagine,' he said, both his hands over mine. 'If you ever need to talk, you know where to find me.'

I almost told him – there and then, just blurted it all out. Instead, I smiled weakly and thanked him.

Stepping fully outside into the sun, I saw little pockets of villagers gathered, leisurely talking. About to go and say hello to Mr Jenkins, I found myself being pulled to one side by Parker, who had just appeared. June and Abigail hung round behind him looking awkward. 'Eh, Searight, I wanted to ask you something?'

'What's that?' I said, trying to disguise the weariness in my voice.

He pulled Abigail towards him. With an arm round her waist, he asked, 'Have you seen this one's lover boy?' Abigail, clearly uncomfortable, crossed her arms, the gaze falling to the ground. 'Where is he, eh?'

'Dad, he won't know.'

'He might.'

'She's right – I don't.'

'Pity that. See, him and me still need words. We haven't got to the bottom of what happened that night.'

'Nothing happened,' said Abigail.

He let her go of her. 'I'm not talking to you. God, typical woman, thinks she knows best. Anyway, that's not how I'm hearing it. Torn shirt and all that, the little bastard.'

'Dad…'

'What? Oh, sorry, my sweetness, my language.' Turning to me, he added, 'She don't like it if I swear. Fair enough, shouldn't swear in front of the kids.' He patted her on the bottom. 'Now, you go home with mum and get lunch ready.'

Glad to get away, she joined her mother talking to a friend. 'She's a good girl but she needs a firm hand. She can twist her mum round her finger, but not me.'

'So I gather you haven't found Dan.'

'You gather right, mate. The little git. Once I get my hands on him…'

'Well, I ought to–'

'Coming to the game this afternoon?'

'Of course.'

He leant towards me. 'I've got a couple bob riding on it. Quite a lot on it actually. So your mate better be ready. Shame you're not playing.'

'The doctor told me—'

'Yeah, you said.' He spat on the ground. 'Good do last night, wasn't it?'

'Yes, lovely,' I replied, trying to disguise my lack of enthusiasm.

'You had a knees-up like that, yeah?'

'It was a total surprise.'

'The likes of you and me, we have friends, don't we? And that's what friends do for each other.' A couple of his mates, as if on cue, turned up. The men exchanged handshakes. 'We're off to the pub again before lunch. Bit of pre-match training. Come with us, if you want. You can tell us all about your grand adventure out on the high seas.'

'I won't. Thanks all the same.'

'We'll get your Greg over. He was good on the old ivories last night. Just a shame about the t-t-t-talking.' I hated him for that. He got the cheap laugh he was looking for and his companions copied him, all of them talking to each other in stutters, trying to outdo each other. I hated myself even more for not saying anything.

I watched them saunter down the road, heading towards the pub, their mutual bond, forged during childhood, made that much stronger by prejudice. 'Hey, June,' he shouted. 'Hurry up and get lunch on, will you?'

She responded with an exasperated look that said 'can't you see I'm talking?'

Turning round, I caught sight of William holding his mother's hand as they headed home. I saw her ruffle his hair which pleased me. Whatever was going through his young mind, at least he still had his mother. As they walked away, he glanced over his shoulder. For the briefest of moments, our eyes met, but, however hard I tried, I couldn't read anything in his expression.

'How are you, Robert?' It was June. Abigail had found a friend to talk to.

'Yeah, fine. And you? Are you pleased to have your husband back?'

'It's only for a few days.'

I wasn't sure what she meant by that but felt it wasn't the time or place to push her. Instead, sensing her awkwardness, I asked, 'Tell me, what do you know about that boy?'

'William?' She leant towards me, talking in a whisper. 'He's a strange one, that one. Don't know why – just is. Anyhow, I'd better go – I've got to get his lordship's lunch on.'

'Nice talking to you.'

She glanced at me, as if trying to read my mind.

Gregory chose that moment to come out of the church. I noticed the vicar slip a coin or two into his hand, his informal payment for Gregory's services as an organist. On seeing me, he came to say hello. 'Got the f-f-football match this afternoon,' he said glumly.

'Looking forward to it?'

'W-what do you think?'

'Come, I'll buy you a drink if you like. Cheer you up a bit.'

'No. No, t-thanks.'

He walked briskly away. There goes an unhappy man, I thought.

Chapter 25

The football pitch belonged to the school, the grass pitted with holes from numerous sets of football boot studs. The grey school buildings with their slate roofs lay to one side looking almost attractive under the sun. Villagers gathered round the touchline as an assorted batch of men and boys warmed up while waiting for Jenkins, the referee for the day, with the orange ball at his feet to bring them together. Angie lay behind me. I stood next to Rebecca who was fanning herself with her straw hat. 'It must be the hottest day of the year,' she said.

'Call this hot? You should try the Indian Ocean.'

She laughed. 'Poor Gregory, he's been dreading this. Look at them all. The men Churchill didn't want. They've either got bad eyesight, asthma or a limp. Most of them have all three.'

'Apart from Parker.' I waved at June and Abigail further down the touchline but they didn't see me. Old Fraser, further along, had brought his own chair and now sat in it drawing on his pipe.

She leant towards me. 'Rumour has it there's a lot riding on this game for him.'

'Pete Parker? Doesn't strike me as a man too concerned with the church roof.'

'Robert, keep your voice down,' she said, nudging her elbow into my ribs. 'No, he's got a bet against someone on the other team. Apparently, it's a…' She lowered her voice, 'large – sum – of – money.'

'Yes, I know. Should spice things up a bit then. Luckily, it's only twenty minutes each half. So, you looking forward to starting your new job?'

'Yes, very much.'

'Have you any family in the area?'

'No. They're in Wales.'

'Ah, so is that where you've come from?'

'Originally but I was abroad for a while. I was married to a… *foreigner*,' she said, mocking the word.

'Where were you living?'

'Oh look, I think we're about to start.'

Jenkins, wearing a black shirt and shorts, blew his whistle and with a muted cheer the game kicked off. The game was seven a side. Our village boys were playing in red, the opposition in blue. Between them, every conceivable shade of red and blue was represented. Some had long-sleeved shirts, others had short; some had V-neck shirts, some crew neck. Parker had placed himself up front, and had taken it upon himself to shout at his teammates. Gregory, hovering in defence, never far from the goalkeeper, looked especially ridiculous in his oversized shorts and his blond hair falling over his glasses, ridiculous and vulnerable. I hoped our players would play well enough so that Gregory's services wouldn't be called upon too often. There seemed to be no structure to either side's playing, and the ball spent much of its time in the air, being hoofed from one end of the pitch to the other. The game was meant to be a friendly affair, but as so often the case when you pit quick-tempered young men against each other, it escalated into something rather vicious. Men fell and shouted at each other every minute or so. But, based on the first ten minutes, if I was a betting man, like Parker, I'd put my money on us, the Reds.

'So, why aren't you playing?' asked Rebecca as Parker got ready to take a free kick.

'I'm not fit enough yet, or strong enough.'

We watched as Parker took a shot on goal, missing by some distance.

'Your future boss is doing well as referee. He's no spring chicken.'

The first half finished nil-nil. The teams dispersed to opposite ends of the pitch as two women in aprons appeared carrying large trays of orange slices for them. I spied Parker at the centre of his team punching his palm, making his point as he tried to galvanise them. Gregory looked like a man on trial for his life.

Ten minutes later, the game re-started with the teams having swapped ends. Now we were close to where Gregory paced up and down, looking distinctly uncomfortable, his face bright red, his hair flattened by sweat. 'Keep going, Gregory,' I shouted. 'You're doing well.'

He threw me a distasteful look.

'Has he touched the ball yet?' asked Rebecca.

'Don't think so.'

Whatever pep talk the blue team gave themselves at

half-time worked for they came out far stronger. As a defender, Gregory was as useful as a sapling, swaying this way and that but utterly impotent and incapable of stopping the opposition. It was only a matter of time before they scored and sure enough, after five minutes, they duly did. Parker, taking out his frustration, yelled and screamed at Gregory. Having realised it, the Blues now exploited Gregory's weakness and scored again and again while Parker almost melted with rage.

'He shouldn't be allowed to talk to him like that,' said Rebecca. 'Who does he think he is?'

'Ted Drake.'

The final whistle couldn't come quickly enough. Finally, Jenkins blew. Our team traipsed off having lost 4-0. Or was it 5-0? Gregory hung back, unable to face anyone. While all the other players, from both sides, shook hands and patted each other on the back, having re-established friendly relations, Parker ran halfway across the pitch to remonstrate with Gregory. 'You b-b-bloody i-i-i-idiot,' he screamed, mimicking Gregory's stutter, pushing him in the chest. 'You just cost me two quid. Two bloody quid. What sort of man are you, you poof?'

Gregory, regaining his balance, glared at him. People nearby stopped to watch. No one, least of all I, expected what happened next. Gregory swung for him, hitting Parker squarely on the jaw.

Jenkins and I ran to try and intervene. Rebecca screamed. 'What do you think you're doing?' shouted the headmaster. Recovering quickly, Parker punched Gregory, causing Gregory to stagger back, his glasses to fly off.

'Parker, leave him be,' I shouted, stepping in between them.

Jenkins followed my lead. 'Both of you, stop this now. You're a disgrace.'

'He started it,' said Parker in the tone of a schoolchild.

Gregory dabbed his nose with his shirt, trying to stem the flow of blood. 'You hooligan,' he muttered.

'Go tell it to your girlfriend. Oh, sorry, forgot – you're still a virgin.'

At this, Gregory lunged at him again. I caught him, my arms round his chest, pulling him back. 'Forget it, Gregory, forget it.'

'That's enough now,' said Jenkins with little conviction.

'Don't worry, *sir*,' said Parker. 'I'm off.' He shot me a filthy look, strode passed Gregory and, for good measure, stamped on his glasses.

Chapter 26

I'd only known Alice for a month but I proposed in a restaurant on a Saturday night in May 1943. Drancy's, it was called. Drancy's in Plymouth. Round tables, white tablecloths, candles, half-oval mirrors on the walls and low-hung lights with orange lampshades. On the wall, behind Alice, was a framed print of Seurat's *Bathers at Asnières* upon a white-bricked wall. 'I love this painting,' said Alice, once we'd ordered. 'It always makes me think of a perfect Sunday, lazing on the riverbank, not a care in the world. Have you ever been to Paris?'

I hadn't even been abroad. Nor had she.

'You ought to join the navy,' she said. 'Then you'd see the world. Imagine, Robert, all the places you might go. Egypt, India, South Africa...'

'The Isle of Wight.'

'Oh now, that's a bit too exotic.'

Dinner at Drancy's was delicious considering wartime supplies – mushroom soup followed by roast pork. But, not surprisingly, considering what I had planned, I had no appetite. I kept checking my jacket pocket, making sure the little box was there. After cheese and biscuits, I had to have a cigarette to calm my nerves. 'Are you all right, darling?' she asked. 'You barely touched your food. There's nothing wrong, is there?'

'Alice, there's something… something I wanted to, well, to tell you.'

'Now, this sounds intriguing. You're not going to tell me you're one of them, are you?'

'One of them?'

'You know.' She leant forward, glancing left and right. 'Catholic.'

I tried not to laugh. 'No, I don't mean tell you, I mean ask you. Well, both really.'

'Robert, the suspense is too much. Fire away, I'm all ears.'

'I'm being serious.'

'Oh, it's like that.' She ran her finger across her lips, as if to remove her smile.

'Alice, I… I love you and–'

'Robert…' She reached over and took my hand. 'I love you too.'

'And – you do?'

'Yes.' She tightened her grip on my hand. 'Yes, I do.'

I reached inside my pocket. Silently, I placed the velvet box on the table in front of her, next to the cheese board.

'Robert, you're not…?'

'Alice, would you be my wife?'

She placed her hand over her heart. Carefully, she took the box and opened it. 'Oh, Robert, it's… it's beautiful.' It was nothing grand – a simple gold band with the smallest of rubies nestled on a layer of silver leaves.

'I know it might seem a bit soon; I know we haven't–'

'Yes.'

'Yes? – it's too soon or…'

'No, silly, yes, I'm saying yes.' I realised she was quietly crying. With her mascara running, she said, 'I'll be your wife.'

*

The following day, I invited Alice over and together we visited my parents to tell them the good news. This was something, I decided, that couldn't be done over the telephone. My mother screeched and hugged us both. My father shook me by the hand and pecked Alice on the cheek. 'I'm pleased,' he said. 'You'll make a lovely couple. I'm sure.'

'Why, thank you, Father,' I said, taken aback by his uncharacteristic show of affection.

Clarence, on hearing the news later that day, said, rather gushingly, 'Great stuff. I'll be hoping for lots of little nephews and nieces.'

'Give us chance,' I laughed.

'I rather see myself as Uncle Clarence.'

'Yes,' said Alice. 'I'm sure you'll make a lovely uncle. Not all uncles are necessarily loathsome creatures.'

'I should hope not,' said Clarence, slightly affronted.

And so, my fiancée and I began to make arrangements. We met the vicar from Alice's village and set a date for a church wedding. My mother, according to my father, was pulling out her every dress and trying them on. I went round in a happy daze, unencumbered by thoughts of war and death. I'd met the woman I wanted to spend the rest of my life with, and I couldn't have been happier.

213

*

About a month later, on a Thursday afternoon in June, I received a phone call at work. It was Alice's father. 'Robert,' he said, his voice sounding breathless. 'There's been an accident. It's Alice.' My heart stopped. 'She's driven into a tree.'

'Oh Lord. Is she all right?'

'Yes, she's fine – all things considered. It could've been a lot worse.'

Clarence shouted from the kitchen. 'Fancy a cuppa, Robert?'

'Shh, be quiet, man.'

'I beg your pardon?'

'No, not you, Mr Redman. Is she hurt?'

'Nothing long term, and nothing broken, thank heavens.'

'Where is she?'

'She's in City Hospital in Plymouth. Her mother and I have just come back from seeing her.' I heard him suck on his pipe. 'She's in shock still and awfully weak, and in quite a bit of pain, I fear.'

'I'll go and see her now.'

'No, steady on, old boy. Visiting times will have finished by the time you get there. And… well, the thing is… she told me to say… try not to take this too personally, but she said she'd rather not see you for a while.'

'Oh.' I felt myself slump. 'Oh. W-why… why is that? Did – did she say?'

'I'm afraid she didn't. Mrs Redman reckons it's probably a vanity thing. You know, not wanting you to see

214

her in such a state. She's badly bruised up, the poor love.'

'Yes, I… I suppose. Of course that's probably it.'

'Absolutely. Now, I know it's been a bit of a shock, it's been a shock for all of us, but she's being well looked after. She'll be fine. Which is more than I can say about the car,' he added quietly.

'Tony!' came a voice in the background. 'Is that all you can think about?'

'No, of course not, dear.' Mr Redman's voice had become muffled as he placed his hand over the receiver.

'Mr Redman? Mr Redman?' I said louder.

'Hmm? Sorry, what was that?'

'Mr Redman, will she be OK for the wedding?'

'Oh that.' Yes, that, I thought. 'That's another couple months off, isn't it? She'll be fine by then. I'll let you know if there's any updates. Cheerio for now.'

'Will you send my…'

Too late; he'd hung up.

'Bad news, I take it,' said Clarence, bearing two mugs of tea.

*

The following day, I called the hospital from the village phone box to enquire about visiting times, then rang work and told them I had an emergency to see to. I donned one of my finer suits, combed my hair, and went to catch the bus to Plymouth. With my brother's encouragement, I'd decided I would visit, whatever she or her father had said. 'She's your fiancée, damn it,' Clarence had said. 'You have every right to see her for yourself.'

I bought a bunch of flowers from a street seller outside the hospital on Lipson Road.

215

From reception, I was told I would find Miss Redman on Ward Six on the third floor. I paused outside the swing doors, took a deep breath and felt my fingers tighten round the stems of the flowers. I almost lost my nerve when the door swung open and a nurse walked straight into me. 'Can I help you, sir?'

'No, I mean, well… yes.'

'Who have you come to see?'

'A Miss Redman.'

'Follow me.'

I had to skip a step or two across the linoleum floor merely to keep up as I was marched through the ward past rows of beds occupied by women of various ages. She delivered me to a bed at the far end near a large window overlooking a patio courtyard. Beneath the window a radiator, cold to the touch, and at the end of the bed a clipboard. 'A visitor, Miss Redman,' she announced loudly.

'Thank you, nurse,' I muttered.

'Sister, if you please,' she said before making a brisk exit.

'Robert?' Lifelessly, she lay propped up by several pillows. Over her knees a bed tray on which rested her uneaten breakfast of tea and toast.

'Alice, my love, how are you?' She had a white bandage wrapped several times round her head almost obscuring her eyes, from which streaks of matted hair poked out. Her left eye was black and swollen, her cheeks red and puffy, her lips were thin and devoid of colour.

'I've been better,' she muttered.

'I know you said… that I wasn't to come but…'

'It's OK,' she said slowly. 'It's good to see you.' She reached out her hand but then dropped it again as if the

216

effort was too much.

'I simply had to come see you.'

She patted the bed. I sat and took her hand. Above her on the wall a poster depicting a pair of hands washing proclaimed 'Cleanliness is our best friend'.

'Your father rang me last night. He told me what happened; that you'd had an accident. I've been worried sick. You look… you look terribly tired, darling.'

'I am. I can't talk. Tell me what you've been up to.'

'Me? Well, erm… there's not much to say really…' Nonetheless, I prattled on about work, about life in the village, about what was happening in the news, but I could tell she was too weak to listen. After a while, aware I was tiring her out too much, I ran out of steam. I stroked her hand. 'I'll come back – when you're stronger, yeah?'

She nodded, her eyes half closed. 'Yes, I'd like that. I'm sorry. Perhaps the day after tomorrow.'

Chapter 27

I'd just fed Angie when I heard the knock on my door. There, I found Gregory, visibly wrought, his face flushed. 'Something's wrong?' I asked as, without waiting to be asked, he barged past me into the house. I noticed the crack in the right lens of his glasses – a result of Parker's football boot.

'Something's wrong all r-right,' he said. 'Some reprobate's thrown rubbish all over my front garden.'

'What? Are you sure?'

'Of course I'm bloody sure – you can't exactly miss it. Litter strewn all over the place. Must be about three binfulls of the stuff. It's disgusting. I know he's an idiot, but why would he do that?'

'He?'

'Oh come on, Robert, it's obvious. We know it's Parker, or one of his henchmen.'

'And the neighbours, have they–'

'No, just me.' He sat down at my kitchen table and pushed Angie away.

'You should call the police,' I suggested, knowing his response.

'What would be the point in that? It's only litter, after all. And I've no proof. I know it was him but I didn't see him do it. The man's a thug as well as an idiot.' He stood to leave. 'Anyway, I'm not staying. The real reason I came was to tell you I've just had a visit from Rebecca. She's cancelled all her lessons.'

'Has she? What for?'

'I've put her off, haven't I? I always put women off. It's not right. How is it a thug like Parker can attract a lovely woman like June while me… lovely Gregory, who's so nice and kind, Gregory who wouldn't hurt a fly, Gregory who's nice to old ladies, and so polite. It doesn't get me anywhere though, does it? I can't attract a woman for all the t-tea in China.'

'You're being too harsh on yourself. She won't have cancelled because of you – she's probably too busy or realised she's not good enough or something, or…'

'No, it's because of me. Yesterday, I tried to… I can't tell you, it's too embarrassing.' He thumped himself on the thigh with frustration. 'You didn't help either.'

'Me?'

'Come on, Robert; don't play the innocent with me. You know I like her but it didn't stop you, did it? Flirting with her like that. She was all over you at Parker's do.'

'No, Gregory, listen, you misunderstand–'

'Oh, I always misunderstand. I'm incapable of reading the signals. I'm just the village idiot.'

'That's quite a claim.'

He glared at me. 'Sorry,' I muttered.

'Yeah, not funny, Robert; not funny at all.'

It was only after he'd left that I realised in his anger he'd lost his stutter.

*

I decided to explore. I wanted to work out where William went to on his bike. Leaving Angie at home, I took my bicycle and headed towards where I'd seen him go a couple days before. The sun was out but there was still a chill in the breeze as I cycled through the village and down the lane. Finding the rutted track, I pushed my bike up the steep incline, and around the corner. On reaching the top, I spied in the distance a barn, a lone building amongst the fields. Remounting, I cycled along the bumpy track. Leaving the bike propped up outside, I pushed open the heavy barn doors and peered inside. Lines of sun slanted through the slats, catching the motes of dust. The place felt deserted. The mud-packed floor was strewn with cardboard boxes, old brown newspapers and rusty cans. In the middle was an ancient car, a Ford, one of its windows smashed, its bonnet open revealing a rusted engine. Looking inside the car, I could see the seats had been ripped, exposing the springs inside. Elsewhere, planks of wood lay around in higgledy-piggledy piles, an old wheelbarrow, mounds of discarded tools, a coil of rope and, propped up against the barn wall, a long ladder.

From out of the dimness, someone, a woman, spoke. Whoa, I clutched my heart – I wasn't alone. 'Hello? William?' said the voice from the far end of the barn.

'Hello?' I called out hesitantly. 'Hello? Who's there?' I heard a scuttling. 'Hello? I'm Robert. Robert Searight.'

'Robert? Is that really you?'

With a jolt, I realised I recognised the German accent.

'*Joanna?*'

She appeared before me. 'It is you. Robert.' She came towards me. She looked bedraggled in a brown cardigan, a grey skirt, a long red scarf, her hair long and unkempt, her face gaunt. She stopped a few feet from me. We looked at each other, disbelieving.

'Why aren't you at home? What – what are you doing here?'

'It's a long story.' She tried to smile. 'It's so good to see you. Owen – is he back too?'

She didn't know; I'd have to tell her. 'No. I'm sorry.'

'He's dead, isn't he?'

I nodded.

She shut her eyes. 'Let's sit down,' she whispered.

She led me to a corner of the barn where, to my surprise, she'd made herself a little hideaway – a battered-looking armchair, a chair with a broken leg, a small rug even, and a camping stove. 'Welcome to my new home.'

'What happened, Joanna? I don't understand. Why are you here?'

She had always had bulging eyes, which gave the impression of always being in a state of constant surprise, but now, her face so thin, her eyes were even more prominent. 'I've got everything I need. Look…' She showed me a cardboard box and inside were various tins, mainly of soup, chocolate bars and a couple of bananas. 'I can't offer you a drink though. Water and that's about it. There's a water pump round the back. I'm dying for a coffee. Take a seat. Here, sit on the armchair.'

I sat down. Looking around, I thought if one had to live as a fugitive, then this place was as good as it could get – it was dry, protected from the wind, and warm enough.

Nonetheless, it wasn't right for a woman such as Joanna to be living like this.

'Joanna, I don't understand…'

'You must tell me – what happened to Owen? How did it happen?'

I shook my head. 'He didn't make it. I'm sorry.'

Tears formed in her eyes as I tried briefly to tell her the story. She sat perched on the edge of the chair with its broken leg, and listened intently. 'He talked of you often. It was obvious how much he loved you.'

'Oh no, my poor, poor Owen. I feared this,' she said, bowing her head. I noticed she was wearing her wedding ring.

'He wanted you to have his wedding ring. It was important to him. I'll bring it over later this afternoon.'

'Thank you,' she murmured.

'He was a good man, your Owen. I liked him a lot. When I returned to the village, I felt it was the one thing I had to do – to give you his ring. When I found out you'd gone, I felt as though I had failed him.'

'How did you find me?'

'I followed that boy – William.'

'William. He's been my saviour. What did people say about me?' she asked, fishing a handkerchief out of her cardigan pocket.

'That you'd just left one day. That was it.'

She rolled her eyes. 'They make it sound as if I had a choice.'

'You do want to tell me about it?'

She sighed. She blew her nose and wiped her eyes. 'I never felt comfortable here, Robert. I was fine in Plymouth, even after my first husband died – no one noticed me there. But here… As soon as the war started, people were civil, but I could see it in their eyes – they saw me as a wolf in sheep's clothing, ready to turn on them at any moment. But then, things got a little better. We may have been at war but of course nothing happened during those early months. It still seemed far away. Life in the village carried on as normal. And I had Owen. You know Owen; like you say, he loved me very much and he looked after me. He was a good husband. But then you left, both of you. And then we had Dunkirk and suddenly the war felt very real. Things got worse again after the bombs started falling. Plymouth was badly hit. People cursed Hitler and his aeroplanes that brought death from the skies. And that's when it began. The first incident, I remember, was a letter through the door. It didn't have a stamp on it. Inside, on a single sheet of paper, the words 'German bitch'. Robert, I was so upset. But that was nothing to what came later. No one spoke to me. Even my friend Sylvie. Do you know her – Sylvie Jenkins, the headmaster's wife? I was still teaching. The kids were fine, at first, but the other teachers… No one talked to me in the staffroom. Only Mr Jenkins showed me any decency.

'One day, someone posted a large envelope through my letterbox. I knew I shouldn't have looked inside because, again, there was no stamp. But I did. Inside was a stool. Yes, I know. I knew it was human. Can you believe that, someone had taken the effort to defecate inside an envelope for my benefit? I was sick. I felt so hurt – my husband, my English husband, was out there, with you, fighting for his country – their country, *our* country, and they were doing this to me. My only friend was Jet. You remember Jet? My little black cat.

'One morning I got up to find someone had painted a swastika over my front door. I tried to clean it off with turpentine. A crowd of people gathered to watch me as I scrubbed, jeering at me, calling me a Nazi scrubber. How amusing. People I had known for years, laughing at me, calling me the foulest names, as if I was personally responsible for the Blitz in Plymouth. I was frightened, Robert. After they all left, having had their morning's entertainment, that little boy, William, came up to me. I knew him from school. I waited for him to call me some horrible name – as usually happened now with the kids. Instead, without saying anything, he handed me a piece of chocolate. I collapsed into tears. For the first time in months, someone had shown me a little kindness.

'I went to see Reverend Pritchard. He advised me to leave, said it might be for the best. Best for whom, I asked. Them or me? I said no, I refused to be hounded out by the mob. I returned home from church and my house had been broken into. Nothing was taken, as I far as I could see, but they had ransacked the place. The contents of my larder scattered on the floor, broken crockery, upturned furniture. On the mirror in the bathroom, they'd written 'Death to Hitler' in red lipstick. My lipstick. I went to the police. They didn't say it directly, but the message I got was what did I expect? I knew now that the vicar was right – I had to leave. But where, Robert? I have nowhere to go.

'One night, I was treated to a recital of sorts. It was gone midnight, a group of men gathered and clanged dustbin lids loudly outside my window. Poor old Jet – he disappeared sharply and didn't return for hours. They kept it up all night, taking turns, as if they were on shifts. I cried, Robert; I cried for myself and for Owen. They wouldn't have done this had Owen been around; if he hadn't been fighting for their liberty. The following night, they returned. And the night after that. Every night starting at twelve. They would have kept all my neighbours awake too, but they didn't complain. Perhaps they felt it was in a good cause – to harass the enemy living beside them.

'And then they killed Jet. That was the final straw. I found him in the garden. They'd broken his neck. On his little body, another note, warning me I'd be next. How could they do such things, Robert? The cruelty of it took my breath away. That night, before the dustbin lid players arrived, I packed my bags, and carrying as much as I could, I disappeared into the night. I came here. And I've been here ever since, trying to work out what to do. I've still got my keys, but I've no money and no access to my bank account. Stupidly, it's all under Owen's name. I saw William one day, flying a kite in the field just there. I begged him to help me, and he did. He came back the following day with a can of soup. I had to wait another day though before I could ask him to bring me a tin opener. It's almost funny. I've had soup everyday now. I can't tell him I'd like something else for a change. The boy's been an angel.'

'Who were they?'

'I don't know – no one, everyone. I still have my faith, and I tell myself that, at heart, they're good people who lost their senses for a while, their sense of proportion. Tell me, Robert, tell me what to do.'

'I'll take you home, you can't–'

'No, I can't.'

'You could stay with me.'

225

'I can't go back there, you must understand.'

I tried to think, where could I take her? 'Perhaps... Listen, Joanna, tomorrow we'll catch a bus into Plymouth, and we'll go to the HQ of the merchant navy there. I'll buy you lunch–'

'I have nothing to wear.'

'Give me your keys, I'll bring you a set of fresh clothes. We'll throw ourselves on their mercy. They'll sort you out with something, I'm sure. After all, Owen was one of theirs. It's the least they could do.'

'Owen. My lovely Owen.' She clasped her hands together, as if in prayer. 'I'll never see him again, will I? I know I'm stating the obvious, but it doesn't seem real. I'll never hear his voice again, that lovely Devonian accent he had. He's in a better place, of that I'm sure. Oh, Owen, Owen...' She rose to her feet and, turning her back on me, started crying. She strolled away towards the centre of the barn, her shoulders shaking. Leaning against the Ford, caught in a shaft of sunlight, she raised her eyes to the roof, as if seeking God's explanation.

*

I cycled home, Joanna's house keys in my pocket. Ignoring Angie, I ran upstairs and opened the drawer to my bedside table. The ring was still there alongside the crucifix.

From home, I walked briskly to Joanna's house carrying a small suitcase. Yes, there on the front door, was an outline of the swastika. I hadn't noticed it before but now, on seeing it, it was obvious. She'd repainted the door but not with enough layers to obliterate the graffiti. Looking behind me, hoping no one would see me, I unlocked her front door and entered the dark hallway. The stench of staleness and neglect hit me. Locking the door behind me, I switched on a light. There was a hat stand and, on the wall, a sepia photograph of a middle-aged couple and a framed map of Devon. A dustpan and broom leant in the corner. The house seemed deeply quiet, I hadn't expected otherwise, but it was the depth of silence that unnerved me, as if the house itself had known that no one had talked within these walls for weeks. Stepping into the living room, the light bulb blew as soon as I tried turning it on. Upstairs I found Joanna's bedroom. Its fussy, floral-patterned wallpaper made the room feel smaller than it was, the bed was neatly made, a teddy bear snug under the blanket, propped up against the pillow. A dusty copy of *Lady Chatterley's Lover* on the bedside table on her side; and on Owen's side, a motoring magazine and a book on Victorian ships. A scratching noise made me jump. 'Hello?' I said nervously. Turning round, I realised it was the branches of the apple tree scraping against the window pane.

There was no sign here, or elsewhere, of the break-in Joanna had described. Whatever mess they'd made, she'd thoroughly cleared up after them.

On her chest of drawers was a framed photograph of them both. The image of the two of them together stopped me short. It was taken perhaps a year or two before the war, on a beach, the sea and a couple of distant bathers behind them. Leaning in towards each other, their shoulders touching, they looked so happy. Together with its frame, I slipped the photo into the pocket of the suitcase I'd brought with me. I quickly chose a number of items from her wardrobe. I had no idea what she'd prefer, so, having quickly scanned the small array of clothes in front of me, I chose things that I thought would prove practical – jumpers, woollen skirts, a couple of nice blouses and so forth.

Propped up against the dressing table mirror, I noticed an envelope. Hesitating only a moment, I opened it. Inside were a couple of letters in German, a photograph of an elderly couple, perhaps her parents, and her marriage certificate. She and Owen had got married in Plymouth in January 1939, a few months before the war. Her maiden name, it said, was Johanna (not Joanna) Gräfe, she was twenty-nine at the time, a good seven years older than Owen.

Looking through a chest of drawers, I fished out a few pairs of undergarments, trying to overcome my inherent sense of embarrassment at rifling through a lady's underwear drawer. I also took a hairbrush and a small bottle of perfume. The latter, although not practical or essential, I thought might help cheer her up a little. Folding everything neatly into the suitcase, I crept downstairs, still conscious of making too much noise, and had a quick look around. Opening a small cupboard in the kitchen, the intense, foul stench hit me – fruit flies took flight, as I staggered back. The bowl of fruit was blackened. I found a washing up bowl, and with a long wooden spoon, dragged the stinking mess into the bowl, and threw it into her dustbin outside. Returning to the kitchen, I took some cans of food and made to leave. Locking the door firmly behind me, I left, relieved that no one had seen me during my little escapade.

*

I cycled the mile or so back to the barn, this time taking

Angie – I thought she might cheer Joanna up a little. I found Joanna much as I had left her. Sitting in the armchair, her eyes closed, as if relaxing in her living room at home. A standard lamp and a radio was all that was missing.

'Hello, I arrive bearing gifts,' I said, presenting the suitcase. Angie trotted around, delighted at so many new smells.

'Oh, Robert, this is wonderful,' she said, shifting through the contents. 'Oh…'

'Anything the matter?'

'The photo.'

'I thought…'

She sat down and resting the photograph on her lap looked at it intently. 'Such happy times,' she said to herself. 'And now Owen's gone, and I'm living like a fugitive with only the mice for company.'

I knelt beside her and took her hand. 'We'll sort something out, Joanna, I promise.'

'I don't think I can face it; it's all too much.'

'I'll help. I'll do everything I can. Oh, and I brought you this…' From my trouser pocket, I gave her the ring.

She took it and held it up to the light, a faint smile on her lips. 'With this ring… Thank you, Robert.'

'I think it was perhaps the last thing he said – to make sure that whatever happened, I stayed alive in order to give you this ring.'

'And now you have.'

'Yes, and now I have.'

I watched her as she slipped it on, trying out different fingers. Admiring it, she said, 'None of my fingers are big enough, but I shall still wear it.' She held up her hand admiring the two wedding rings. 'How could it have gone so wrong?' she said. 'We were so happy. We'd always wanted children but once the war started, we felt the time wasn't right. Perhaps it was a good thing – how could I have looked after a child with all this happening around me? But I wish now…' She wiped her eyes.

'He would have made a great father, I'm sure.'

Angie started growling, her tail erect.

'Angie, stop it.'

'There's a lot to interest her here. Will you tell me about it?'

'About Owen?'

'I know you told me but I want to know more. What happened to your ship, and Owen, how did it happen? How did he die? I want you to tell me everything.'

'If you're sure.'

She stroked Angie, who licked her hand. 'Yes,' she said, 'I'm sure.'

And so I told her my story.

*

It was almost dark by the time I returned home. I'd tried to persuade Joanna to come with me. It didn't seem right to leave her there, in that barn at night-time. But no, she said she preferred the barn to the village, saying that she'd never want to step foot in it ever again. I offered to stay the night with her. Again, she said no; she had a lot of thinking to do; she needed time, she said, to absorb the story I'd told her. And so, reluctantly, I left her, promising her I'd return the following day. I left her with her husband's ring on her finger and still clutching the photo of her and Owen.

Chapter 28

Two days after seeing Alice in hospital, I returned. I found her sitting up in bed, flicking through a glossy magazine, looking much stronger. The bandage around her head had been removed; her hair, quite gleaming, had been washed. 'Robert, hello.' Her voice had come back but none of her usual cheeriness. I asked her how she was and she said fine in a voice that implied she was anything but. We talked about the food and the nurses and the old woman opposite who kept crying out at night, keeping everyone awake.

'So, what happened? How did you crash the car?'

'I'll tell you. Let's go sit in the courtyard.'

'Are you allowed?'

'They're fine about it. They say a little exercise and the fresh air will do me good.'

I helped her slip her dressing gown on. To my surprise, she had to walk with the aid of a walking stick. Holding onto my arm, we hobbled slowly, very slowly, down the stairs and out into the courtyard. A few benches and a number of tables, chairs and sun umbrellas were dotted round a rectangular patch of freshly-cut grass, along with little statues of cupids. Bushes in large pots added to the greenery. This little haven had been spared of bombs. We found ourselves alone and sat on a bench overlooking the grass.

'Are you warm enough?'

'Just about.' She lit herself a cigarette and, closing her eyes, breathed in the smoke. 'Robert, I need to tell you about something, something I've never spoken about before – to anyone. I don't want you to interrupt. In fact, I rather you didn't look at me either.'

'OK, as you wish.' Self-consciously, I fixed my attention on a lawnmower next to a cupid on the other side of the courtyard.

'This is not easy for me. I'd swore I would never tell anyone but… but if we're to have a future together, you need to know what you're letting yourself in for. The accident last week… I'm not even sure it was an accident. I was driving too fast as usual. Far too fast. I wasn't concentrating; my mind was so clouded in anger. I took a bend too quickly. Lost control. The next thing I knew I woke up in hospital. Apparently, I hit a tree.

'Your father said–'

'No, please, darling, you mustn't interrupt. You'll think me strange but I need to pretend you're not here otherwise I won't be able to finish this, and I must. I have to tell you. Last week, my parents went to Exeter to see my father's brother, his twin in fact, Victor, Uncle Vic. They spent the day there. I knew he was ill but they came back and told me he had cancer of the kidneys. The doctors reckoned he hadn't long to go. Possibly just days. He desperately wanted to see me, Father told me; I had to go see him; you know, one last time. I said no, I didn't want to.' Fishing a handkerchief from her dressing gown pocket, she blew her nose. A plump man in brown overalls appeared, checked the bins and returned back indoors.

'Father tried appealing to my better nature, using words like duty and family. He even tried to threaten me with words like disinheritance. In the end, I decided to go. Not because of anything Father said but because I wanted to. This was on Thursday. I went straightaway before I changed my mind, or rather before I lost my nerve. Uncle Vic's always lived alone, never married. Lives in a small cottage outside Exeter – ivy on the outside walls, little gravel path, that sort of thing. All very quaint. And inside, its low beams and horse brasses and logs in a basket by the fire. There was a nurse downstairs, a woman in her fifties, I guess, very tall for a woman, and gangly. "Are you Alice?" she asked. "Oh, how lovely. Your uncle's been talking about you such a lot. We weren't expecting you but I know he'll be delighted to see you." She told me he needed round-the-clock care now. "He gets tired very easily, so you won't be able to stay for long, I'm afraid." The shorter the better, I thought. "We're expecting the vicar." She looked at her upside-down watch on her starched white uniform. "Quite soon, in fact. If I'd known you were coming… Well, you're here now. Let me go wake your uncle up and make him look a little more presentable for you." And off she went.

'I waited about ten minutes, sitting in a squashy armchair being pawed at by a ginger tom, horrible beast. I almost turned tail and ran but, I thought, I've come this far, I'm not leaving now. I'd been to the house before but only a couple times and not for many years. It reeked of cats and stale smoke.

'The nurse came down and told me I could go see him. The bedroom was bathed in sunlight, giving it an almost ethereal feel. It was uncomfortably warm – the windows were closed despite it being so hot outside. I saw the tail of a cat disappear beneath the bed. The sound of the ticking clock on the bedside table, next to a vase of irises, seemed very loud. The bed itself, a single, was unusually high. I was taken aback by the man in the bed. My throat went dry on seeing him. He was my father's twin and he looked like him. Not any more. He'd lost so much weight and looked deathly pale, his cheeks had sunk in, and what was left of his hair had turned white and wispy, the bags under his eyes were like huge rubbery sacks. So, this is what death looks like, I thought to myself. He was wearing a pair of stripped purple pyjamas. "Alice, oh, how lovely, lovely, to see you. Come in, come in, my dear. Take a pew." With a bony finger he pointed to a chair next to his bed. I noticed how long his fingernails had grown. The thought of touching him made me shudder. "How are you?" he asked. Even his voice had changed. Gone was the booming voice he had, now it was all thin and raspy. I took my coat off and put it on the back of the chair.

'"Fine," I said. I glanced round the room. There was a painting of a waterfall above his bed; and there was a copy of *Don Quixote* on the bedside table next to a glass of water, its bookmark was only a few pages from the beginning. There was a mauve dressing gown with oversized tassels hanging off the back of his wardrobe. "Father said you'll be dead within a few days." I hoped to shock him by my callousness but he just laughed it off.

"'Always the master of stating the obvious, was my brother. I think by the mere fact of living longer than me, he thinks he's won in some way. Life has always been one big competition for your father.'

"'He's a competitive man; that's why he's always done well for himself.'

"'You're right; he always had to be better than me – faster, richer, better dressed, nicer house. I always reckoned it was because I was older than him. I was the first one out, you see. Twins, eh? He's done well, I give him that, but I put it down to me – his perpetual need to be more successful drove him all his life." He shook his head. "I was never like that, never felt the need to prove myself all the time.'

"'You got your own back, though, didn't you, Uncle Vic? You had something of his. He never knew it but it was enough for you.'

'He sighed heavily. "Perhaps you're right." He looked at me pitifully with his grey, dead man eyes. "Alice…" He reached out his bony hand for me. He saw me recoil, sitting on my hands. "Alice, thank you so much for coming to see me, to hear me out. I didn't think you would and I wouldn't have blamed you if you hadn't. As your father says, I'll soon be dead. And I know I can fall off this mortal coil quite happily if… if I had your forgiveness.'

"'Forgiveness? Forgiveness for what, Uncle Vic?'

'He swallowed. I watched his bony Adam's apple bob up and down. "Please, Alice, don't make this more difficult than it already is. Please… tell me you forgive me.'

"'Forgive you for what, Uncle Vic?'

"'You mean to punish me. I understand." He rubbed his eyes. "To forgive me for coming to your room at night."

"'Oh, that? I forget; how many times was it? Once, twice maybe?'"

"'No, many times over the years. I'm sorry. It was wrong of me, I know that now. Wrong and depraved.'"

"'Why? I've always wanted to know – why?' I had to stop myself from screaming the word out.

"'It's a question I've asked myself repeatedly. I don't know why. I used to enjoy my stays in your house, especially as your mother was such a good cook and your father bought expensive and very nice beers, but then I would come away full of self-loathing, hating myself. Perhaps it was my inferiority complex; I was always such a failure next to your father and his work and his lovely family and his big house and his new cars.'"

"'So you thought you'd get your own back by coming to his daughter's bed at night and lying on top of her, suffocating her, letting your hands wander to places no decent man should go, and making sure she felt your–'"

"'Stop!' Tears rolled down his sunken cheeks. "Stop, please, Alice, just stop. I'm sorry, believe me when I say it. If I could turn back time–'"

"'But you can't, can you, Uncle Vic? You can't.'"

"'No. I can't. I'm sorry. I truly am. Just say you forgive me and I can die a happy man; I beg you.'"

"'The worst part was that you looked so much like my father. It felt as if Dad was doing this to me, these unspeakable things. At least you smelt differently. I love the smell of his piped tobacco, always will.'"

"'I understand.'"

"'I've met someone.'"

"'You have? I am pleased.' He wiped his tears with the

236

back of his hand.

"'He's very nice. Decent. I'm a grown woman now – I want him to touch me; I want him to take me to bed and fuck me." I watched him grimace. "But he doesn't because he's a decent man. Perhaps he fears he'd be taking advantage of me. Something that never stopped you. We're engaged. Engaged to be married. Shame you won't be around to be there, Uncle Vic. You'll be in some dark, fiery place where men like you go to rot for the rest of eternity. He's different from all the others. I say 'all the others' because, believe me, there were many."

"'Stop, Alice, you don't need to tell me this.'"

"'Oh, but I do. It's why I came. So you would know. I lost my virginity, the second time, mind you, when I was fifteen. A boy at school. Piers, his name. After school one day. The bike shed, would you believe? What a cliché. He was the first. By the time I was seventeen, I'd lost count. And it continued. By the time I was twenty, I'd slept with so many strangers, I reckoned I deserved a medal – for services to mankind, at least every man, young and old, within a ten-mile radius of home. I was always careful, mind you. Always careful. After all, wouldn't want to shame the family, now would we?"

"'Did it… help?'"

"'Did it help? That's exactly the question I used to ask myself – did it help? No, it didn't. Did I find love? No. Did it purge me of your memory, the smell of sweat, the beer on your breath? No. Today, still, if I smell beer, it makes me sick. And I mean, throwing up sick. So I stopped going with men. I decided – the next man I sleep with will be my husband – wherever he may be. For years, I hated my father. I thought, being twins, you'd be the same. I thought he too wanted to lie on top of young girls and suffocate them. I hated him so much, the poor man."

"'We were nothing alike."

"'No, he's a good, hardworking man; you're a filthy, despicable man. Like you say, Uncle Vic, nothing alike. I know why you never married now – you never wanted a woman, you just wanted a girl. A girl like me. Well, you had her for a while, didn't you? I tried to tell my mother once. First, she tried to laugh it off. When I persisted, she slapped me across the face and sent me to my room. I wanted to tell Father. But I couldn't; I felt too dirty."

'We were interrupted by a knock on the door. It was Uncle Vic's nurse. "Is everything all right in here?" she asked. "It's just I thought I heard raised voices, and we wouldn't want that, not in Mr Redman's condition."

"'It's fine, nurse," said my uncle. "Thank you."

"'We're just reminiscing," I added with an exaggerated smile.

'She looked at me suspiciously. "Well, if you're sure, Mr Redman. You look a little drawn. I wouldn't want you to tire yourself out."

"'Quite sure. Thank you, nurse."

'She was so tall she had to duck as she went out the door. I waited until I could hear her rummaging around downstairs. Rising from the chair, I said, "You ruined my childhood; you almost ruined my relationship with my parents; you almost ruined my relationship with men. And now you want me to forgive you?"

"'Believe me, I've wanted to ask you for years. But I felt I didn't have the right; I knew I'd... well... that I'd damaged you. But now, Alice, now that I am here, on my deathbed... surely, death wipes the slate clean; it makes

238

good men of us all. Until I was confined to this bed, I used to go to church, two, three times a week, and beg God's forgiveness until I was in tears."

'I stood up, ready to go. Holding my coat over my arm, I asked, "And did He? Did God forgive you?"

'"Yes, God forgave me, of that I am sure. He would have seen how sincere I was. And that is why, before you go, you have to say you forgive me, Alice. This will be the last time you'll see me. I beg you."

'I tapped his *Don Quixote* with my finger. "I should read this one day," I said quietly. I walked towards the door, feeling his eyes on my back. The thought of it made me tremble, tremble like a little girl in bed, hiding under her bedclothes, looking at the sliver of light under the bedroom door, waiting for that door to edge open, waiting for the inevitable. I turned the doorknob.

'"Alice, please…"

'I turned to face him one last time – a man on the edge of death, about to slip into oblivion, his leaden eyes beseeching me. "Hell's not good enough for you. I hope you rot, you bastard."

'"No, Alice, nooo!" The effort of screaming after me left him convulsed in a fit of coughing, fighting for breath. Gently, I closed the bedroom door.

'"What's going on, what's happening?" On hearing the commotion, the nurse had come running up the stairs. She charged into the bedroom, shooting me a filthy look as she passed me on the landing. "Mr Redman, what on earth…" Turning to me, she snarled. "What have you done to him?" I watched from outside the bedroom as she patted him rigorously on the back, reaching for the glass of water. "What has that wicked woman done to you, you poor man? I knew she was trouble."

'I walked back down the stairs, passing another cat, and left.

'As I walked out of the front door, I saw someone hurrying up the gravel path. Looking up, I saw that it was the vicar they'd been expecting, a tall, thin man with brown-framed glasses. "You'll find the patient upstairs," I said.

'"Yes, thank you," he said, slowing down.

'"You'd better hurry," I said. "He's in need of your God."

'He seemed rather bemused by my comment. "Right. Yes, thank you." Throwing me another bemused glance, I watched him enter the cottage, closing the front door behind him.

'Robert, are you OK? Robert? You look rather pale.'

Chapter 29

I had so many fitful dreams during the first few days back at home – of being on that boat. I dreamt that we were in the midst of a storm, our little boat being tossed about on the waves. Ahead of us, we could see a shaft of light descending from the heavens. Owen, on his feet, had his arms raised towards it as the rain and wind swirled around him, shouting, his voice lost to the storm. However hard we tried to reach it, to seek the sanctuary of the light, the further the waves pushed us away from it. I awoke with a start. Angie crawled up the bed to say hello, her short tail wagging. The weather outside was dismal.

Having dressed, I went to the shop, braving the drizzle, and bought a few more provisions for Joanna. 'Expecting guests, are we?' asked Mr Hamilton.

'Something like that.'

I had no room for Angie in the basket, thus I left her at home as I cycled back to the barn. By the time I got there, there was a hint of sun breaking through the dense clouds. Leaning against the hedge, was William's bike. As I cycled and slipped up the muddy track, William passed, running, as if escaping something. 'Hey, William, stop a minute.'

I'd taken him by surprise; he hadn't seen me until I spoke. He faltered for a moment, skidded to a halt, almost losing his footing. He looked frightened, as if I'd caught him doing something wrong. He seemed to be crying. 'What's the matter, William?'

For a moment, I thought he might speak, but then, instead, he ran off. I turned the bike round, slipping on the mud. 'William,' I called after him, trying to keep my balance. A can of tinned pears fell out of the basket. Cursing, I had to dismount to retrieve it by which time I'd lost the will to chase after him. I had to go see Joanna. But the boy's expression had worried me – something was wrong; I could feel it.

I pushed my bike to the top of the hill, then cycled the last bit as the track flattened out. Dropping the bike, not caring about the shopping, I pushed open the barn door, shouting Joanna's name. Quickly, I ran to the far end where she'd set up her little home. She wasn't there. But lying on the seat of the armchair, the frame and the glass from the photograph. The photo itself was gone. 'Joanna? Joanna!'

I dashed back outside and ran round the whole building, scanning the fields all around. Nothing. I returned inside the barn, now short of breath, and it was only then that I noticed for the first time, to one side in a darkened corner, a second ladder, this one reaching up to a sort of loft. Peering up into the space above me, I knew she was up there. Repeating her name quietly, I slowly climbed up the ladder, testing each rung, wanting to delay having to confront what I knew lay ahead of me. With my heart beating wildly, I felt myself tense up as my eyes reached the floor of the loft. There, suspended above me, a shadow, a figure. 'No, Joanna, no.' Scrambling up the last few rungs, I ran over to her, only to fall as my leg went through a rotten floorboard. Sprawled on the dusty floor, my left leg dangling through the hole, I forced myself to look up. Using her scarf, Joanna had hung herself from a roof beam. On the floor beneath her, the photograph of her and her husband.

Chapter 30

'So this was what time exactly?' The policeman, whose name I had already forgotten, peered down at me from his great height, his pencil and notepad in hand. We were standing in my living room – two policemen and myself. Another two waited outside in their car.

'I told you; it was about half past nine. I don't know the exact time.'

'And the last time you saw her alive was last night? How did she seem then?'

'She was upset. Wouldn't you be? Hounded out of your home by people you thought were your friends?'

'But you don't know who exactly these people were, you said so yourself, sir.'

'No,' I sighed. 'I don't know. She seemed unwilling to tell me.'

The four policemen had arrived in the village by car, its siren blaring, screeching to a halt outside my cottage. I'd rang them from the village phone box the moment I'd returned. Their appearance inside sent Angie into a fit of frenzied barking. One of them tried to stroke her only to have his hand almost bitten off. Back outside, I squeezed onto the backseat of their car. I directed them to the field but not without a number of villagers noticing. I waited outside the barn while they went in. I had no desire to see Joanna again. One of them gave me the photograph. The tallest one asked me a few questions. What was she doing there? How long? Why? How did I find her? Did I know her? Having padlocked the barn door and on returning to the cottage, he asked me the same questions again. I decided against telling him about William. By now, a small crowd had gathered outside my door. As I showed the policemen out, everyone took a step back as if fearing contamination. The tall policeman told me he'd arrange for the body to be picked up straightaway, and that'd there be a post-mortem. He told me also that he would be back within a couple of days to question the villagers. 'All of them?' I asked. 'All of them,' he replied for everyone to hear.

'Have you been arrested?' asked Mrs James. 'Post-mortem on who?' asked another. 'Why do they want to question us?' 'What's happening, Robert?' asked Mr Jenkins.

'OK, let me speak, I'll tell you.' I did wonder whether announcing it like this was wise but, I thought, they'd find out soon enough, and it wasn't as if there was anyone who needed to know first. Looking at them, their number increasing by the minute, I spied Pete and June Parker amongst them. And so I told them. There were gasps all round. People shook their heads and said 'poor woman'.

'Hanging, you say?' asked Jenkins. 'How awful, how terribly awful.'

*

I went to find Reverend Pritchard. His wife at the vicarage told me he was at the church. Turning the ring-handle, I pushed open the church door, momentarily pleased by the satisfying creak of the door hinges. My shoes echoed on the stone floor as I approached the altar. The hymn numbers from the previous Sunday's service were still on display, above a papier mâché model of Jesus in his white gown with a vivid pink face. The vicar appeared from the back at the church. 'Ah, Robert,' he shouted, waving at me. Still wearing his dog collar under a grey jumper, he beckoned me over.

'I need to speak to you, Reverend, that is, if you're not too busy.'

'No, not at all. Come, let's sit down,' he said, offering me a pew.

Sitting in the pew in front, he turned round to face me as I told him about Joanna and the visit from the police.

'This is shocking news,' he said. 'I'm truly sorry to hear this. You know, she came to see me once. Her husband had just gone to sea, and she was suffering because of her nationality. It's strange how people get. Sometimes they need to vent their anger, and in this instance it was Joanna who became the focus of their viciousness. These people, they must have known she was German by birth only. She told me she'd been married before – that's what brought her to England in the first place.'

'She still had her accent.'

'Yes, and people didn't like that. Prejudice, Robert, is a difficult thing to break down. I told her to go to the police, but she had no wish to.'

'Didn't you advise her to leave?'

'Leave?'

'The village.'

'Me? No. Oh, no, I wouldn't have done that.'

'No.' I didn't believe him.

'I've no idea how long these post-mortems take, do you? In the meantime, I shall arrange a funeral. It's the least I can do.'

'Yes, that'd be good. Thank you.'

'What day did Owen die on?'

'I don't know exactly. June eleventh, twelfth? He was the last to go. By then I'd lost track of the days.'

'Yes, I understand.'

No, I thought, you don't understand. No one could.

Chapter 31

After I returned home from visiting Alice in hospital, I sat for hours in a daze. I couldn't understand any of it. Why would a man, a grown man, do such a thing, to exploit a young girl, his niece, his own flesh and blood, for his own devious means? It made me ashamed to be a man. Angie sat on my lap. I felt proud of Alice for standing up to him, for refusing to offer him absolution. And what of the accident? The thought she may have done it on purpose chilled me. She was my future wife and there'd never been a sign that she was anything but a happy, carefree woman, enjoying life and all it had to offer. Did it change the way I felt about her? She'd been with so many men. It didn't matter. I visualised her in my mind, remembered her laugh, the feel of her hand in mine, and I knew, if anything, I loved her more intensely than before.

I'd wanted to go visit Alice again but she'd said she needed to be alone; to come to terms with what had happened. I had to swallow my disappointment but I understood.

On Tuesday, I received a phone call at work. It was Mr Redman, Alice's father. She was back, he told me, she was home. Still rather gaga, he said, but if I wanted to visit, say Thursday, that'd be fine.

And so, on Thursday, I went. The Redmans certainly lived in a fine Victorian house in the middle of nowhere. At the front of the house, in the middle of the drive, stood a dried-out fountain. Mr Redman welcomed me in. We stood in the hallway with its black and white diamond floor and its heavy wooden doors. Mrs Redman, he said, was out but he could just about rustle up a cup of coffee if I wanted. 'I'm not normally allowed in the kitchen,' he said with a wink. 'Sugar?'

'Just the one. Thank you.' I couldn't help but look at him and think of his twin brother. 'How's your brother?' I asked. 'Alice told me–'

'I'll let her tell you. You'll find her at the back of the garden.'

The garden had a throwaway look about it, everything was overgrown and disorganised; I knew somehow it wasn't for the lack of care but instead it had been cultivated as such – allowing nature to assert itself with minimal interference. Following Mr Redman's instructions, I found Alice at the far end sitting on a bench wearing a yellow summery dress and a pair of sunglasses, reading beneath the shadow of a weeping willow.

'What are you reading?'

'Oh, Robert, you made me jump.'

She made to get up. I noticed her walking stick leaning against the bench. 'No, don't stand.' I leant down and kissed her cheek.

'Sherlock Holmes,' she said, removing her sunglasses.

'I'm sorry?' I sat next to her.

'The book – *Hound of the Baskervilles*. You know, our local master of the hounds names every one of his dogs with a name beginning with an R. Can you imagine?'

'I don't think I could think of that many names beginning with R.'

'Exactly. Funny to think he might have a dog called Robert.'

'How are you?'

'He's dead.'

'Uncle Vic?'

'Yes, he's dead. He died earlier this week.'

'Good.'

'Yes. Yes, it is.'

We sat quietly listening to the silence of the garden – the bees, the rustle of the wind in the leaves of the willow tree, the singing of a sparrow. 'Funeral's tomorrow,' she said after a while. 'I'm feeling a lot better but...' She lowered her voice. 'I'm pretending not to be so I have an excuse not to go. Not that I mind seeing his coffin being lowered into his grave – in fact, I'd be happy to see that; no, it's all the reminiscing afterwards. What a fine chap he was; oh, how we shall miss him, what a shame he never had any children. All that claptrap. It's bad enough here at mealtimes – Dad can't stop waxing lyrical about him, conveniently forgetting that most of the time they hardly got on. Uncle Vic was right – death wipes the slate clean. But not as far as I'm concerned. I hate him; I shall never stop hating him. I was doing all right – I invented my new persona, became the cheeriest girl one could meet, the one with the sharp tongue and the high heels but that was all it was – an invented persona, a disguise. Last week, seeing him again, made me realise that. Do you know, there's not been a single night when I haven't gone to sleep without that man on my mind. He may be dead but he'll continue to haunt me for the rest of my life, I know that now.'

'Perhaps…' I wasn't sure whether I could say this, whether it might sound glib. 'Perhaps, when we're together, living as man and wife…'

'Robert…' She took my hand. 'This is the hardest bit at all… I love you, I really do, but I can't marry you.'

Something hit my heart. I tried to breathe, tried to catch my breath. 'What… what do you mean?'

'I can't marry you.' Tears sprung to her eyes. 'I'm so, so sorry, but I can't; not now, not after all this.'

'But… I don't understand–'

'I don't expect you to.'

'I'll look after you, I'll help you get better, however long it–'

'No.' She wiped her eyes. 'No, I can't do it to you. You're a good man, Robert, a kind, decent human being. You deserve better. You deserve a lovely, uncomplicated wife who'll love you very much.'

'But I love you, Alice; it's you I love. I don't–'

'Please, Robert, no. I just… Believe me, I love you too but I can't love you, not properly, not when my heart is so full of hate. It's self-pitying, I know, but I can't help it.'

I put my hand to my chest, felt my heart pounding. 'You're letting him beat you,' I said, my voice coming from somewhere faraway.

'I know that. But if we marry, he'll beat you too, one day. He'll destroy us and I can't let that happen – not to you. I'm not sure you'd be strong enough to cope.'

'Alice, please…'

251

'I've decided I want to leave.'

'Leave?'

'Devon.'

'You want to… but where? Where would you go?'

'London. I have an aunt in Charlton, my mother's sister, and a couple of friends, so I won't be alone. I need to start afresh, Robert; I need to put everything behind me.'

'Including me?'

I became aware of a shadow looming. Looking up, I saw Mr Redman with a cup and saucer in his hand. 'Sorry it took me so long. I warned you I wasn't any good in the kitchen.' He glanced at his daughter. 'Oh dear, I'm interrupting something, aren't I? Are you all right, my girl?'

'Fine. Robert's been a tonic, but he's leaving now.' She shoved her Sherlock Holmes further to one side, accidently pushing the sunglasses off the bench.

'Oh. So soon?' He looked at both of us, puzzled. 'Won't you at least have your coffee before you go?'

I stood up and felt the earth tremble beneath my feet. 'No, I won't. Thank you all the same. I'm sorry to have put you to the effort.'

'No, not at all. Not at all.'

'I'd… Yes, well, I'd better be off, I suppose.'

'If you say so.'

I picked up the sunglasses and handed them back to her. She took them. 'Thank you, Mr Redman. Alice, I'll… I'll say goodbye then.'

She shook her head, her eyes clenched shut, her fingers toying with the sunglasses, unable to speak.

I wanted to reach down and kiss her, to put my arms round her, to hold her. But I knew if I did, I'd never let go.

Chapter 32

The day after finding Joanna, with the sun out, I finally did make a start on sanding the fence. I needed a distraction. Various people passed and wished me good day and commented on the weather. The work, though tiresome, was therapeutic. Angie, flaked out, was lying in the shade on her side, occasionally lifting her head to half-heartedly bark at people. I realised I didn't know how long Joanna had hidden away – she never said. It could have been weeks; it could have been months. Yet, when I replayed our conversations in my mind, she'd shown no bitterness at those who had treated her so foully. I knew if I hadn't had found her, she'd still be alive. And yet, she had to know what had happened to Owen. What thoughts must have passed through her head during that last night? Had she died with her faith intact – had she hoped that in death she might be reunited with him? Lost in my thoughts, I hadn't noticed Pete Parker's approach until he spoke.

'You say you found her in Morgan's barn? Sorry, mate, did I make you jump?'

I was on my knees, tackling the fence. Angie, too tired to bark any more, merely growled, stretched and dozed off again. Straightening myself up, I asked who was Morgan.

'The old bloke who owns those fields – and that barn. June told me him and his wife left a few months back. Went to stay with their son's wife up in Barnstable. Their son was killed, you see. They haven't been back since.'

'I didn't know.'

'No, don't suppose you did. So what was she doing there? I heard she got chased out of town.'

I had to hold my hand up to shield my eyes. 'Yes. But why? Do you know?'

'You asking me? I wasn't here, was I? I don't know.'

'Was it because people turned against her? She was German.'

'You tell me.'

We considered each other for a few seconds.

'My mates in the army, they used to say the only good German is a dead German.'

'Is that what you think?'

He shrugged his shoulders. 'Perhaps. What of it? You're telling me that you didn't think that, out on the seas, watching out for those U-boats?'

'This was different.'

'Not to everyone, it isn't.'

'She wasn't a Nazi.'

'I guess not all of them on those subs were either.'

'She lived here, she was one of us.'

'I know that. She was alright with me. Decent bloke as well was Owen.'

He considered my handiwork for a while. 'I still haven't caught up with that Dan. Maybe he's hiding out at that barn too. Didn't see him, did you?'

'I'd better get on.'

'And how's your mate Greggers? If you see him, tell him he owes me two quid. That sandpaper you're using – it's too fine, you oughta be using something coarser.'

'It seems to be doing the job.'

'Suit yourself.' He turned to leave. This time, belatedly, Angie got to her feet and barked at him. 'I guess there'll be a funeral and all that.'

'Yes.'

He looked around him. Lowering his voice, he asked, 'Are you going to the funeral?'

'Of course.'

'You're going to the funeral of a German.' He spat. 'You disgust me.'

*

Ten days later, a firm of undertakers brought Joanna's body back to the village, depositing the coffin with the church. The funeral took place on a bright Monday morning. In attendance, along with Reverend Pritchard, were just myself, an undertaker, Gregory and Mr Jenkins. We wore black, of course. During those ten days, the vicar had ordered a headstone, which had already arrived and been put in place.

With no one to help, the four of us carried the coffin outside to the plot assigned by the vicar, a plot near the outer wall of the graveyard. We admired the new headstone. Reverend Pritchard had opted for the simplest of inscriptions on a basic stone slab. No angels or cherubs here, I thought, as with so many of the older gravestones nearer the church itself. What I hadn't expected though, was that he'd added Owen's details, taking my guess of June twelfth as the day he died on. Beneath their names and the dates, were the words *By their love, reunited in Heaven.* Most apt, I thought. I didn't point out that he'd spelt Joanna the English way, without the 'h' in the middle.

The service was brief. I cast my mind back to the even briefer service we had for John Clair. Nine men died on that boat; John, being the first, was the only one afforded a service.

Afterwards, I thanked the vicar.

'You know, the police came to see me,' he said.

'They spoke to everyone, didn't they?'

'Yes, I believe they did. No one admitted to seeing the mob she told you about.'

'N-no surprise there,' said Gregory. 'I w-wonder w-who c-could have urged them on.'

'No, he wasn't here at the time,' I replied.

'Yeah, b-but those boys who h-hang out with him, it'd be them.'

'Possibly, but they would have done it under their own steam. It had nothing to do with Parker.'

'Well, whoever it was,' said the vicar, 'I hope they truly repent.'

'Bit late for that now.'

'Yes, I suppose it is. Well, gentlemen, if you'll excuse me…' Together with the undertaker, Reverend Pritchard returned to the church. Passing them, coming towards us, were William and his mother.

'We weren't going to come,' said Rita. 'But William wanted to. He'd…' The boy circled round the grave, peering in, his face creased with concern. We watched him as he wandered off deeper into the graveyard, stopping occasionally to read an inscription.

Rita sighed. 'It was important to him; he had to come see for himself. I had no idea, you know. I kept wondering why food was missing from the larder. I'd think "tonight, we'll have leftover chicken… oh, it's gone." It never occurred to me that William was taking it until the shopkeeper came to see me. William had been stealing things from the shop. I was furious with him. I had to pay it back. But he wouldn't tell me, however much I threatened him. He only told me the day she… well, you know. He came back and went straight to his bed. He was so upset. He's hardly eaten since. He's always been very quiet, has William, he's always kept things to himself. A bit of a loner. Like his father. He can't understand why she's dead. Robert, will you speak to him? Tell him what she was like.'

'I've tried speaking to him before.'

'He'll listen to you now. Now that he knows that you were also her friend.'

'I'll try my best.'

William had stopped to look at a headstone, bending down and running his finger over the letters. I left Rita and Gregory standing over Joanna's grave. 'Hello, William,' I said, approaching him. He looked up at me. 'You know, Joanna was a good woman. But not everyone realised that. She was German so, I suppose, people thought that made her bad. But it wasn't true – we both know that.' He rose to his feet. He'd been examining a grave to a woman, a councillor's wife, who'd died in eighteen-something. 'She was frightened of those people, but she liked you, William. She told me what a good boy you were and how kind you were to her. She was married to a friend of mine, a very good friend. But he died – in the war – like your father. He loved her very much. She didn't know he'd died; I had to tell her. But just because she… she wanted to be with him in heaven, it doesn't mean your mother would do that. You know that, don't you?' He nodded. 'Your mother wouldn't leave you. She loves you too much to leave you.'

He looked at me inquisitively. 'Do you think there is a heaven?' He spoke in a surprisingly deep voice for an eight-year-old, slowly, as if he thought about each word before saying it.

'Yes, I do. Look at all these graves round here,' I said, waving my hand. 'Each one a person. I believe that each and every one of them is in Heaven, alongside Joanna and her husband. Alongside your dad.'

'Yes, that's what I thought.'

He smiled briefly before making his way back to his mother, his hands in his pocket.

Chapter 33

'Don't you smoke any more, Robert?'

Uncle Guy and I met in a small café in Argyll Street near the Barbican in Plymouth. The place with its yellow wallpaper was small, its round tables and chairs squeezed in. A large blackboard offered the menu and a poster on the wall depicting two small children declared, *Children are safer in the country. Leave them there.* Guy had come in ten minutes late, his trilby and the shoulders of his mackintosh darkened by rain.

'No,' I said. 'I lost the habit while at sea. Haven't taken it up since.'

'Very sensible.'

I ordered him a cup of tea and a slice of Victoria Sponge which he insisted on paying for.

'So, how are you?' he asked, stirring two spoonfuls of sugar into his tea, spilling a little on the oil tablecloth.

'Oh, fine, just fine.' I didn't like to tell him that I'd found my best friend's wife hanging from a beam in a dusty barn. Instead, I told him about my dog and how I was enjoying my leave, away from the sea.

'It'll be difficult for you when you go back.'

'Yes, I'm dreading it and looking forward to it at the same time. It's coming round all too soon. In some ways I feel nothing could be as bad. Surely, I won't experience anything like that again.'

'Yes. From what I hear, the Germans' ability to knock out our convoys has been greatly reduced. Tell me, Robert, was Clarence on the boat with you?'

'No, he went down with the ship.'

He shook his head. 'The poor chap. It's been hard on your parents, very hard. He was a good lad.'

'I've lost my brother, you lost yours.'

'Yes. I did. I still miss him, you know. He was a jolly lad, irritatingly so at times, but still, after almost thirty years, I miss him very much. I often wonder what he'd be doing now. Whether he'd be married, what job he'd be doing, that sort of thing. You'll think the same about Clarence for years to come. Possibly for the rest of your life.' The café door swung open bringing with it a breeze. Two young women in long camel coats and wide-brimmed hats, their arms linked, staggered in, giggling. They sat on a table behind me and, talking loudly, lit up cigarettes. 'I was on a ship that was hit once.'

'Yes, you said.'

'Hmm.' He swallowed a large chunk of cake, waving his hand in front of his mouth. 'Excuse me. Yes, 17th November 1917. Nice cake this. You sure you won't have some?'

'No, I'm fine.'

'Me and a whole load of poor buggers like me were being evacuated from France across the Channel. I'd just lost my leg and was still in some pain. We were caught by a mine not far out from Dover. The ship, the *Derby* she was called, went down like a potato. A bit like you experienced, I imagine. But then I was straight onto a lifeboat, onto another ship and home. I didn't have to endure weeks out in the middle of the ocean without a bite to eat. It must've been terrible for you.'

'It wasn't easy.'

'I bet. Did anyone survive? Apart from yourself?'

'No. Most went down with the ship.' My mind flashed to Smithy, trapped against a wall by a truck, screaming at me not to leave him, the utter fear in his eyes knowing he was down to his last moments and could do nothing to prevent it.

'Robert, you OK?'

'Hmm? Yes, sorry.'

He took a sip of tea, then stirred in another half spoonful of sugar. 'Your mother was on the *Derby*.'

'What? My *mother*?'

He laughed at my disbelief. 'Yes, she was a nurse. A very good nurse.'

'My mother? A nurse during the war? I never knew.'

'It's strange how war does that do a person. We do these incredible things, see terrible things, sometimes do the most heroic deeds, yet we never talk about it. Like you, Robert – a moment ago. You just remembered something, didn't you? I saw it in your eyes. But you can't talk about it – not even to an ex-soldier like me. And it'll always be there, I warn you now. You never forget these things, however much you want to. You can't rid your mind of the dead but, I warn you, you mustn't let them rule your life.'

'Yes, I suppose.' I finished my tea, placing the cup back down carefully on its saucer. 'My father – he's another who never talks about the war.'

'Well, no, he wouldn't. He wasn't there.'

The two giggly friends burst out laughing, drawing the attention of everyone in the café.

'Yes, he was. He told me – the Essex Regiment.'

'No, I was in the Essex, fourth battalion. Your father did his bit, mind you, but he did it behind the lines, so to speak. He was based in London, something to do with logistics and transport. Then just after the war, he was moved to Manchester. You were still a baby. Then, he moved down here. Well, that was mainly Mary's doing. Me and Josephine were already here; we came in '25, just after we were married, and your mother wanted to be near her sister. So your father worked in Plymouth for a long while, perhaps twenty years or so, then retired.'

'I... I don't understand. Logistics and transport? But he said... No, you must be wrong, he has the medals. He has them... framed.' I remembered how they had disappeared from my parents' dining room when we all had lunch in there.

'No, no. You've got confused, Robert. I've seen those medals. He just bought those, like a collector. They're behind glass, so you won't be able to see, but they'd have the recipient's name written on the rims.'

'Are you... are you sure?'

'Of course.'

My father had lied to me, to us. The women on the table behind burst out laughing again. I felt like yelling at them, telling them to shut up. All this time, he'd had lied to me.

'Robert, I ought to be going.'

'What? Yes, OK.'

'I'm tired. And when I get tired, my leg begins to hurt. It starts to throb and it's rather unpleasant. So, if you don't mind…'

'No, no, you go, Uncle Guy. It's been nice talking to you. Yes, very… nice.'

Chapter 34

'I understand, you're no longer taking piano lessons with Gregory.'

I had come to see Rebecca and was sitting in her kitchen, sipping black tea. The kitchen was large, covered with a dark red rug and sporting a hefty black stove on which sat a couple of dirty pans. At my feet, a tabby ginger cat rubbed itself against my leg, purring loudly. Propped up on the dresser were a couple of framed photos of Rebecca and a young, good-looking man with a sweep of dark hair. Drying in the corner, my umbrella lay opened. The sunny morning had turned wet.

She covered the pans with a couple of tea towels, as if hoping to make them disappear. 'I just felt as if I was getting nowhere. I'm not that good, if I'm honest.' Behind her, stacked on an ironing board, a pile of clothes waiting attention.

'I'm sure that's not true.'

She sat down on the other side of the kitchen table and started rearranging a vase of flowers. 'Do push her away if she's bothering you.'

'The cat? What's her name?'

'Tiddles.'

'Angie will smell her on me. Gregory said you were making progress.'

'It's the practising. When school starts again, I won't have the time. How's the tea? Sorry about the lack of milk.'

'It's fine. It's a shame – about the piano, I mean. Are you sure there's no other reason?'

'What? No. It's nothing against Gregory – he's a lovely man.' She plucked a couple of petals off. 'I mean, when I say he's… not in that way. He's not the sort for me. Not that…'

'Who's the man?' I asked nodding at the photos. 'If you don't mind me asking?'

She looked at them as if seeing them for the first time. 'My husband.'

As if anticipating my next question, she said, 'I'm thirty-four, Robert, and I am a widow.'

'I'm sorry to hear that.'

She shrugged.

'Why don't you give the piano another go? Just until school starts – see how you get on.'

'I don't know…' She squashed a petal leaving a smear of red on her fingertips.

'He knows where he stands.'

'What? Does he? Yes, well. I don't know. Look, I'll think about it.'

I finished my tea. 'Excellent.'

'Don't say anything yet. To Gregory, I mean.'

'My lips are sealed.'

'And what about you, Robert? Don't you get a bit

lonely in that place of–'

'No, not at all. I'd better go.'

'Oh yes, of course. Tiddles – stop being a nuisance. Get away now. Don't forget your umbrella.'

She showed me out. In her hallway, I stopped to admire a framed print of Winston Churchill. 'A fine man,' I said politely.

'Isn't he just?'

*

It was still raining. On my way home, umbrella aloft, I heard a familiar voice calling out my name. I turned to see Parker jogging to catch me up, splashing through the puddles, wearing a cap with a long peak, and a pair of dungarees.

'I've just been to the church,' he said, slightly out of breath. 'June told me. She went to see the new headstone. And I've had a look myself.'

'And?'

He narrowed his eyes. 'You'd better go see for yourself, mate. You won't like what you see, I warn you now.'

'What do you mean? Parker, what have you done?'

'Eh, eh,' he said, putting his hands up in submission. 'Don't you go jumping to no conclusions. You don't even know what I'm talking about yet.'

I turned on my heels and headed straight to the church. I followed the gravelled path round the side and to the back. The graves closest to the church dated back to centuries past, the lichen-stained stones weathered, the letters faded, the mounds covered in grass. I followed the path to the outer edges of the graveyard. Here, the headstones were of more recent times, featuring lead lettering, solid and black, a few adorned with bunches of wilting flowers. Rounding the corner, I saw Reverend Pritchard in the rain standing next to Joanna's grave, shaking his head. He looked up on hearing me approach. 'Robert, what brings you here?'

'I got word that something wasn't right.'

'You could say that. Look…'

I stood next to him, sharing my umbrella. 'Oh, my word.' Glistening in the rain, someone had painted a red swastika over Joanna's headstone.

'Horrible, isn't it?'

Poor woman, even in death she hadn't escaped the prejudices of the small-minded. 'You didn't see anyone?' I asked.

'No, no one.'

We continued staring at the desecration. The red was so deep to be almost purple. Eventually, the vicar asked, 'Who'd do something like this?'

'I don't know,' I said. 'But I've got a feeling.'

*

It wasn't difficult to find Parker. He was just leaving his house, heading the way of the pub. 'You saw it then?' he asked on seeing me.

'Why? That's what I want to know – why?'

'No, you wait there, matey. That weren't me, and you better not go round telling people it was.'

'Someone else, was it?'

'Yeah, guess it must've been. I wouldn't do that, not in my own backyard, so to speak.' He stepped towards me, purposefully making me feel uncomfortable. 'You went to her funeral. I thought I'd advised against it.' He was so close I could smell the cigarettes on his breath.

I tried to sidestep him. He blocked my way, first one way then the other. 'Oh, for pity's sake, Parker, what is this?'

'People are upset. I'm upset. She was a Nazi–'

'She was not–'

'Oh, I know what you're gonna say – but you're wrong. All Germans are Nazis. Don't you forget, they voted him in. What would your mates on the *Academic* say, eh? All those men killed. All those poor women – widows because of the Nazis.'

'She was more English than German. She was married to an Englishman, for God's sake. And he loved her very much.'

'Once a German always a German. I lost me dad in the last war. I've seen mates of mine killed by the bastards in this war.'

'That's nothing to do with her.'

'You don't know; she could have been one of those who voted for him.'

'You're despicable, Parker, you know that?'

He laughed. 'Despicable, eh? I was wrong about you, Searight – you *are* just as bad as your old man; you do go round as if you had a spoon stuck up your arse. You act all proper, but I know what you're like.'

'And what is that, Parker. What am I like?'

'You do and say the right things, but you're no better than anyone else. Take my daughter – oh, you act all proper and gentleman-like, protecting her from hooligans like Danny boy, but given half a chance.'

'You–'

'She likes you. Taken quite a shine to you.'

We heard the bell on the shop door tinkle. 'Is everything all right out here?' Hamilton had appeared, a look of concern on his face.

Parker stepped back. 'Just a chat, Hamilton, not that it's got anything to do with you.'

'Yes, well…'

'Anyways, I'd better be off.' As he sauntered off, his thumbs hooked in his dungarees, he stopped and turned, adding, 'I'm keeping my eye on you, Searight.'

Hamilton and I watched him go. 'Are you OK, Robert?'

'Me? Yes, of course.'

Hamilton shook his head. 'Wherever that man goes, trouble is sure to follow.'

'Yes.' I realised my heart was thumping. I could never admit it to Hamilton, but Parker had shaken me.

'Thank God he's off,' he said, drying his hands on his apron. 'Day after tomorrow, I believe.'

'Not soon enough.' I turned to leave, Hamilton watching me.

*

'My God, what's happened here?'

I was standing in Gregory's living room. The place had been ransacked – the drawers from his chest on the floor, their contents tipped out, the standard lamp pushed over, a mirror broken, books pulled off the bookcase and scattered all over the floor.

'I was b-broken into,' said Gregory, standing at the centre of the devastation. 'They didn't t-touch the p-piano, thank God.'

'Did they take anything?'

'Yeah, a p-pair of candlesticks – that was it.'

'Were they worth anything?'

He shrugged. 'No.'

'What about the other rooms?'

'No – they only t-touched this room for s-some reason.'

'You have to tell the police this time, Gregory.'

'I know.'

'Come on, old man, I'll give you a hand clear the place up.'

It didn't take us long – the mess was superficial. In no time, we had his living room looking as old, everything tidied-up.

'It must've h-have been P-Parker,' said Gregory. We were standing in his kitchen gazing out of the window at his chickens. 'I w-wouldn't p-put it p-past him.'

'Listen, do you have any sandpaper you could spare?' Parker's suggestion was, I had to admit, correct – I needed a coarser grain.

'Don't think so. H-have a look in the shed.'

The shed had almost nothing in it. A large dustbin full of chicken grain, a few gardening tools and that was about it. I rooted round, looking for the sandpaper but found nothing except.... except a tin of red paint. It'd been opened, the lid prised off but still full. I sighed. I visualised the swastika on Joanna's grave. Surely not, I thought, not Gregory. He wouldn't do such a thing. Yet it was definitely the same colour, the same deep shade of red. But who knows what happened here during my absence. Perhaps Gregory had been drawn in. He was above that – surely. But then, I thought of his petty jealously over Rebecca and me. I wasn't sure.

Chapter 35

The following day, I made an unannounced call on my parents. I found my mother in the kitchen, ironing her way through a pile of clothes while listening to an operetta on the radio. The place smelt of burnt onions. 'Robert, what a surprise. How lovely to see you. What's the matter?' she asked on seeing the less than congenial expression on my face.

'Where's Father?'

'Oh, let me think.' Reaching behind her, she turned down the volume on the radio. 'I like a bit of Gilbert and Sullivan every now and then. Your father, he was out this morning. He had to go and see–'

'Doesn't matter about this morning. Is he in now?'

'Y-yes. Erm, let me see, he's in the shed at the bottom of the garden, having a sort out, I believe. Do you want me to call him?'

'No.'

'Is anything wrong, Robbie? You seem a little… Has something happened?'

'Nothing's happened. I'm fine. Mum, you're burning that shirt.'

'Oh my! Oh, no, what have I done? Blast it.'

'I'll leave you to it.'

I marched into the dining room. Mother had opened the French windows – a light breeze blew the net curtains. They were there; he'd put them back up. I'd never really looked at them before – three medals from the Great War – nicknamed Pip, Squeak and Wilfred, a colourful display of medals in a gold frame, about nine inches by seven. As Guy had said, the medals were too embedded into the black cloth background to see the rims. Shaking the frame, trying to dislodge them, made no difference. 'Damn it,' I said aloud, laying the frame on the dining room table. Looking in the top drawer of the dresser, I found a carving knife and sharpener. That'll do, I thought. Taking the knife sharpener, I hesitated a moment before smashing its handle against the display glass. Holding the frame upside down, I shook the loosened glass into a wastepaper bin, and with my fingers eased out the remaining shards. Two round medals, one silver, one gold, and, on the left, a star with three points and criss-crossed with a pair of swords. On the rim of the former and on the back of the star was written the same name.

The dining room door opened. It was my father, wearing a gardening smock and wellingtons. He opened his mouth to say hello, but then, on seeing the discarded frame on the table and the medals in my hand, he blanched. Good, I thought, so you should. I held the medals up. 'Nice medals, Dad. Very nice.'

'What are you doing? What the blazes is happening here?'

'Private G. Reilly, Royal Fusiliers. Number…' I held up the star.

'What is the meaning of this?'

'Number 28741.'

'How dare you? What right…'

My mother came running. 'Lawrence, Robert. What on earth…' She put her hand to her heart. 'Robbie, what are you doing?'

'You knew, didn't you, Mum? But you were happy to go along with it. So, who is he, Father, this Private Reilly, who gave up his youth for this country and whose medals you've stolen?'

'He didn't *steal* them, Robert–'

'He might as well have, claiming them for himself. It's like that shotgun you have, pretending to have shot the pheasants that mum bought in the market. It's all fake.'

My father stumbled towards a chair at the dining room table, crunching a piece of glass underfoot, and slumped onto it, his head in his hand. Mum looked from him to me, her face etched with concern. 'Robbie, you didn't have to…'

'So, why, Father? That's what I want to know. Why are you masquerading as a soldier?'

'Leave him be, Robbie…'

'It's obvious, isn't it?' said my father, his eyes shut. 'There was Guy, there was Jack, and there was me, the one who stayed away.'

'That's not a good enough reason. This brings everything home, doesn't it? I always felt you were ashamed of me for some reason but now I'm the one who's ashamed.'

'And you have every right to be. But I wasn't ashamed

273

of you, Robert.'

My mother stood behind father's chair, resting a hand on his shoulder. 'It was my idea,' she said quietly. 'You have to blame me. Like your father says, his cousins fought but he didn't. But I've always thought that what he did was terribly important. Without men like your father, the army in Flanders would never have got the equipment they needed and at the point when they needed it. Machine guns, rifles, canons, lorries, carts, tanks, even the food and medicine, the lot.' She flattened down a piece of Father's stray hair. 'He was just as much a hero, in his own way. I bought the medals; it was me that first told someone they were Lawrence's.'

'But to tell your own sons? That I don't understand.'

'I never told you that,' said my father. 'You assumed.'

'Fair assumption, I would have thought.'

'Yes, I know. I wanted… I don't know.' He seemed deflated. 'I wanted Clarence, both of you, to be proud of me. The job I had was considered a "starred occupation" which meant I was exempt from active service, even when they introduced conscription. Your mother's right in a way, but, in the end, I was still little more than a pen pusher. Not much to reflect on, nothing much to be proud of. And now, with Clarence gone… It's made me realise. You're right, Robert, I have been unfair on you over the years. I don't know how to say sorry. Too late now, I know. The medals – yes, it was your mother's idea but I take the blame – I could have said no. But I didn't. Your uncles were brave boys, both of them. And I tried to bask in their reflected glory, trying to claim some of it as my own. Pathetic when you think of it. You're right, it's shameful.'

He sat there in his chair and I suddenly, and for the first time, saw him for what he was – a man growing old before his time, a man without friends, lost in a county that had never been his own. A man with precious few memories, a man who hadn't left any mark on the world and who knew that he wasn't going to now. I placed the medals carefully on the table. 'Clarence may be gone but I'm still here, you know, and...'

He looked up at me, his eyes dulled by a life of disappointment. 'Yes?'

'I suppose... When I think about it, I'm proud of you.'

'What? Are you? How... how can you be?'

'You and mum – you gave us a happy childhood, strict sometimes...' I tried not to laugh. 'But happy nonetheless. You taught us right from wrong. We were never in need of anything. And we had this lovely house, the garden. You don't realise these things when you're young. But by God, you try floating round in the Indian Ocean for two weeks, you soon start to appreciate things. And I'm grateful to you both for making me who I am.'

Father tilted his head as if he couldn't understand. 'Do you mean all that?'

'Of course.'

He exchanged glances with my mother. She smiled at him, her hand resting on his shoulder. His eyes filled with tears. 'Thank you, Robert. Thank you, my son.'

*

Angie was restless. She hadn't been out on a walk for a couple of days and I knew by the way she kept dropping her ball at my feet that she needed some exercise. It was late, past eleven, and I couldn't be bothered but I felt sorry for her. 'OK,' I said. 'Just a quick run around the square and back.' She tilted her head, listening. As soon as I reached for her lead, she knew. Amidst great excitement, leaping and barking, I put on my coat and headed out.

It was a mild evening, a full moon illuminating the way. I saw Pearce, the blacksmith, returning from the pub. We waved. I heard the chattering of voices, giggly with too much drink.

I was heading home, passing along the stone wall at the back of the church when I heard something – the sound of an iron gate being closed. Angie growled. Rounding the corner, I saw a figure shrouded in a cape dashing away.

'Hey,' I shouted. 'Stop.' The darkened figure picked up speed. I gave chase, Angie running alongside me, yelping. The figure turned the corner, their cape flapping behind them. I let go of Angie's lead, and willed my legs to go faster. Running at full pelt now, I was gaining ground. They glanced behind and suddenly drew to a stop. I slowed down, catching my breath. 'You were in the graveyard. Why?'

The figure turned round.

'You? I don't… I don't understand. What's the matter? It was you, wasn't it? The swastika.'

'The what?'

'Come on, Rebecca, don't play the innocent with me. What were you doing in the graveyard at this time of night? What are you hiding behind your back?'

'Nothing. I was just…'

'Is that a bottle of white spirit?'

She sighed; her shoulders slumped. 'Yes. I was trying… You wouldn't understand.'

'Try me.'

She looked up at the sky, at the moon disappearing behind a cloud. Angie returned to me. Rebecca rubbed her eyes and, to my surprise, began crying.

'Come on,' I said. 'I'll take you home.'

Removing the hood of her cape, she said, 'I'll tell you. I want to. Don't you hate the Germans for what they did to you?'

'Not really.'

'No, perhaps you don't. Respect for your enemy, and all that rubbish. I told you I was a widow. I was married to a German. We lived in Hamburg. My husband was a communist. He was arrested in thirty-four. They put him in a concentration camp. Protective custody, they called it. All my friends shunned me. I had become a pariah overnight. They released him for a while. Oh, Robert, he was a broken man; they'd crushed his spirit. The things he told me – the beatings, the cruelty. And then, a few weeks later, they came for him again. And that was it. I never saw him again; he didn't survive. They wrote to me. Shot while trying to escape, they told me. I had no one to turn to, no friends, no family, and so I came back to England. I shall never forgive them for what they did.'

'But Joanna wasn't–'

'I know, I know. I'm sorry.' Slowly, we started walking. 'I was angry. It was just, well, the other day it was the anniversary of my husband's death, and I felt so wretched, so angry. So, I got some paint–'

'From Gregory.'

She stopped. 'Oh no, he doesn't know, does he?'

'No.'

'You won't tell him, will you? Please, don't tell anyone.'

'If you promise not to do it again.'

'Of course. I borrowed the paint from him and returned it the following day. He didn't ask why I needed it.'

'You know, she was married to a good friend of mine. He was on the lifeboat with me. He didn't make it.'

'I didn't know. I'm sorry; you must hate me.'

'No. I'm not sure I hate anyone really, not even the Germans.'

'How can you fight and kill if you don't hate?'

'I'm in the merchant navy – our job is not to kill. But you're right – I think I did hate the Germans, simply because they were the enemy, for what they've done to our cities, for allowing themselves to vote for a madman. But I survived the boat. And for that I'm eternally grateful…'

'To whom? The Germans?'

'No, not the Germans. I don't know.'

'To God?'

'Certainly not God. I look around me, I look at the sky, at the moor, and I see everything differently now. I'm too full of appreciation and gratitude. I have no room within me for hate. Not any more.'

'You're a good man, Robert. And I'm a good person too.' She laughed awkwardly. 'Really, I am. As soon as I'd done it, I regretted it. The stain of red paint on my fingers, it was like the stain of blood. I felt as if I had her blood on my hands, and I felt ashamed of myself.'

'So, what were you doing just now?'

'I went to see the headstone. I wanted to see how much damage I'd done. That's why I had the white spirit – I wanted to remove it. Of course, I wouldn't do it again. I feel bad enough as it is.'

'You weren't the first.'

278

'I'm sorry?'

'Before she left, someone painted a swastika on her front door.'

'Now, that wasn't me.'

'I know. Before your time here. Come on, let's get you home before anyone sees us. I'm tired.'

Chapter 36

I stayed away from Parker's leaving do at the pub. As did Gregory, who came to see me. Together, we sat in my living room, Angie on my lap, reading the papers, idly talking. 'Didn't Parker want you to play the piano tonight?' I asked.

'He can take a running j-jump as far as I'm concerned. H-he c-came to see me yesterday. He was up-upset because I went to the f-funeral.'

'Funny that, he came to see me too.'

'The man is a b-bully. He c-called me a Nazi.'

'I don't think it was him who vandalised Joanna's headstone though.'

'Of course it was. W-who else w-would do such a thing?'

'Hmm.'

'Hey, g-guess what? Rebecca came see me today. She's going to r-resume her piano lessons.'

'Really? That's great news.'

'I know she doesn't l-like me – in t-that way. That's fine

280

though. Still, it'll be nice to s-see her every now and then.'

'Of course. And what about the police? Have you been to see them yet?'

'No.'

'Gregory – you really should. Did you find anything else missing apart from the candlesticks?'

He shook his head. We returned to our reading.

A couple of hours later, after an evening of companionable silence, Gregory declared he was going home. As he put on his coat, he asked whether I was looking forward to returning to sea. Our conversation was cut short by an urgent rap on the door.

'That doesn't sound good,' I said, my words lost beneath the sound of Angie's frenzied barking.

A second knock was soon followed by a third. 'All right,' I shouted. 'Coming.'

On opening the door, I found an agitated-looking Abigail in front of me and, lurking behind her, Dan, a large haversack swung round his shoulder. 'Can I come in?' she said, barging past me, not waiting for a reply.

'You might as well come in too, Dan.'

'Thanks.'

'H-hello, Abbie,' said Gregory. 'Oh, hello,' he added on seeing Dan.

'Are you OK?' I asked. 'Get down, Angie. Is something wrong?'

'It's dad,' she said, falling into my armchair. 'Someone told him that they saw me with Dan.'

'I thought you'd gone,' I said to Dan.

'I came back.' He crouched down to pat the dog.

'He went mad. And now he's at the pub getting drunk. When he gets back, he's going to kill me.' She produced a

281

handkerchief from her pocket.

'Surely–'

'No, you don't know him. When he's got the drink inside him…' She coughed.

'He's capable of anything,' added Dan.

'He's right there,' said Gregory.

'He said if he ever caught up with Dan…'

'But what do you want me to do?'

'Can we stay here – just for the night?'

'Stay here? I'm… I'm not sure.'

Rising to his feet, Dan said, 'Just one night, Mr Searight.'

'One?'

The two of them exchanged worried glances. 'Dan's found a place in town. We can move in tomorrow.'

'You're running away? Why? Your father goes back tomorrow?'

She blew her nose. 'It's not just that. I hate it here. I want to live in town, with Dan, get a job.' She began coughing again.

'Are you all right?' I asked her.

She waved my concerns away, her hand easing her throat.

'W-what about your mother?' asked Gregory.

'I don't want to be like my mum – wasting her life in a dead village like this.'

'No, I meant, won't s-she miss you?'

'Yeah, but she'd understand.'

'I reckon she'd come with us if she could,' said Dan. 'Anything to get away from *him*.'

'You want to stay the night? I'm really not sure if this is a good idea.'

'Please, Mr Searight,' said Abigail. 'I'm…'

'Yes?'

'I'm frightened of him. I'm frightened of what he'll do to Dan – and me.'

'Especially when he's tanked up,' added Dan.

'He n-need never know,' said Gregory, turning to me. 'OK, I suppose. One night, yes?'

'We'd be gone first light, Mr Searight.'

'You'd have to camp down here on the sofa, Dan. Abigail, you can have the spare room.'

They both thanked me, their relief pouring out of them. 'I'll make you a cup of tea, if you like, Mr Searight.'

Five minutes later, we all sat in the living room, nursing cups of tea, not sure what to say. Gregory, inviting Angie to sit on his lap, had forgotten he was about to leave. Abigail had another coughing fit. She'd been poorly, she told me. I asked her about their new place. They both described it, talking animatedly about their future, their plans. Dan, she told me, had already got a job – working in construction. Demand was high, he said, 'what with all the bombings.'

We were still talking about life in Plymouth, when we heard loud shouts from outside.

'Oh my God, it's Dad. Listen.'

Sure enough, I could hear him now, calling out Abigail's name. Peering through the side of the curtain, I could see him outside the house, staggering, waving a bottle in the air. 'Oh, Lord, he's heading this way.'

Abigail rose to her feet, her face streaked with fright. 'Don't let him in, please.'

'Don't worry – I'll get rid of him.'

Dan took his place next to Abigail, taking her hand.

283

'Oi, Searight, you in?' shouted Parker outside. He pummelled my front door. Angie barked. I had no choice but to see him and try get rid of him as quickly as possible.

'Ha, you are in. Thought as much. Seen Abbie?'

'You're drunk.' Angie yelped behind me.

He shrugged his shoulders. 'And can you blame me? Tomorrow I go back to war. You know what it's like. While idiots like Dan the Man and G-G-Greggers sit pretty on their fat arses away from it all, I'll be donning my uniform taking orders from some toff who doesn't know his arse from his elbow and getting my head blown off. So, yeah, I've had a drink or two; there's no law against it.'

'But perhaps you should–'

'I asked you a question. Have you seen Abbie?'

'No, I'm afraid not.'

'I'm afraid not. God, you sound like your old man.'

'Be that–'

'She didn't come to the pub tonight. You'd have thought she'd want to see her old man off in style, wouldn't you? But no, she's got other things on her mind. I thought she might come round see you. I know she's got a soft spot for you,' he said adapting a sing-song voice.

'What can I do?'

He stood there, his eyes narrowing. I could feel his hatred emanating from every pore. He shook his head, as if trying to free himself from such thoughts. 'Well, listen, if you see her…'

'I'll tell her to go home.'

'Yeah. Right.'

He heard it. Immediately, he stood erect. 'That's her. That's her cough; she's had it all week.'

'No.'

He grabbed me by my collar, pushing me back against the doorframe. 'What's she doing here? That's what I want to know,' he growled in my ear.

I followed him through to the living room, Angie dancing round us.

Everyone was on their feet. We stood in silence for a few moments – Parker, his daughter, Dan, Gregory and myself in a large circle, Parker his eyes darting from one to the other. I realised then just how intimidated we all were by this man. Abigail shrank a little behind Dan.

'What the hell's going on?' said Parker. 'Quite the chimps' tea party, eh? Alright, Greggers? Not fixed your glasses yet?' He stepped up to Dan, who towered above him. Looking up into his eyes, he said, 'So, caught you at last; the bastard who tried to rape my daughter.'

'Dad, it wasn't like that–'

'Shut up; I'm not talking to you,' he said without taking his eyes off Dan. 'I'll deal with you later, you little slut.'

'S-s-steady on, P-Parker.'

'Stay out of it, you freak. You still owe me two quid.'

'The candlesticks weren't worth much then, eh?'

He glared at me and I knew I'd hit the target. 'Piss off, Searight. So Dan, Dan, the rapist man, you're not good enough for the army but you think you're good enough for my daughter.'

'We love each other, Mr Parker,' said Dan quickly. 'We want–'

'"We love each other, Mr Parker,"' he said in a high-pitched sing-along voice. 'I don't give a shit what you want. Now listen here, you sod, I'm going tomorrow. If I hear you've even so much as looked at her, I'll kill you, you get me?'

'Mr Parker—'

The crack of bone against bone shocked me. Abigail screamed, Angie barked. Dan fell in a heap, yelling in pain, clutching his nose.

'That's enough, Parker,' I cried. Looking down at Dan, I saw the blood seeping through his fingers. Parker had head-butted him hard.

Gregory and Abigail went to Dan. Gently, Gregory pulled his hand back while Abigail, now crying, put an arm round Dan's shoulders. Dan groaned, his eyes circling. Standing up, Gregory tried to speak: 'You've b-broken h-his his…'

'Nose?' finished Parker. 'Is that the w-w-word you're looking f-f-for?'

'Get out,' I shouted, pointing, unnecessarily, at the door. 'Get out now.'

'I'm leaving all right, don't you worry. Abbie, come.' He put his hand out for her.

'No,' she said between sobs, holding Dan, stroking his hair.

'What did you say, young miss?'

'S-she s-s-said no.'

He spun to face Gregory, spitting out his words. 'One more word from you, you wimp, you'll get what he got.' I could see Gregory wilt with fright. He then seemed to find a strength, glared at Parker, and marched out of the house.

'Gregory?' I called after him as I heard the front door

slam. Angie kept up her constant barking.

'Two gone, one to go, eh, Searight?'

'Proud of yourself, are you, Parker? A good example to set your daughter?'

'I don't have to justify myself to the likes of you. Can't you shut that bloody dog up? Abbie – now!' he shouted.

'Look what you've done to his nose. We need to get a doctor.' Propping Dan up against her, she'd given him a handkerchief now coloured stark red as he tried to stem the flow of blood.

She was right, we needed to call the doctor from the neighbouring village, but I couldn't leave, not while Parker remained.

'He'll live,' said Parker. 'Now, I've said it twice…' He strode towards her, grabbing her arm.

'I'm not leaving him,' she screamed as she tried to wrestle her arm free of her father's grip.

'He got what he deserved. Now, get up. Get up.'

Dan, his eyes clenched shut, groaned.

'Get off me, let me go!'

Conscious of my fear, I tried to intervene. 'Let her go, Parker. You heard her.'

'Come on, Abbie, you're my daughter. Leave him, you can do better than that.'

Still draped with Dan's head now on her lap, she looked up at him, and quietly said, 'I hate you.'

Her words caused Parker to step back. 'Abbie, no, you don't mean that. I'm your father, for Christ's sake, your dad. I… I love you, you know that.'

'You have a funny way of showing it then, don't you?' she screamed. 'Shouting, cursing, hitting. It's all you do.'

Clasping his temples, Parker began mumbling. 'For Christ's sake…' He stomped round the room, kicking out at Angie who darted beneath the table. 'Maybe you're right. It's the war, Abbie, it's messed me up. I've seen things, horrible things. It's affected my brain; I know that. It's not my fault.'

'So you take it out on us? Me and mum, we were OK while you were away. You come back and it's been hell. I can't wait for you to leave.'

He stared at her, open-mouthed, absorbing her words.

'Parker,' I said quietly. 'Go home now. It's time you left.'

Ignoring me, he stepped up to her. I knew what was coming from the look of utter loathing in his eyes. I reached out my arm to try and stop him but like a drunken man I was too slow. Raising his right arm, he brought his hand down, slapping her hard against the side of the face. Her head jerked back. 'You bitch!' he screamed. 'You bitch, you fucking slut.'

He raised his arm again but this time I gripped it. 'That's enough, Parker.' From the corner of my eye, I saw Dan trying but failing to get to his feet, while Abigail, holding her face, sobbed.

I didn't see it coming. With his free arm, Parker punched me in the stomach. Doubling over, he punched me again, catching me on the cheek. I fell to my knees, preparing myself for another blow but from behind me, I heard the living room door fly open.

'P-Parker!'

Parker laughed raucously.

I turned to see Gregory, standing at the door, his legs

astride, pointing his father's hunting gun at Parker while Angie yapped at him, her tail wagging.

'Gregory, nooo!'

Too late. He pulled the trigger. I clenched shut my eyes as the sound of a primeval, ear-piercing scream filled my ears.

Chapter 37

I had failed him. I had failed Gregory as much as I had failed Owen and Joanna. For days at an end, I lay in my bed until late. I didn't leave the house. I answered the door just once, didn't eat, didn't wash or shave. Angie suffered with me, cooped up indoors for hours at an end. Their faces kept coming into view – Gregory's, Owen's, Joanna's… and Alice's. They were all gone. I had lost them all. I kept reliving the days at sea, on that boat. I had hoped to rebuild my life – instead I felt more at sea than ever.

The one time I answered the door was when I heard the voice of a policeman shouting through the letterbox. Two of them came in, I recognised them both from their visit following Joanna's death. Angie almost had a fit on seeing these men in black and in the end I had to lock her in the kitchen.

'Makes a good guard dog, don't he?' said the tall one.
'She.'
'Makes a good guard dog, don't she?' he repeated

with exactly the same intonation.

Having sat down and removed their helmets, they made me replay the events of Parker's shooting minute by minute. Parker apparently was well. Gregory must have fired with the intention of missing otherwise, said the first policeman, 'from that distance, Parker was as good as dead.' He was in shock for a while, they said, but was now back at home.

'Are you charging him?'

'Greggers? Of course. What else would you have us do, sir?'

'It's Gregory, not Greggers.'

'Begging your pardon, sir. Intent to cause bodily harm. He's fully admitting it, so you won't have to appear in court but he'll be sent down for it, that's for sure.'

'Sent down? But he'd been goaded by Parker for… for years.'

'Had it coming to him, did he then, sir?'

'Well… no. But… How long will he get?'

'Depends whether the judge is feeling in a good mood or not. Eighteen months probably.'

'Eighteen months?'

'Out within the year if he keeps his nose clean, and he don't look the type to be wanting to cause the prison authorities any problems.'

'That's still too much. He's not a strong man; prison could destroy him.'

'He should have thought of that before he went round shooting at people. Now, if we could have a bit more detail about the night in question…'

Twenty minutes later they finally seemed satisfied

with what they had, thanked me, and left. I slumped on the settee, exhausted, Angie on my lap.

A year in prison. I dreaded what it might do to him. I should have protected him more; I should have stood up to Parker. But I couldn't have – I was still too weak both mentally and physically. Perhaps, I shouldn't have encouraged Rebecca so much – but I wasn't aware that I had until it was too late.

Then, if I wasn't thinking about Gregory, I was thinking about Owen. I knew I could have kept him alive, I knew that; I could have allowed him to use Beckett's body as sustenance. Beckett, the despicable man, would not have cared a jot. I would regret it for the rest of my life. I could have brought Owen home to be reunited with his wife. Instead, both were dead, and the more I turned events around in my mind, the more certain I was that it was my fault. He needed my permission; he needed me to be party to the act. I had denied him and he, not I, had paid for my morality. I knew now that my obsession over the ring was merely a means of apologising to Owen, of trying to make good the bad I had done. I had killed him with my squeamish objections as surely as if I had hit him with a rowlock.

I remembered how the debriefing panel looked at me – Major Bryant and the doctor at his side. How did this man survive when all the others had succumbed? I couldn't tell them; how could I when I'd shut it off in the darkest corner of my mind?

Oh, Alice – if only you were here now. You'd understand. But she wasn't here. She was as lost to me as Owen.

There was only one person who could help me now.

Finally, after about three days locked away, I washed and dressed. Life outside had not changed – I had expected everything to be different. It'd been raining, the road was wet, but the sun had come out. The world smelt fresh. I saw Fraser but, not wanting to talk, managed to avoid him. I made my way to the church. I saw Abigail and Dan at a distance, holding hands. They hadn't made it to Plymouth yet.

Before going inside, I circled round the church into the graveyard. Joanna's headstone had been cleaned; not a single trace remained of the hateful sign. I was pleased. 'I'm sorry,' I said.

I found Reverend Pritchard inside the church, still wearing his cassock, rearranging some flowers at the end of a pew.

'Oh, Robert, you caught me.'

'Caught you doing what?'

'I'm just redoing the flowers. Mrs Hamilton does them, but she and I have… let's call it a difference of opinion on how they should look.'

'Can I talk to you, Reverend?'

He caught my tone. 'Yes, of course; anytime, Robert.'

'I meant now.'

He glanced at his watch and I could tell he felt embarrassed at having done so. 'Why, of course. Now would be as good time as any. There's no one here, shall we sit in the pews?'

We sat in the pew nearest the front. It meant I could talk to him without having to see his eyes. Instead I focussed on the altar and the unlit candles upon the table catching the rays of sun piercing the stained glass window above it.

'Something's troubling you, I know,' said the vicar. 'I can see it in your eyes. And I've seen it before.'

'Yes.'

'You know anything you tell me will be in the strictest confidence.'

'I know. Thank you.'

'So go on, how can I help?'

'It's not easy for me to talk about this. It's… it's about my time on the boat…'

'That much I guessed.'

'I'll have to start at the beginning… otherwise you won't understand the strain I was under, we were all under. There were ten of us…' And so I began. I could feel the salt on my skin, could smell it in the air. I could feel the sun burning my back, the lack of moisture in my mouth. I could see all around us the sea, the unforgiving sea. I could see their faces, all of them changing day by day as hunger and thirst took its toll – Palmer, Davison, Hodgkin, the rest of them. The strange thing is I rather missed them all now. I wondered whether Beckett's wife was still seeing her butcher. I thought of Palmer and all the kids he and his wife were planning on having. I thought of John Clair's mother, grieving for her young boy dead at just nineteen. So many lives. What a waste, such a terrible waste. I remembered the storm and the utter feeling of vulnerability, being at the mercy of the sea as it tossed us around like a cork. And I knew as I told Reverend Pritchard my story I would never finish it. It was too much. I'd tried too soon; I hadn't left enough time to come to terms with what happened on that boat. Christ looked down at me, an orange glow round his head, the nails riven into his palms; Mary to his left, St

Paul to his right, their hands clasped in prayer kneeling prostate before his figure on the cross. *Behold the Lamb of God who takes away the sin of the world.*

I felt a hand on my wrist. 'Slow down, Robert.'

I realised I was crying. 'I can't… I can't do it.'

He turned to look at me. 'Can't do what, Robert?'

'I'm sorry; I've wasted your time. Nothing can take away the sins I have committed. I can't tell you.'

A streak of disappointment flashed across his face. He tried to hide it but it was too late – I'd seen it. I knew then that this had been a mistake; for I saw next to me not a man who could absolve my sins but just an ordinary, plain man, a man as fragile, as impotent and as weak as myself.

'I have to go.'

He made to reach for me. 'No, don't, Robert, whatever is troubling you, you can tell me.'

'I can't. I'm sorry.'

I stumbled back down the aisle, holding onto the side of the pews as I headed towards the main doors, feeling dizzy, feeling relief that I had avoided telling a man who could do nothing for me, feeling the mournful eyes of Christ on my back.

*

I'd been dreading reporting back to duty but now it was almost upon me, I was rather looking forward to it. I needed to get away from the village; I felt suffocated here. I felt conscious of my every move, especially since the incident. I knew I'd been judged guilty by association. I may have been a victim of the war and of the sea, but first, through Abigail and now through her father, I was again viewed with barely-concealed hostility. I wanted to be somewhere where I could blend in and go by unnoticed, away from unspoken prejudices and unfounded accusations.

The following day, I went to visit Gregory at his home. He was on bail with strict instructions not to leave the village. Both he and Parker, he told me, were to have no interaction whatsoever. 'Suits me fine,' he said. The courts had yet to set a date for his appearance. Considering he was fully expecting a custodial sentence, he seemed in fine fettle. His shooting of Parker had purged him of some of his insecurities. Rebecca, he told me, had just been and gone. 'Her piano playing is still fairly atrocious,' he said, 'but I'm not going to disillusion her. Hey, R-Robert, if… I mean when I g-go to prison, you will c-c-come visit me, won't you? They're b-bound to send me to Princetown. It's not too f-far.'

'Of course, old man. You try keeping me away.'

He smiled.

I left with a deep well of affection for him.

*

Later that afternoon, there was another knock on the door. Thinking it might be the policemen returning, I thought it best to answer it. It wasn't the police – it was Mr Redman, Alice's father, standing there. Now this, as they would say, was a turn up for the books. He looked sprightly, wearing a linen jacket and a pink shirt. I showed him through to the living room and offered him a cup of tea, which he politely declined. He made friends with Angie and asked how I was. I'd been better, I told him.

'I'm afraid I've come to discharge a rather unpleasant

duty,' he said.

'I don't like the sound of this.'

'No, well, you won't,' he said fishing inside his jacket. 'I've come to return you this.'

He held it out for me in the palm of his hand. I recognised it immediately – it was the box with my engagement ring to Alice. I sighed.

'I told you you wouldn't like it. Here, take it.'

I flicked open the box and gazed at the gold ring with its ruby on a nest of silver leaves. It seemed no time ago I was buying it. 'She doesn't have to return it.'

'I know but I think she felt it was the right and proper thing to do. My condolences, Robert; I would've liked having you as my son-in-law. I don't think my daughter's covered herself in glory over this. It beats me why she broke it off. She's not told me. Even if she had, I'd probably still be no nearer to understanding. She's a woman, after all, isn't she?' he said loudly to Angie, patting her rigorously on the back. Angie gazed up at him, her head tilted to one side. 'You're a girl, aren't you? Life's much simpler with dogs, eh? My wife reckons it was something to do with that accident she had but I'm not so convinced. She was very upset when her uncle died, my brother, but I wouldn't have thought that'd be grounds for breaking off her engagement to a thoroughly decent egg like yourself.'

'Thank you, Mr Redman. She didn't want to come herself?'

He grimaced. 'No, afraid not.'

'Are you sure you won't have that cup of tea?'

'No, much as I would like to.' He glanced at his watch. 'In fact, I ought to be getting back. I need to keep Alice on an even keel.'

'Even keel?'

'Ah, yes. I knew there was something else. She's spending the day packing and she's got into a right old flap about it. She's leaving us, Robert.'

The words hit me in the stomach. 'Leaving? Where?'

He sighed. 'London.'

'London?'

'She's got some friends there. You can imagine what me and the wife think of it. If Herr Hitler starts bombing us again, we all know what will be his first port of call. I think she's mad and I've told her so. But I'm the last person in the world she listens to. Honestly, if the milkman told her she was mad, she'd listen to him. But not me. No.'

'London.' It wasn't so far but she might as well have said Shanghai. I knew that was truly it – that I would never see her again.

'You all right, Robert? It's a bit of a shock, I know.'

'She did tell me once she had a couple of friends there who were trying to persuade her to join them.'

'Ah, there you are then. You know more than I do. But nothing unusual in that, is there, girl?' he said again addressing Angie.

'When does she go?'

'Tomorrow. I'm taking her to the station in Plymouth. She's catching the 2:22 to Paddington. Oh dear, I fear I've thoroughly depressed you now, as I knew I would. It's not easy being the bearer of bad news. I'd better get back.'

'Thank you anyway, Mr Redman.'

I escorted him to the front door, Angie running between our feet. He paused. 'I suppose you'll be back at sea soon.'

'Yes, another week.'

'I wish you luck.' He shook my hand firmly. 'I shall miss her, you know. I shall miss her very much.'

'Yes,' I said. 'Me too.'

'Yes, I know. I'm sorry it turned out this way.'

I watched him get in his car, his hand shielding his eyes from the sun. The village seemed quiet for once, no one about, not even the children, as if everyone was having a post-lunch nap. Donning a pair of sunglasses, Alice's father revved up his engine, waved cheerily and drove off.

Chapter 38

I had a hideous night. The thought that Alice was leaving, going to London, to start a new life without me, I found hard to bear. I couldn't believe she could forget me so easily. I'd placed the ring in the back of my bedroom drawer, deciding that was where it should remain forever more.

Unable to sleep, I took Angie for a walk even though it was the middle of the night. The moon was as bright as it could be, throwing its eerie light over the village, not a cloud in sight, long shadows at every turn. Walking through to the far side of the village, I could see the moors looming ahead. Incapable of resisting, it drew me in like a magnet. I soon found myself at the moor gate, the beacon in front of me silhouetted against the moonlit sky. Angie darted round, perfectly visible with her white coat. A group of sheep and lambs kept their eyes on us. The night was warm, cooled slightly by a gentle breeze; the smell of bracken and damp grass filled the air. From somewhere I heard the crying of a vixen. I stopped to say hello to the piebald horse, who trotted over to the gate expectantly. I apologised for not having brought any sugar with me. And then I headed up towards the top of the beacon. I think perhaps I thought I was in a dream, labouring up and up the hill. I didn't stop to ask myself what I was doing. A couple of times I slipped on the dew, but still I climbed on, determined to get to the top.

Finally, out of breath, I reached the summit. I gazed upon the landscape below me, the village nestled amongst the trees, the church spire visible. I saw the viaduct, and the neighbouring hamlets and villages beyond. I looked up at the moon. Was it really the same moon I spent so long gazing at from the boat?

I sat down on the grass, crossing my legs. *'I want to be as far away from here as possible. I want to be up there – on the moon.'* Those were among the last words he said before slipping into a sleep from which he never woke. If I had allowed him to nourish himself on Beckett's flesh, he would be here now – asleep in his little house, lying next to his wife, a cat at their feet.

I called for Angie. Obediently, she came and made herself comfortable in my lap. Would he have lived with the remorse? No, a man does what he has to do to stay alive. Would he have replayed it in his mind every moment? Probably. Would he regret that his existence had depended on the flesh of a comrade? No. 'After all,' I said aloud to the dog, 'I did it. I did, Angie, I did.' She looked up at me. I could see the whites of her eyes. I stroked her. 'I stopped Owen but I didn't stop myself.'

I remember I stared at him for hours, his body laid out on the bottom of the boat, the bilge water lapping round him. I remember struggling to my feet and finding a tin lid.

Every movement hurt like hell. But I had a purpose now. Oh, Angie, you're a good dog. May God forgive me. It wasn't easy. Morally, it wasn't easy – that is obvious, but physically it wasn't easy either; I was so, so weak. With shaking hands, I sliced a small piece of his flesh from his thigh. I gagged as I placed this minute sliver of a man's flesh against my lips. I prayed. Muttering, trying to hold back my tears, I said the words, 'Take, eat; this is my body, which is given for you. Do this in remembrance of me.' Taking a mouthful of water from the little that remained, I gulped the flesh down. The act of swallowing caused such pain, my gullet had seized up. I could feel the insides of my stomach rebelling. Fearing I would be sick, it took me a while before I could take a second piece. How much more I ate I cannot remember. All I know was that those little morsels of nourishment kept me alive for a few hours longer; long enough for that plane to appear.

Major Bryant knew. He could see it in my eyes. He knew all right.

This was the first time I had allowed myself to remember. I retched. Pushing the dog away, I turned onto my side and vomited. I puked until there was no more to give. I stumbled up onto my knees but then, exhausted, I fell onto my front onto the wet moorland grass and sobbed.

'Owen, if you can hear me, please forgive me. I failed you. I'm sorry. May God forgive me. May you, my friend, forgive me.'

*

I awoke with a start. I thought I could hear the creaking of the boat. I shuddered at the memory. I looked at the clock

– it was almost one in the afternoon. Pulling back the curtain to a bright, sunny day, I saw old Fraser pushing a wheelbarrow up the road. So that was the creaking sound. I almost laughed. Angie stretched and wagged her tail. I realised I felt lighthearted. I opened the drawer of my bedside table and pulled out the metal figurine of Christ on the cross. I remembered I'd hidden it away my first day back in the village. I hadn't wanted to see it every day. Now, I felt different. One could still see the shadow of the cross on the wallpaper. I returned it to its former place on the wall, hitching the little hook onto the nail. The house felt different somehow – airier, lighter. I felt different too. I placed my hand against my heart. Something within me had changed. A pigeon landed on the windowsill, its wing beating against the glass. Angie leapt at it, and the pigeon flew away. 'It's gone, you silly dog.'

I reached for my dressing gown hanging from a bedpost. I froze. In that moment, reaching for my dressing gown, I realised why I felt different. Since coming back to the village I had, without knowing it, a pain inside of me, like a hand gripped round my heart – but it had gone. The pain I had endured without realising had vanished. Owen had forgiven me. I knew it. I had gone to the top of the beacon a broken man, burdened by the weight of guilt, and had come back down it a forgiven man. In the course of one night, my life had been returned to me. I had been granted a future.

But first, I had to do something.

*

I rushed over to Mr Jenkins, knocking violently on his door.

He answered with an empty milk bottle in his hand. 'Robert, what in the... Has something happened?'

'Mr Jenkins, I need to borrow your car.'

'My car? You're not insured; I can't just–'

'Please, Mr Jenkins. It's urgent; I wouldn't ask you otherwise. My... my future depends on it.'

He guffawed. 'Sounds rather dramatic, if you don't mind–'

'I need to get to the train station in Plymouth by 2:22. Please, Mr Jenkins.'

'If you're catching a train, how will I get the car back?'

'I'm not catching a train but I need to stop someone else from doing so.'

'Well...' A tabby cat appeared at his feet. 'Mirabel, no you don't,' he said, shoving it back inside with his foot.

'I'll pay for any damages – not that there'll be any.'

'It's a bit sudden. Oh, what the heck. OK, but just this once, mind you. Hang on.'

Thank God, I thought, glancing at my watch. I had forty minutes. Just enough time.

'Here you are,' he said, reappearing, handing me the keys. 'You'll find it near the bus shelter.'

'Thanks, Mr J. I'll have it back to you by this afternoon.'

'Less of the Mr J, if you don't mind.'

I ran to the bus shelter. William was playing football with a couple of other boys. He waved to me. I found the headmaster's car – an Austin, its otherwise shiny hood splattered with bird shit. I hadn't driven a car in years but one doesn't forget. It started first time. The petrol tank was almost full. William picked up the ball while I reversed out. I winked at him.

It was a good ten-mile drive to Plymouth and this dilapidated old thing was incapable of going over thirty miles an hour. Nevertheless, I thought, I still had plenty of time. That was, at least, until I got stuck behind a tractor as soon as I passed the neighbouring village. The road was far too narrow to pass. I honked on the horn, eliciting no response. If anything the driver, in annoyance, was slowing down. 'Come on, please, come on,' I shouted. We were moving at walking pace. The minutes ticked by. Covered in sweat, I could feel my heart pounding. Clods of mud flew off the tractor's back wheels splattering the car bonnet. 'I don't believe this,' I muttered, close to tears. 'Oh, please, just disappear.' I felt weak with the heat and frustration. Could I go back, take a different route? No, the road was too narrow to reverse. I was stuck. They'd be arriving at the station any minute – Alice and Mr Redman, parking up their car. 'Let me pass, you old…' Then, just at that moment, without slowing down, the tractor swung left into a field, through an open gate, juddering up a muddy track. I thought of Joanna's barn. 'Thank God for that.' As soon as I could, I slammed my foot on the accelerator and speeded down the road.

The Devonian roads passed in a haze. I could imagine Mr Redman fussing. 'Now, Alice, are you sure you've got everything? Your suitcases, your purse, the ticket?' 'Daddy, of course I have; I'm not an imbecile.' He slips some money into her hand. 'Here, take this.' 'Oh, Daddy, really, there's no need…' 'It'll help you get going. Just until you find a job.' 'But I've got a job to go to–' 'Just in case. You never know.' 'Oh, Daddy.' She flings her arms round him and kisses him on the cheek, breathing in his odour of piped tobacco. 'Come on now,' he says, 'we mustn't miss that train.'

I'd reached the outskirts of Plymouth. The time was two twelve; I had exactly ten minutes. Fortunately, the train station was on the northern edge of the city, meaning I didn't have to get snarled up in the city centre. The station had been the subject of bombing during the Blitz but now, three years on, things were almost back to normal.

I careered into the car park, coming to an abrupt halt right next to Mr Redman's car. That meant they were there – inside the station. I ran from the car park into the coolness of the terminal. I felt drenched in sweat. A policeman near the entrance eyed me suspiciously. The clock inside showed two eighteen. Four minutes. I ran past the ticket office, zigzagging round passengers, trolleys and cases. Glancing again at the clock, I tripped over someone's suitcase. 'Oi, look where you're going,' shouted a middle-aged woman. Ignoring her, I darted onto the nearest platform. Looking up and down its length, I saw no sign of them. But then I heard my name being called. 'Robert? Robert?' My heart jumped on hearing Alice's voice. Squinting against the glare of the sun, I saw her next to her father in the shade of the platform opposite.

'Alice, wait there,' I shouted.

I sprinted up the steps of the platform bridge, rushing past a couple and their small child, just as the stationmaster announced the imminent arrival of the London-bound train. I bounded down the other side, taking two steps at a time.

'Robert, what on earth are you…'

'Alice.' I had to pause to catch my breath. 'Alice…' I realised I had no idea what to say. I cursed myself for not having prepared something.

'Hello, Mr Redman,' I said breathlessly.

'Hello, Robert. Didn't expect you to come say goodbye.'

'I haven't.' We heard the sound of the train approaching. I turned to see its great billows of smoke heralding its arrival, the sun reflecting off its engine.

Alice led me to one side. 'Robert, why are you here?'

Mr Redman discreetly took a few steps back.

I tried to read her eyes – trying to work out whether she was pleased to see me. All I saw was confusion and a touch of fear.

'I've come to stop you from getting on this train.' From the corner of my eye I could see the train easing into the shadow of the platform. People behind me gathered their things. Mothers pulled their children in. A young couple fell into an embrace.

She stared at me as if she didn't understand. 'But, Robert, I'm all set; they're expecting me. I can't just...'

'What? What can't you do?'

'I came to see you.'

'You did?'

'I heard you were back. I wanted to see if you were OK. I knocked. But you were out. A young girl saw me. She told me you had had a terrible time; that you were "recuperating". She had difficulty saying the word. You look a lot thinner.' She glanced at the incoming train. Great swirls of smoke filled the station platform.

'Don't do it, Alice.'

'Oh, Robert, it's too late; how can I not? Tell me, I've been worried about you, are you OK?'

'I tell everyone that I am. But I'm not. The

307

experience… it tainted me.'

'So that makes two of us. Tainted.'

Mr Redman had stepped out of view. He had her cases and bags on a trolley. Someone, a woman, shouted my name, making me jump. I realised she was shouting for her son, another Robert. He was behind her, sucking his thumb. On spinning round and finding him, she burst out laughing. 'There you are, you cheeky beggar,' she shrieked.

The train had come to a halt. Doors swung open. A few people unencumbered by luggage jumped out. The stationmaster confirmed the train's arrival. Alice's eyes kept darting from me to the train.

'Alice, it's been a year since you left. I have thought of you every hour since. I couldn't understand why you left me. Why should your uncle have affected the way you felt about me. You'd been through hell. I hadn't. But believe me – I have now. I understand now. You get to the point you can't live with yourself, with the memories. A wise man told me not to let the dead rule my life, and he was right.'

'A wise man?'

'He wore a pointy hat.'

She laughed and thumped me on the chest. People were boarding the train. A middle-aged man helped an elderly woman with swollen ankles on board. The guard appeared with his green and red flags, his whistle already between his lips.

'I brought you this.' I held out the ring within its box. 'I think you should take it back.'

She smiled, slipping the box into her coat pocket. 'The girl outside your house told me you're going back to sea soon. Is that right?'

'The day after tomorrow.'

'I can't bear it down here any more, Robert. There's nothing here. I need to go to London.'

'All aboard for London,' shouted the guard.

Mr Redman came into view. Clearing his throat, he said, 'Don't mean to pressurize you, girl, but if you're getting on that train I need to get these cases on now.'

'I'm getting on, Daddy.' She took my hand. 'I'm going to London. But when my fiancé here gets back from sea, he'll be joining me. Won't you, my love?'

I threw my arms round her and kissed her until the sounds of the station, the snorting of the train, the slamming doors, the announcements, children screaming, receded into a faraway distance. I breathed in her smell; a smell of warmth, light perfume and hair lacquer.

'Will you join me?' she whispered in my ear.

'You know I will. I'd join you on the moon if I had to.'

'This train ain't going to be held up for you two lovebirds,' shouted the guard. 'If you're getting on, you have to get on now.'

'Alice, please,' urged Mr Redman. 'Everything's on board, above your seat.'

Letting go of me, she quickly hugged her father. 'Thank you, Daddy. I'll miss you.'

Mr Redman and I watched her climb the steps onto the train. I closed the door behind her. Lowering the window, she reached out and took my hand. 'I love you,' she mouthed.

'I love you too.'

The guard blew his whistle and waved his green flag. With a snort and a fresh puff of smoke, the train creaked into motion and gently eased away. 'I'll be waiting for you,' she said, as our hands were pulled apart.

'I love you,' I shouted.

She blew me a kiss.

The train chugged away from me and into the sun. Rooted to the spot, I watched as it turned a bend and, picking up speed, disappeared from view. Soon there was nothing left but a few wisps of grey smoke curling up into the bright sky.

Silently, Mr Redman passed me a handkerchief. I hadn't realised but there were tears in my eyes.

'You planned this, didn't you, Mr Redman. You came to see me yesterday wanting me to do this.'

'No, no. What on earth makes you think that?' he said, unable to suppress a grin.

I tried to hand back his handkerchief. 'Thank you, Mr Redman.'

'Keep it,' he said, waving it away. 'And I think from now on, you should call me Tony.' He slapped me on the shoulder. 'Because by the looks of it, you'll soon be my son-in-law after all.'

Epilogue

Dartmoor in Devon,

June 1945

Dartmoor, eleven o'clock on a blustery June morning. It may be summer but the fact has bypassed this desolate part of the world. Sitting in my parents' car affords me no respite from the cold. I turn my collar up against the wind blowing in from across the hills. I'm expecting him to appear any moment now. I just have to be patient and wait.

The view is beautiful in its own bleak way. The hills covered in mist, the gathering of sheep, the bracken, the outcrops of granite. A blackbird sits on the fence at the far side of the car park and squawks.

I have returned to Devon specifically for this occasion, arriving last night. I have been a resident of London for only the last four weeks, since the end of the war, at least the end of the war in Europe. I am no longer a serving member of the merchant navy; I am a humble civilian once again, working in a London bank. Not the most ideal of professions and certainly not one to stir any passion, but it's a job and for that I have to be thankful. I'm a married man now. Have been for all of two weeks. I often find myself smiling for no particular reason beyond the fact that I am happy at last; happier than I ever thought I would be; happier than I deserve to be. I enjoy living in

London with my new wife. We rent one floor of a house in the southern suburbs in a street that was half demolished by German bombs. The work of rebuilding has already begun. Alice, having been in London for a year, is quite the girl about town. She works as a typist for a local newspaper. And I still have Angie, my little Jack Russell.

It feels rather strange returning to Devon and its sleepy ways. I'm staying a couple of nights with my parents. It's the first time I've seen them since I left almost a year ago to return to sea. My father, at last, has finally decided to join the world, and has ingratiated himself into various local committees. He's bought a dog, a golden retriever he calls Bunty, and takes her for long walks every day. He has been injected with an energy I've not seen since his working days. My mother too looks better than I've seen for years. She and the village vicar are in discussion, planning a church plaque in memory of my brother. There are photographs of Clarence all over the house. His presence is still very much part of the fabric in my parents' home. I'm sleeping in my childhood bedroom. Nothing much has changed. Still the same fake-Turkish rug of all shades red, the toy soldiers lined up on a shelf in order of their era, a seagull mobile hangs from the ceiling, a framed map of the British Isles and of course my books – Sherlock Holmes being my favourite as a boy. Clarence and I were lucky – we each had a room, something we didn't have when we still lived in Manchester.

My final year at sea passed without incident, the U-boat menace, as it had been called, had been reduced to the point of almost non-existence as the German navy had been rendered virtually powerless. The work however remained vitally important to the war effort – shipping supplies across the oceans. Not that I ever saw another mule. We were, perhaps, the unsung heroes of the war.

A car draws up near me. I watch as a tall man in a mackintosh and a trilby steps out. He looks like a policeman. Tipping his hat at me, he walks off towards the prison entrance.

I still think of the boys on the boat and I wonder how their loved ones are getting on. I think of John Clair's mother, Charlie Palmer's wife, and wonder whether Harris Beckett's wife settled down with the butcher. I do hope not. Beckett may have turned nasty in the end, but, then, who was I to judge? We all had, in our own way. It was like an illness – it affected different men in different ways. All I know is I survived when, perhaps, I didn't deserve to; I have a wife and I have a future, and occasionally, when the night is at its darkest, I hate myself for it. I twist my wedding ring round my finger. I can't help Owen, I can't help Joanna, but I am helping Alice. She too has her dark days but they become fewer and fewer. And there's someone else I can help. Not for long but I can take him home and settle him in. This is why I am here today.

Leaving the car, I decide to wait near the entrance, a stone archway set in a solid, stone wall leading to another archway further along with a large wooden door. The door opens with a satisfying groan and the man in the mackintosh comes out. He strides past me, tipping his hat. I nod in return. I look at my watch. 11:15. He's late but I imagine there's much paperwork to be done and forms to be signed. A poster encased in a glass frame on the wall tells me that Princetown Prison was originally opened in 1809, designed to cater for French prisoners of war from the Napoleonic Wars. I'm about to read more when the heavy doors open again. And there he is, clutching a small suitcase, his hair caught by the wind, his jacket, also, flapping in the breeze. The door closes behind him. I hear the key turn in the lock. He glances back at it, as if surprised he should be left outside to fend for himself. He waves on seeing me. We approach each other, meeting halfway between the two arches.

'Robert,' he says, shaking my hand. 'It's g-good to s-see you.'

'And you, Gregory. How are you?'

'N-not too bad. All things considered. Not too b-bad. T-thank you for doing this.'

'It's the least I can do.'

We walk to the outer archway where he stops to gaze around at the surrounding countryside. He breathes in the fresh air which carries the scent of heather and damp grass, taking in the moors and the silence. 'So, this is what p-peace looks like.'

'It most certainly is.'

'I'd quite forgotten.'

'Let's go embrace it then.' I take his suitcase for him. 'Come on, you ex-jailbird, let's get you home.'

THE END

Other novels by Rupert Colley:

This Time Tomorrow – 'Two brothers. One woman. A nation at war.' Part One of *The Searight Saga*, involving Guy, Lawrence and Mary, whom we met in this story. A compelling story of war, brotherly love, passion and betrayal during World War One. Vast in scope and intimate in the portrayal of three lives swept along by circumstances.

The White Venus – 'When the ties of loyalty are severed, whom do you trust?' Set in Nazi-occupied France during World War Two, a coming-of-age tale of divided loyalties, trust and a tragedy never forgotten but never mentioned.

The Woman on the Train – 'Someone saves your life. How far will you go to repay the debt?' A war-time debt threatens to ruin a musician's career and much more.

The Black Maria – 'When love becomes your greatest enemy.' A love story set in 1930s Soviet Union, a novel about fear: fear of each other, fear of being denounced, fear of Stalin's secret police; and, ultimately, the fear of falling in love.

My Brother the Enemy – 'Fear on the streets. Death on every corner. But the real enemy is the brother at his side.' A story of jealousy, sibling rivalry and betrayal, and a desperate bid for freedom, set against the backdrop of Nazi oppression and war.

The Torn Flag – 'Sometimes the simplest of choices can have the most devastating of consequences.' Set during the Hungarian Revolution, an epic tale of people caught in the machinations of history, where the choices you make determine your fate.

Historyinanhour.com
Rupertcolley.com

Printed in Great Britain
by Amazon.co.uk, Ltd.,
Marston Gate.